OPEN SEASON

Open Season

A Novel

Jim Moriarty

SMG
SPORTS
MEDIA
GROUP

All inquiries should be addressed to:
Sports Media Group
An imprint of Ann Arbor Media Group, LLC
2500 S. State Street
Ann Arbor, MI 48104

Printed and bound in the United States of America
by Edwards Brothers, Inc.

Moriarty, Jim.
    Open season / by Jim Moriarty.
        p. cm.
    ISBN 1-58726-180-4 (alk. paper)
    1. Golf--Tournaments--Fiction. 2. Serial murders--Fiction. 3. Photographers--Fiction.
I. Title.

    PS3613.07497064 2005
    813'.6--dc22

                                        2004022732

                    ISBN-13: 978-1-58726-180-0
                    ISBN-10: 1-58726-180-4

        10   09   08   07   06   05   10 9 8 7 6 5 4 3 2 1

Acknowledgments

This book would not have been possible without the generous help of Danny Freels, in the editing and rewriting phases and in steering it into the hands of a publisher. The staff at Sports Media Group have added valuable suggestions to the story and, of course, made it a reality. A special thanks goes to Andie Rose who created the cover and to Linda Tufts who solved a thorny issue in the narrative with a simple suggestion. Lastly, I thank my wife, Audrey.

PART ONE

April

1

My legs were curled up and cramping. My knees had that familiar ache from the old days when I played catcher on a small college baseball team in Iowa. My back felt like someone had stuck a sharp knife between two lower vertebrae. Sweat was rolling off my chin and I wiped it off with the back of my hand and felt the scratch of an afternoon stubble. My whole body hurt like two days after a car wreck. I changed the film in my cameras and tried not to drip sweat inside the black bodies. Almost no one used film anymore. I still did because I had the luxury of a little extra time and I hadn't shot golf in a while and, besides, I'm stubborn. I hate change. A Brit photographer was crouched in front of me, his six-foot-four frame twisted into a position even more contorted than mine. "For God sakes, just get *on* with it," he mumbled.

The man at the podium began the tiresome custom of introducing the people seated behind him, gesturing to his left and his right without bothering to look, like he was pointing out potted plants in his living room.

"From the European Tour," he announced in a slow, Southern monotone. Several people rose.

"The Ladies Professional Golf Association," he continued. Two leathery-skinned women in lime green blazers got up.

"The Argentinean Golf Association." One short, dark man.

"The Spanish Golf Association." An old man with his gray hair combed straight back across the top of his head like the figure on the prow of a sailing ship.

"The Japanese Golf Association." Two very serious Japanese waved appropriately.

"The Canadian Golf Association." The back row.

"The PGA Tour." Four men rose, one short athletic-looking man with salt-and-pepper hair whom I recognized as the commissioner, Jacob Pierce. When he stood he never quite straightened all the way up, fidgeting with a rolled-up paper, tapping it against the palm of his left hand until it slid all the way through the fist of his right. He seemed to be surveying the crowd as if he was looking for someone he was supposed to meet but who hadn't arrived yet. I didn't recognize the tour representatives on either side of Pierce but the fourth man was Colt Reeves, the head of their rules officials. I hadn't seen Reeves in years but my dislike, maybe even hatred, for him was still just as strong. He worked the 13th hole every year for the Masters rules committee and took delight in telling players their options after disastrous shots into the little creek in front of the green. That wasn't, of course, why I loathed him. That had everything to do with my wife. Well, ex-wife.

"The PGA of America." A half-dozen overweight men dressed in clown-colored plaid jackets wobbled uncertainly to their feet.

"The United States Golf Association." It was the largest group yet, all men with the exception of one dainty woman who had a long blonde ponytail. The men all wore blue blazers with insignias on the breast pocket and red-and-gray striped ties. The woman had the same kind of coat, except tailored to show her figure, and a simple white blouse with the top buttons undone.

"And the members of Augusta National." A large group of elderly gentlemen, all wearing green jackets, gathered their old bones, helping each other rise, more or less, in unison. The spectators ringing the giant practice putting green applauded politely. Virtually none of the Patrons, as Augusta National likes to refer to them, knew who any of the green coats were. It didn't matter. These were the producers, the men in charge. Some of them owned banks. Some were CEOs of Fortune 500 corporations. One or two owned small Southern states or, at the very least, the mineral rights to them. A few were just plain rich and spent their days enjoying the fruits of their trust funds. This was the one week of the year that even this handful of members allowed themselves to be seen on site. And even they were mere window dressing. Most of the members preferred to stay as far away from the club as possible during the tournament. The green coats acknowledged the applause of the crowd with a few desultory waves, secure in the knowledge that within a few hours' time all these people would be gone and, within a few days, every vestige of the tournament would be relegated to cold storage. If they could, they would have made the entire crowd disappear instantaneously. The fact is, no one is welcome at Augusta National except the members and the people who serve at their pleasure. Everyone else is granted admittance once a year to help overflow the club's coffers with TV rights fees, ticket money, and souvenir profits. It's pretty, all right, but it's a business just the same.

I was there to photograph the Masters for *Current* magazine, fulfilling my role as just another necessary evil allowed to come in through the servants' entrance on a temporary pass. In the past year *Current* had increased its sports and celebrity coverage in hopes of reversing a disturbing decline in circulation and advertising. Justin Pound, the irascible old art director, knew I'd done some golf once upon a time so he pulled my name out of his freelance hat. It had been a while since I'd shot golf, though, and I'd forgotten what a physical ordeal the Masters could be, carrying all those heavy lenses up and down the Georgia hills and then jousting with the half-drunk mob of spectators to get a position to take a picture.

"Could he bloody well take any longer?" the British photographer asked over his shoulder as the tournament chairman droned on and on about the pink and red azaleas and the immaculate green grass.

"Nick," a panicked woman shooter from *Sports Illustrated* called to me in a whisper from further down the line. "Were you at fourteen?"

"No," I replied under my breath. "I was in the wrong place all fucking day."

"Shit," she said. "How about Killets?"

"You'll have to ask her," I replied, though I knew she hadn't been there either.

Jennifer Killets was my coworker, the other photographer assigned to the tournament by *Current*. Even though Killets and I made a strategic plan before we went out on Sunday afternoon, I knew it was an exercise in futility. It always was with Killets. All she cared about was getting a cover shot, if there was a possible cover at all. I couldn't count on her being anywhere she was supposed to be when she was supposed to be there. Killets was going to do whatever Killets wanted. She knew it. I knew it. Everyone knew it. The difference was, I was supposed to plan for it.

The Brit smiled. The decisive shot of the tournament had come at one of the most unexpected places on the course, the green on the 14th. The winner, a hot young Italian named Francisco Pietro, had played his approach shot a foot shy of perfect. It thudded into the up slope of the green and rolled backward down the false front into a deep valley. Three-putting from there was a virtual certainty. At that moment he was tied with Tiger Woods, who was playing with Billy Ray Toomey two twosomes in front of him. When Pietro left his second in such a precarious position all the photographers, including my partner, abandoned him and ran to catch up with Woods, who was about to play his second into the par-5 15th. I was already down there waiting. According to the "plan," the 15th and 16th holes were my responsibility. The 14th and 17th belonged to Killets. We had two-way radios to talk to one another but, through a bizarre coincidence, Killets's radio always seemed to go dead at times like these. Jenny figured surely Tiger would make a birdie at the 15th, maybe even an eagle, and give up one of his famous Sunday pictures. She saw a cover in her future.

Instead, Pietro rolled his impossible putt up the hill, taking the hard right break along the screamingly fast flat at the top of the plateau, where it fell into the cup for a birdie three. He threw his Alfa Romeo cap into the air, leapt off the ground, fell backward on the turf, and did the Italian version of the Gator. He got to his feet, staggered up the hill with his hand on his heart, picked the ball out of the cup, kissed it, and then knelt down and kissed the ground just for good measure. Woods, with the crowd at the 14th screaming behind him, hit the ball into the water at the 15th and bogeyed, parred the 16th, and bogeyed the 17th from the front bunker to fall out of contention.

Pietro steadily finished out with a two-putt birdie at the 15th, followed by three routine pars. When he was through the 16th, I double-timed it up the hill to my position at the back of the 18th green, where I had an assistant saving a spot for me in the crowd. The photographers who want to be on the ground instead of in a cramped tower to the left of the green buy a couple of metal folding chairs and hire a kid to sit there all day and hold the spot. With Woods out of it, the only player who still had a shot at Pietro was Toomey, who needed to birdie the last. He hit it six feet above the hole on the 18th to give himself a chance but then did the unthinkable and left the putt short. As I shoved and apologized my way through the thick crowd, I nearly ran smack into Toomey's wife, Sandi, behind the green where the players come out of the scoring tent. She was waiting there with her sister, Soozi, who's married to another tour player, Jimmy Wildheart. They all met when Toomey and Wildheart were roommates and All-Americans at Texas Tech and Sandi and Soozi were impressively endowed Red Raider flag girls.

"How could he *do* that to me?" Sandi yelled at her sister. It looked like Billy Ray Toomey was about to be the main brisket in a West Texas barbecue.

Sweaty and tired, I crawled and pushed my way up to where my assistant was sitting. I got there in time to shoot Pietro walking up onto the 18th green, waving and bowing, but it didn't matter. I had missed the picture five holes ago. So had Jenny. More important, so had *Current*.

We all missed it, except the tall Brit kneeling in front of me, who could hardly contain his pleasure at being the only photographer to capture Pietro's theatrics. The success wouldn't make him rich—it wasn't Tiger Woods, after all— but his photos would do wonders for his reputation. And every art director of every other newspaper and magazine in the world would want to know why their photographer had missed it. Justin Pound would be at the front of that line, too. And Jennifer Killets would be blameless. She was bulletproof. The knot in my stomach told me it was a phone call I wasn't looking forward to making.

Just as the sun began to reach the tops of the Georgia pines on the hills behind us, the tournament chairman finished his endless acknowledgments and allowed the champion from the year before, Woods, to put the green jacket on the beaming Italian. The line of photographers began yelping like jackals. "Over here, Tiger! Francisco, look this way!" Some of the European shooters even yelled in Italian. Woods, wearing his best commercial smile, and the euphoric Pietro worked their way along the line of photographers, taking the coat off and slipping it back on, over and over, looking this way and that as countless strobes fired bolts of light. All the while the Patrons around the green yelled, "Down in front!" in Southern accents, trying to take pictures of their own with cameras they weren't supposed to have.

When I'd had enough, I gathered up my gear, slowly straightened my aching legs, and made my way through the crowd down the hill past the big scoreboard and into the press center where the photographers were assigned lockers, in the bowels of the building, next to the bathrooms. Before everyone switched to digital, the debris of photography would have been scattered everywhere. Used gaffer tape. Cardboard film boxes. Plastic film canisters. Discarded wrapping for batteries. Now, most shooters worked with a few squares of flash memory in their pockets. Some things hadn't changed, though. Pimply-faced assistants who had taken the week off from high school were leaning against the white cinderblock walls with exhausted and fearful looks on their faces. They were a part of our collective failure. The hallway filled with pungent, sweaty bodies scrambling in from the presentation. In a matter of minutes photographers were everywhere on their hands and knees, rendering the narrow hallway nearly impassable. One or two were counting their rolls of film, making sure everything was marked properly. Writing Push One, Normal, Push Two on envelopes. Others were kneeling, reviewing the last few pictures on screens on the backs of their digital cameras and carefully looking through their fanny packs to make certain all their memory cards were there, that nothing had fallen out during the scrambling and the chaos. A few were already breaking down their equipment, packing lenses and camera bodies into foam-filled cases for transport home or to the next assignment. Some just sat on the floor, drinking beer out of green cups. Everyone, though, was silently rehearsing an excuse.

"How was it mate?" one of the Australian photographers asked as I gingerly stepped over his back to get to my locker, being careful to set my feet down between his expensive Nikons.

"Awful. Couldn't have been worse."

"Well, I'll wager you're not alone. If you weren't at fourteen, there wasn't much reason to be here this week now was there?"

"I suppose not."

"Who got it anyway?"

"The only one I know for sure was the Brit, David Hailey. Who does he work for anyway?" I asked.

"The *Sunday Telegraph*, of all people. Probably the only publication on the face of the globe that doesn't need the bloody pictures right away. You can be sure those pics will be fetching a pretty penny with the Fleet Street boys. Lucky bugger."

I'd met Hailey before. He wasn't very popular among the European shooters but he seemed like a decent sort. He was the son of a British peer whose family owned Murphy's Irish Stout and he'd inherited something in the neighborhood of seventy million pounds. Anyway, it was a high-class neighborhood. A couple of years ago he decided he was going to be golf's Lord Snowdon, which didn't sit too well with the working-class stiffs who were trying to scratch out a living, stabbing each other in the back over euros and pence. The rumor was he was willing to work for almost nothing just to be out there. The other British photographers took to calling him "Christmas Tree" behind his back because of all the gaudy bits of expensive equipment he had dangling from every appendage. But from what I'd been able to see, he worked hard at it and turned out some good stuff. He certainly had that day.

The skinny woman photographer from *Sports Illustrated* was working her way down the smelly hallway having quiet conversation with one shooter after another. She was looking for someone who had THE shot. There would be a lot of pressure from New York to buy it, exclusively if possible, but to get it one way or another.

"Hey, Oliver," an anonymous voice down the line yelled.

"Yeah?"

"You got a message."

Shit, it had to be Pound calling about Pietro. I was going to have to tell the son of a bitch we missed it. I missed it. Damn Killets. Art directors and editors don't understand how it's possible to completely miss a picture. After all, they saw it on TV, didn't they? Why the hell weren't you there?

I figured I might as well get it over with so I put my cell phone in my pocket and sidestepped through all the photographers to the front desk. My name was scrolling past in red dots on the electronic message board. I asked a woman in a flower print dress with reading glasses hanging on a silver chain around her neck if she knew anything about it.

"Shhhh," she cautioned me with a finger to her bright red lips. "They're interviewin' tha champion."

"Yes, ma'am, I know they're interviewin' tha champion," I whispered. "It says there's a message for me. Nick Oliver."

"Yes. I do believe there is, Nicholas. Here you are." I hated it when people called me Nicholas and I'd had about all the Southern hospitality I could stand for one year.

It was an envelope with an Augusta National logo on the front. I tore it open and there was a note inside:

Call immediately.

— Pound

I got a drink of water from the cooler by the door and began to walk outside when I was stopped by a blue-shirted Pinkerton guard the size of a Volkswagen Beetle.

"I'm sorry, sir, but ya'll have to drink that in h'yar." I'd forgotten one of the many little bullshit rules of the Augusta Masters. If you get a drink in the press center, you aren't allowed to take it outside. I guess they figured we were going to feed bootleg water to the masses.

"Sorry," I said. I chugged what was left and threw the paper cup in the trash.

Outside the door the television reporters were breaking down their cameras and tripods. They had already finished with Pietro. I strolled up the hill toward the old, white clubhouse trying to find a strong enough signal to make a call. It was getting dark. I figured by now no one would care I was packing a forbidden cell phone. Underneath the oak trees Woods was bathed in klieg lights, a solitary figure granting a final interview to a Japanese TV station. He looked bored and pissed off and anxious to escape on his private jet. The air still had the acrid smell of the fertilizer mix the ground crew spread on the slippery hillside early in the week when it rained. Through the clubhouse windows I watched the black waiters in gold waistcoats serving tall drinks to white men in green coats and elderly women in tailored dresses.

I punched the art director's number on the cell directory.

"Pound."

"Justin, it's Nick Oliver."

"Where the hell have you been?"

"The presentation just got over."

"You get what's his name?"

"Pietro?"

"Yeah, whatever. You get him?"

"You mean on fourteen?"

"Fucking, yes, I mean on fourteen. The guy kissed the ground, for God sake."

"I missed it. I was on the fifteenth with Tiger," I explained, though explanations were neither required nor desired.

"Killets?"

"Nope."

I heard him sigh.

"Fuck it all. They're crawling all over my ass about the Italian. What the hell am I supposed to do?"

"I got some decent stuff of him. He made a good reaction picture when he eagled the eighth," I offered. "And there was some good stuff on the eighteenth green." I knew Pound would never go for it. Nothing less than "the" picture would do.

"But not fourteen," he said.

"Not fourteen."

"Shit."

The line went dead.

When a magazine sends a shooter to an event, they're taking a gamble. That's why art directors try to match the right photographer with the right job. Still, the outcome is uncertain. Film can get ruined, it might get lost in transit, or the pictures might just suck. But as long as the photographer shows up clean and sober and makes a reasonable effort to do his job, he earns his day rate and expenses. Of course, the better job you do, the better chance you'll be hired again. The Masters was a plum assignment. Pound thought he'd picked the right guy to team up with Killets. I'd done it before. It turned out, this time he hadn't. In the photography business, you're only as good as your last screw up.

I knew he'd be pissed off for a couple of weeks, probably try to punish me by not calling and not returning my calls, maybe withhold assignments until he absolutely needed me again. But as far as I was concerned he could go to hell. I'd busted my ass all day in the hot sun running up and down the goddamn hills. I'd made an honest mistake, that's all. I'd counted on Killets when I knew better. I clicked the phone shut and slipped it in my pocket before a Pinkerton could see it. By the time I got back to my locker most of the photographers had scattered like palmetto bugs when someone flicks on a porch light. The digital shooters had scurried off to transmit pictures from laptops in their dungeon cubicles or on broadband lines back at their hotels. Some would burn CDs and ship them just like the film-using dinosaurs like myself, running to catch a flight. At the end of the day, the drill was simple—stuff the equipment into travel cases, say a few goodbyes, and fire up the rental cars.

Once I put my film together with Killets's CDs, I'd drive to the airport and send the package to New York by Delta Dash. The plane I needed to catch wasn't leaving Augusta until ten o'clock so there was no particular rush. I could let the tournament traffic clear. The package would arrive at LaGuardia a little past 1 A.M. A courier would pick it up and deliver it to *Current*, where my stuff would be processed and put on a CD, too, so Pound could view it all and curse me at the top of his lungs.

The Brit from the *Sunday Telegraph* was still hanging around, basking in the glory of having scooped all of us. Besides, his deadline was six days away. I didn't blame him for puffing up a bit. At a big event, it's rare to get something no one else has. Sure, there was some luck involved in it, but some skill, too. After all, while we were all chasing Tiger down the 15th, he had the balls to hang back. We made the percentage play, he guessed on the pitch and hit it out of the park. Good for him, I say.

"Hailey, isn't it?" I asked.

"That's right." He was sitting on the floor with his back against the cement blocks.

"You the guy who got Pietro at fourteen?"

"I hope so. I haven't downloaded everything yet but what I've seen looks bloody useful."

"I bet. Well, cheers," I said.

"Cheers." He motioned with his beer.

Photographers are a peculiar subspecies. Ill-tempered, ill-mannered, compulsive, aggressive, and highly competitive, we still manage, for the most part, to remain friends. In sports photography there are no do-overs. You get one shot at it. If, for whatever reason, you blow it, you live with it. No second chances. When someone hits a home run, the rest of us appreciate it. We may appreciate it through clenched teeth but it's appreciated nonetheless.

"You going to Hilton Head?" I asked. It was the next tournament.

"No. It's back home for me. Big cricket match with Barbados in three days' time, you know." I nodded as if I just now recalled reading the goddamn cricket schedule that morning in *USA Today*.

I broke down my gear and packed it away carefully in a large black case with wheels on one end. I relieved Killets of her CDs, gave her a kiss on the cheek, and told her not to worry.

"I won't," she said. And she meant it, too.

On the way out of the press building I dropped my armband into a cardboard box overflowing with them and told myself I was glad it was over. The golf is always magical at the Masters but to a photographer it's just a tournament run by old, rich guys who have nothing better to do than make your life miserable one week out of the year.

2

After depositing my package with a cute little redhead at the Delta counter at Bush Field, I stopped at the Tank & Tummy to fill my rental car with gas. Inside I bought a six-pack of Bud Light from a kid with a pierced eyebrow whose short hair was moussed straight up in the air like a quiver of hypodermic needles. He looked at me kind of funny, which I found odd, until I realized I'd neglected to remove my Masters badge. For seven days it becomes a part of you, like the sudden appearance of a wart, except it's so prized that when you pin your badge on in the morning you just about pass the needle through a nipple so you can be certain all day it's still there. I took the badge off and put it in my pants pocket.

From the Tank & Tummy I cruised through the Taco Bell and ordered a Burrito Supreme with hot sauce. I was looking forward to crawling in bed and watching *The Sopranos*, hoping I might get a good night's sleep. It seemed an unlikely prospect since I knew I'd be spending most of the night second-guessing myself. It was typical postmortem bullshit. What else was I supposed to do?

I took Washington Road underneath the interstate, up the hill toward my motel. About the best thing you could say for the room was it had cable and the maid emptied the garbage almost every day. The curtains and carpeting were a stately shade of purple, carrying through the regal theme of the motel chain, the King & Queen Inn. The floors were cheap plywood with a hollow, spring-like effect. Most nights the rooms rented to truckers off the interstate for $29.99 but during the Masters you had to book it for seven nights for $2,250.

When I got into the turning lane, I could see police cruisers with their revolving blue lights parked toward the back of the motel. I pulled in and was stopped immediately by an Augusta cop. I opened the window to talk to him.

"Where you goin'?" He leaned in suspiciously, like he was trying to smell my breath.

"To my room," I replied, backing away a little so I could focus on his face.

"Show me your room key."

"Sure." I stuck my hand down in my pocket and impaled my ring finger on the Masters badge. "Shit." The hand involuntarily shot back out and I stuck the wounded finger into my mouth. When I looked back over at the policeman I was staring at the barrel of a 9 mm revolver. He held the gun on me with one hand and pulled open the car door with the other.

"Out of the car, boy!"

"I jthust sthtuck myself with my badge," I said lamely.

"Out of the car! On the ground. Face down! Face down! Get down!"

"OK," I said. "Jesus, relax will you?"

He pushed me forward on my knees, then roughly down on the blacktop with his foot.

"Hands on your head!"

"Take it easy. I'm cooperating."

I could hear shoes running in our direction.

"Whatta you got, Billy?"

"He went for sumpin'. Probably a knife."

Someone began patting down my legs and chest and feeling around inside my belt. There was a knee pushing painfully down on the middle of my back. Before an officer I couldn't see put his hands in my pants pockets he asked me, "You got anythin' sharp in there?"

"Yeah," I exhaled the word with the little breath I had left. "That's what I've been trying to tell Terminator here. I stuck myself with the pin on my Masters badge."

"Watch your mouth," said the one with the gun. The other officer put his hand in my pocket and turned it inside out, spilling my King & Queen Inn motel key, my Masters badge, and a money clip with twenty-seven dollars wrapped around my Marriott Rewards and American Airlines Advantage Platinum cards.

"Jesus, Billy, he ain't got no knife."

"Well, shit, you cain't be too careful." I could hear him put his gun back in its holster. The officer who searched me helped me up to my feet. He was black and had sergeant stripes.

"What the hell's going on?" I tried not to sound shaken.

"Where were you today?" asked the sergeant.

"At the Masters," I said.

"Tournament's been over quite some time," he said.

"I had to ship my film. I'm a photographer. I went to the airport, then I got some dinner. The Taco Bell bag's in the car. The shipping receipt is in my wallet," I said.

He looked inside the car. The smell of the food and the six-pack of beer seemed enough to convince him I was telling the truth.

"What's all this about?" I asked.

"It doesn't concern you." The sergeant laid the badge, the room key, and the money in the palm of my hand. "Just go on now."

I stared obviously at his badge number but he didn't

seem the least bit intimidated. I got back in my car and pulled into a parking space as close to my room, 152, as I could get.

There was an ambulance backed up to room 160 like it was a loading dock. Scattered nearby were four police cars with their stroboscopic lights flashing out of synch and a Ford station wagon that said "Office of Coroner" in gold letters on the side. A photographer I recognized came out of room 160 and began walking in my direction. He was one of the *Augusta Dispatch* shooters who had been at the Masters that afternoon. His eyes were the size of a full moon in autumn and he seemed unsteady on his feet.

"Hey," I called to him, cursing myself because I couldn't remember his name.

"Yeah?" he answered like he was drunk.

"Weren't you out at the golf today?" He seemed wobbly.

"Yeah." His voice was a whisper.

"Thought so. Nick Oliver." I put out my hand. His hand was freezing cold. "What's going on?"

"She's dead."

"Who?"

"I don't know." He slid down into a crouch, leaning back against the wall of the motel, next to an air conditioner that was dripping condensed water, making a rust stain on the cement. His camera clattered down next to him and he tried to catch his breath. "It's bad."

I put my hand on his shoulder. "You OK?"

He nodded.

"I'm surprised they let you in there," I said.

"I moonlight for the police. I was just leaving the course when I got the page. Jesus, from that to, to this . . ."

"How about a drink of water?"

"I'll be all right." His eyes welled up with tears.

His name came to me. Richard McPhee. I tried to get

him to come inside and sit down but he wouldn't. He didn't want to go back inside one of those rooms.

"There was blood everywhere," he said.

I got him a glass of water and opened a can of beer for myself. It was cold and I drank it in three gulps, dehydrated from the day's work and still shaking from my own encounter with the police. He took slow, steady sips of the water. I wanted to ask him what he'd seen but decided against it. If he wanted to say something, he would.

"They catch whoever did it?"

"I don't think so."

"What was it, robbery?" I asked. Break-ins were common the week of the golf tournament. Thieves knew everyone was at the course during the day.

"Don't know." He took more small sips. "She was taped to the coat rack. Just hanging there. Cut wide open. Her, her . . . She was everywhere."

"God," I said. "Something like that . . . " I shook my head. "A little town like Augusta. It's hard to imagine."

"Man, I'm guessin' it would be hard to imagine pretty much fuckin' anywhere," he said.

After a few minutes he took a deep breath, stood up, put his camera over one shoulder and his camera bag over the other, and walked away as the police car lights illuminated his back, off and on, off and on.

3

I could hear two officers talking outside my door.
"Forget about it," one of them said. "We already done him."

"This the guy just drove in?"

"Yeah." I heard them knock on the next door down. There was no answer. With the tournament over, most of the rooms would be empty now, waiting to be filled up by truck drivers once again. I heard the door open and I walked over to the wall and pressed my ear against it. I could hear the policemen walking around inside the room, opening and closing drawers, sliding the shower curtain aside. In a minute the door closed again.

My cell phone rang.

"Hello," I said quietly, turning away even though I figured they were gone and wouldn't be able to hear me through the thin walls.

"Pound." He bit the word off.

"Justin. Look, I'm sorry about Pietro," I said.

"I know. I know. Let's forget about it," he said. That could only mean one thing—he needed something.

"You got an early flight tomorrow?" he asked.

"No," I said. "All I could get was afternoon."

"Cancel it. I need you to do an assignment at Augusta National tomorrow morning. A quick portrait."

"Killets already leave town?" I asked. Pound grunted. We both knew I wasn't his first choice. He would have preferred to punish me for a while.

"Who is it?" I asked.

"Some TV guy. A Brit. His name is, let's see, his name is Jeremy Howe. Network guy."

"Yeah," I said, "I know him. He does the tower on the fourteenth."

"Apparently he knows Pietro pretty well. He's doing a sidebar on him for us and all we've got is the network headshot," continued Pound. "Howe's playing in the Monday press outing. Said it would be OK to do it before he tees off. His time is . . . here it is, eight-thirty. The club knows you're coming. When you get finished there, I need you to go to Hilton Head." He kept going like it was one continuous thought. "We're hooking up with Pietro on Tuesday afternoon. Everybody's going to be using that picture from the fourteenth so we decided to go a different direction. His agent said we're on for the shoot. I couldn't find anybody else."

"Try not to sound so thrilled," I said.

As Pound rattled it off, I scribbled down Pietro's agent's cell number on the King & Queen notepad on the night table by the musty bed. He gave me a quick description of the set-up photo. I was to pose Francisco Pietro in his polo uniform, which was being shipped from Miami Beach directly to Harbour Town.

"Don't fuck this up," said Pound. "Do the shoot tomorrow morning, then do the Italian on Tuesday, and follow him on the course on Wednesday. I'll pay you for two days."

He was screwing me out of a day rate but I figured, what the hell, at least he was giving me a chance to make good, even if he didn't really want to.

"I don't want to have to make any more excuses," he said, and the phone went dead.

The pulsating blue lights continued to invade my room most of the night, squeezing through the space where the King & Queen's purple curtains didn't quite meet and chasing away sleep until I was too tired to care anymore. The last thing I remembered was *Taxi* on "Nick at Nite." My alarm rang at 7 A.M. I had a headache from almost finishing the six-pack. Two empties had fallen on the floor. I showered, put three aspirin in my mouth, and washed them down with lukewarm water. My legs and back still hurt from a week of climbing up and down the hills at Augusta National and being accosted outside my room by a couple of the city's finest. I threw my dirty clothes into a large green duffel, carried it outside, and put it in the back seat of the rented gray Lumina. The trunk was already full of photo gear. I looked down at room 160 and it was barricaded with bright yellow tape that read, "Police Line—Do Not Enter" in thick, black letters.

On the way to the club I went through the McDonald's drive-through on Washington Road for a cup of coffee. In the end, this was the real legacy the Masters left Augusta, Georgia. It had spawned a four-lane street with wall-to-wall fast food restaurants. I wondered if Howe got to play the course on Monday morning because he was a television personality or if his number had been drawn in the lottery the green coats hold every year to determine which members of the press will be anointed with the privilege. Either way, it didn't matter much to me.

When I got to the Magnolia Lane entrance, I told the guard my name. His finger traced down the sheet on the clipboard until he saw it added in pencil below the approved list. He asked to see my badge. I showed it to him and he waved me in. I had noticed Howe was going to be playing with Gary Yamaguchi, a Japanese writer from Tokyo, and Thomas Peabody, a guy with wavy silver hair who owned a radio station in Menominee, Wisconsin, and used it as an excuse to get a phony press credential to the tournament. He'd been coming every year since 1971 and wore lime green plus fours and pink golf shirts. In all that time, the only reports he ever filed were his expenses.

I was directed away from the members' parking lot to the gravel lot still labeled "Working Press" with block green letters on a white sign. The morning was bright overcast, perfect light for a quick outdoor portrait, so I put a 300 mm lens on a camera body and headed toward the antebellum clubhouse to look for Howe.

The pro shop at Augusta National is a small brick building painted lily white. I thought someone there might have seen Howe so I went inside. The shelves of the one-room shop had been ravaged. All that remained was a Royal Doulton figurine of Clifford Roberts and a set of solid gold ball markers with the Augusta National logo imprinted on them. The woman behind the counter had dark circles under puffy eyes and too much makeup.

"May I help you?" she asked in an exasperated tone.

"Yes, ma'am," I said, "I'm looking for someone playing in the media group this morning. Jeremy Howe."

"Putting green," she said, as if she'd already seen way too many people that morning and way, way too many people in the last week.

I came out of the little white building facing the first tee and walked up the hill. It seemed odd to have the Pinkertons gone. Workmen were busy loosening bolts, tearing apart the TV towers, scoreboard, and press stands around the 18th green. I walked underneath the broad live oaks by the clubhouse. Their limbs were held in place by a webbing of thin steel cable most people never saw. Like all the inner workings of Augusta National, I thought.

I was surprised to see David Hailey, the Brit from the *Sunday Telegraph*, on the putting green. There were a few other writers I recognized, including one from the *New York Times*. Hailey was lagging ten-foot putts 15 feet past the hole. The writers were talking about Pietro and the unusual collapse of Woods. I didn't know if they hadn't heard about the murder at the King & Queen or if they just didn't care. Augusta National is like a parallel universe, completely disconnected from the world outside the gates.

"Still a little quick, are they?" I asked Hailey.

"Like bloody marble. And they haven't even cut them this morning."

"Thought you were headed back across the pond," I said.

"Bit of business. Sold a couple frames to *Sports Illustrated*. Then it turned out the club wanted the Pietro pictures, too, for the book, you know." The Masters is the only one of the four major tournaments that commissions its own book. Others have tried but only the Masters still does it since it's not for sale and money's no object at Augusta National. "I told them sure but I wanted to be a member. They counteroffered with a few quid and two games. Put me in this morning and told me I can pop in the next time I'm in the States, as well." He said it proudly, convinced he had pulled off something.

"How'd they turn out?" I asked about the pictures.

"Everyone seems happy," he said.

"Splendid." I wondered why I tried to talk like a Brit every time I was within ten feet of one.

"You playing today?" he asked as he slithered another one twelve feet past the hole.

"No. I'm actually looking for Jeremy Howe," I said, being careful not to tell him too much. We were, after all, competitors.

"Really?" said Hailey, who stroked another putt that simply refused to stop rolling. "I saw him mucking about earlier," he said, scraping another ball into position at his feet. "Maybe he's in the clubhouse having a little hair of the dog."

"Play well," I said.

"Safe travels," he offered, not straightening up from his stance, just concentrating on trying to keep his stroke short and his hands soft.

Work crews were everywhere. The defining lines of the tournament, the ropes and stakes, were being rolled up on spools and collected in piles. I walked back up underneath the big oaks and saw Jeremy Howe coming out of the double doors of the clubhouse shaded by the porch overhang. He was a portly man with the balance of a bowling pin. His round face seemed to be cradled in a set of bushy pork chop sideburns that were his TV trademark and he sported a woefully bad toupee. The English had managed to spread indoor plumbing and the art of brewing beer across the face of the globe but the two things they absolutely could not pull off were the wearing of baseball caps or toupees. Howe was known for his stabbing wit and his taste for martinis but an early trip to the bar seemed unlikely, even for him. I guessed runny eggs and grits was more like it.

"Jeremy," I said. "Nick Oliver. *Current* magazine. I'm supposed to get a shot of you to go with a piece you've written for us."

"By God, so you are," he said as he looked out over the landscape. "I'd completely forgotten about it. Will this take long? I'm on the tee in a short moment."

"It'll just take a minute. Very simple," I replied.

"Let's get on with it then. Lead the way, Oliver," he gestured toward the course.

Despite Howe's roly-poly figure, he'd been a legendary amateur player in his day, a member of five Walker Cup teams and the captain of the Great Britain and Ireland side once. He'd never lost a singles match in international play and twice won the British Amateur, once at Hoylake and once at St. Andrews. He'd played in seven Masters himself. He was also smart enough to know he didn't have a strong enough game to challenge the pros and instead parlayed his amateur successes into an announcing job with the BBC, and then crossed to America, where his accent alone was worth ten rating points.

I told Howe we'd walk over to the bunker on the front left of the 18th green. I wanted him to stand at the edge of it to get some fill light from underneath radiating off the white feldspar sand. Then I was going to do a head-and-shoulders picture with my 300 mm lens. The perfectly manicured fairway would make a solid green background. The whole thing would take 30 seconds. He understood the lighting gimmick immediately and knew it was going to be quick work. He stopped at the golf cart that had his bag strapped on the back and pulled out his Scotty Cameron putter.

"Haven't seen you around much lately, Oliver," said Howe, who was using his putter as a walking stick as we made our way down the slope next to the 18th green.

"This is the first tournament I've done in a few years," I admitted.

"Just when I think I'm out, they pull me back in, eh?" he said and laughed.

"Something like that," I said. "What did you think of Pietro?"

"Well, he's a fine player. But, my gracious, I was very disappointed in your Mr. Woods, I'll give you that much."

I positioned Howe where I wanted him in front of the bunker and walked back up the hill a few paces to frame the shot. He turned in a practiced way, posed confidently, and we were done.

"Will I see you at Hilton Head?" he asked.

"Could well," I replied. "I'm working with Pietro tomorrow afternoon."

"You tell the fortunate Florentine his was the worst approach shot to the fourteenth green I've ever had the privilege of witnessing," he said as he struggled up the hill back toward the practice putting green. "Ah, David Hailey," he called out, raising his putter in the air. "King of photography." With a pat and a wave to me, Howe waddled off.

I felt the pressing need to get out of Augusta. Back in the parking lot, I called the rental car company and told them I'd be keeping the Lumina another week and dropping it at the airport in Charleston. Savannah was the closest big airport to Hilton Head but I'd lived in Charleston before my divorce and during the tough days after it. I thought it might be therapeutic to visit for a day or two when I finished with Pietro.

Coming out of Magnolia Lane, I was able to turn left for the first time in a week. During the tournament the state troopers make you turn to the right when you exit the parking lot. The morning traffic had dissipated and I pulled out easily. Across the street was an old Piggly Wiggly that, over the years, had morphed into the Open Arms Church of Divine Light. The sun was beginning to heat up. It was supposed to be eighty degrees by one o'clock.

I punched in the number for Pietro's agent. We arranged to meet at the Harbour Town clubhouse the following afternoon. I was hoping the new Masters champion wouldn't be a pain in the ass.

4

The drive from Augusta to the sea might seem like a good way to decompress after the stress of the Masters but when I'm in the car by myself my mind does a walkabout. It's like the milky, disjointed moments before sleep. I can't help thinking about Juli. Most of the time I can hold the thoughts off, occupy myself with other things, but not in the dark and not when I'm driving alone. I'm emotional roadkill.

Sometimes it seems like it just happened, that it wasn't some recurring nightmare from years ago. I was sitting in O'Hare Airport eating a bagel, waiting to board a plane for Phoenix when my phone rang. It was Bridgett Reeves, the wife of Colt Reeves, the head of the tour rules officials. I remember every bit of that morning.

I was at gate K-17 and Bridgett, whom I didn't know then and haven't met since, was crying into my ear and telling me that she was trying to work it out with Colt and wasn't there anything I could do? And I told her I didn't have any idea what she was talking about and she said ohmygod, I thought you knew. I thought they told you. And I said, no I had no idea what she was talking about and that's when she told me that her husband and my wife had been having an affair for three years. I could feel the cold tile floor through the soles of my shoes. She said Juli had left a message on

Colt's cell phone using a fake name but the number was hers all right and that she had thought they had stopped seeing one another but that obviously they hadn't and, ohmygod, I thought you knew, and more tears and wasn't there anything I could do?

I told her I'd talk to Juli about it. I wrapped up the rest of the bagel in my *Chicago Tribune* and dropped it in the trash.

I called Juli at the Phoenix Open. She was, and still is, a press officer for the tour, handling interviews, posting stats on the website, that sort of thing. We first met when I was on assignment for *Golf Digest*. I said I just got a call from Bridgett Reeves and she said you've been having an affair with Colt for three years and I thought we ought to talk about it and she said yes we did need to talk but she couldn't right then because Phil Mickelson was coming in for an interview because he was the defending champion and the hometown boy but surely I must know how she felt about me. I said I'd talk to her when I got to Phoenix.

Only I didn't go to Phoenix. I already knew Bridgett Reeves was telling the truth. I'd seen it weeks before when Juli and I were at home in Charleston in our tiny carriage house apartment in the historic district, near White Point Gardens. We both traveled in our work but we arranged our schedules to be home together when we could. Our life in Charleston was like one of the carefully tended gardens that seem to be everywhere in the old town. We ate at restaurants the tourists didn't know, drank good wine, and slept late in the mornings with the windows open, blowing warm air off the Ashley River.

Juli was my favorite subject to photograph and the camera loved her. She had sharp bones and short, dark hair. I wanted to run a test roll on a new black-and-white Agfa film and asked her to sit for me. She had a dishtowel in her hands and a smudge of dirt on the side of her face from

planting lavender in a hanging basket. Sometimes, when I
look through the lens, I see more than I want to see. Something happens, something completely involuntary. Sometimes I see things. Things that are beyond the light, below
the surface. When I looked at Juli that morning, I knew there
was someone else. When I was at O'Hare Airport, Bridgett
Reeves told me who.

That was a long time ago. I wanted to shut out the pictures my mind created but I couldn't stop them. Being able
to imagine other people together is a curse. In the end, I
decided leaving her was the only way to turn off the slide
show running over and over in my head. Only it turned out
that didn't help much, either. I hadn't seen Juli in over a
year now but I knew she would be working at Hilton Head.
And Colt Reeves would probably be there, too.

There are two ways to get to Hilton Head from Augusta,
three counting the private jets the top players fly. The quick-
est way driving was to take the interstate back to Columbia
and connect with I-26 to Charleston and turn right. The other
way is to take back roads through rural, shit-kicking Georgia until you get to Savannah, then turn left. I decided on
the back country, through Statesboro because of the song
by the Allman Brothers. Besides, I thought a night in Savannah might make it easier for me.

Savannah was the place Juli and I went when we really
didn't want to be found. We stayed at Mrs. Bellamy's, a bed-
and-breakfast in a brick Federal-style home just off Wright
Square. I figured I'd eat at our favorite restaurant, the Moonlight Grill, and smoke a cigar in Twist, the martini bar next
door. I thought I could exorcise my demons by confronting
them for a night.

Savannah is a walking town and in our wanderings Juli
and I stumbled on Queen Street Antiques, near the art college. We always found something there that made us laugh.

Once it was a clay ashtray with baby alligator heads embedded in all four corners. I was remembering how excited she had been to find the silly looking thing when the policeman's lights in the rear view mirror snapped me back to reality.

"Shit," I said to myself. I immediately thought about the police from the night before. Then I looked at the speedometer. There was a simpler explanation. I was doing seventy-five in Blitchton, Georgia. The cop wanted my license, my registration, and my ass.

"It's a rental car," I said, trying to sound apologetic as I handed him the contract and my license.

"This don't look nothing like you," he said. The picture on my license looked more like a white Charles Barkley than me because I'd lost nearly thirty pounds since Juli and I split up.

"Thanks," was all I could think of to say.

"You know how fast you were going, sir?" he asked from behind his sunglasses.

"I honestly don't know, officer," I was trying to sound contrite, hoping I could talk my way out of it. "I was coming from Augusta. The Masters. I wasn't paying attention, I guess. I was daydreaming."

"That supposed to make me feel better?"

He wasted no time writing me up. Shit, I thought. I knew my insurance company would drop me if I got another ticket. I'd have to get a lawyer in Georgia, one of those backwoods guys who has you make out one check to him and another one to the judge's reelection campaign. I threw the ticket down on the seat next to me and pulled back out on the road.

When I got to Savannah I zigzagged through the town squares and was lucky to find a parking space near Mrs. Bellamy's B&B. I rang the bell at the top of the double staircase and she opened the door, all 300 pounds of her, dressed in a colorful shift with large geometric designs. Her thick hair was lashed in a tight bun and her eyebrows were drawn on with bold, slashing pencil strokes. Mrs. Bellamy enjoyed greeting people herself. Her lone employee, Mae, did all the work, including grocery shopping. I doubted Mrs. Bellamy could even fit through the front door anymore but that didn't keep her from dressing up every morning as if she was going to luncheon at the Hibernian Club. Her guests kept her in touch with the world.

"Mr. Oliver, what a pleasant surprise. Haven't seen you in quite some time," she said, putting her bulk into reverse, backing down the hallway. "Where's your adorable wife?"

"We're divorced, Mrs. Bellamy," I confessed.

"Sorry to hear that," she said with just the right touch of sadness in her voice.

"Do you have a room available?" I asked.

"I do," she said as she squeezed into a chair behind the desk just off the hallway. "Do you want your usual room? There's no one in it."

"Why not?" I replied, though I wasn't so sure I did.

"Some folks do, some don't," she said as she scribbled on the guest card in red ink. "Still living in Charleston?" Her Savannah accent was easy and smooth.

"No," I said, "I live in Chicago now. It's more convenient for work."

"I'm sure it must be," she said.

"I thought it might help. To come back," I said.

Mrs. Bellamy looked at me with a certain gentle, maternal resignation. "Sometimes that's the way it is," she said. "Just when you think you've put things behind you, they come up and bite you right in the ass. MasterCard or Visa?" The jowly sacks of flesh underneath her arms swung back and forth as she made an imprint of my card with her old-fashioned machine.

5

Savannah didn't help.

I ate seared ahi alone at a table for four on the second floor of the Moonlight Grill. Afterward, in Twist, the dingy martini bar next door, I smoked a cigar. The walk-in humidor was nearly empty and the cigar I selected crinkled between my fingers. The outside leaf crumbled when I clipped the end. Cigars had apparently lost their cachet and so had the little bar Juli and I used to visit. Nothing seemed to stay in fashion long. I ordered a pint of Guinness that the college-age bartender poured too fast, not understanding he needed to let it settle. A young man in a hurry. It seemed odd when the dark pint arrived unaccompanied by Juli's splashy, red Cosmopolitan. Across the street at the Velvet Elvis the double doors were thrown wide open. I watched as three young men with tattoos and black skullies smoked cigarettes and carried amplifiers inside from the back of a blue Ford van. It would be hours before the music began and I knew I would never be around to hear it. I was nearing middle age, married late in life and unhappily. Much of it was my own fault. Hell, I was no angel. The difference was, I'd figured it out before anybody got hurt. I knew what I had. In the end, I guess Juli realized what she didn't have. When a man cheats it's for sex. For a woman, it's all about upgrading. I was pretty sure Juli never knew about my mistake. If a tree falls in the forest and there's no one there to hear it, what noise does it make? Only the squirrels know. It was easy to convince myself it didn't matter. I believed it, too, until the tree fell on me.

I thought about Charleston and how I had tried to stay there after the divorce. Our Charleston friends had been mostly mine. Juli got the Volvo, I got the friends. I got off the road and opened my own studio but it was a bigger disaster than my marriage. I didn't have the personality for nine to five. Sometimes it felt like I was on assignment to cover my own life, recording it on film, looking at the results through a loupe, hoping to get the light and the composition just right.

I looked down at the pint glass. There was a frosting of brown foam in the bottom. Outside the Velvet Elvis the musicians were closing up the back of the van, all moved in. I knew they wouldn't begin banging on their guitars with their exaggerated windmill arm motions until after I was back at Mrs. Bellamy's in bed alone and wondering why I couldn't sleep.

Walking the town at night without Juli gave me a hollow feeling. There was a comfortable chill in the April air and I stopped to look in the windows of the Ray Ellis gallery, at the watercolors of the Maine coastline and his AME churches. When I got to the river, the uneven steps down the cobblestone walkways beside the ancient cotton warehouses seemed darker and more sinister than I remembered. A tugboat pushed a Korean freighter, heavy with rusty orange and red cargo containers, silently up the Savannah River. Cars bounced along the rough road, cruising the Riverwalk for action. When I'd seen enough of the things we used to see, been enough of the places we used to go, I climbed back up the worn stone stairs and returned to Wright Square.

In the morning I came downstairs with my duffel. Mae asked me how I wanted my eggs. She was a thin, short black woman with thick glasses and her wiry dark hair brushed straight back as if she had dressed in a convertible going 80 miles an hour down I-16.

"You sure you don't want a little something?" She kept trying to push her shrimp and grits on me.

"No, thank you. Honestly, I'm not hungry." I'd been on the divorce diet for longer than I cared to remember.

"You're gonna have to eat something or you'll waste away to nothing. It's not healthy." She turned and walked back into the kitchen.

"You're getting an early start," said Mrs. Bellamy who seemed to fill the whole room as I handed her my key.

"I've got an assignment this afternoon on Hilton Head with one of the golfers," I said.

"We get golfers here sometimes. I tell them I don't care for it," she said as she filled in the cost of the room and the city taxes on the credit card imprint she'd made the day before. Mrs. Bellamy looked at me over her reading glasses and said, "It seems terribly boring. People so absorbed in themselves. Are they that important?"

"I don't guess so," I said. "But, you know, anyone who plays an individual sport is bound to get a little self-absorbed. The thing about golf is the game is very humbling."

"The ones I've seen don't seem the least little bit humble to me, hon. Quite the opposite," she said. "All they do is talk about themselves. What they did here, how many times they hit it there. It just doesn't strike me that whacking a little ball around is all that admirable a way to spend your life."

"So, I guess I won't be seeing you at the tournament?"

"Doll baby, you won't even be seeing me at the Wal-Mart." With great labor she rose up from behind her desk and smoothed her dress down on her expansive hips the way a groom brushes down the flank of a horse.

"Mind if leave the car parked outside for a little bit? I want to walk around town a while."

"Not at all," she said. "Meter maids don't start coming around until nearly ten. Y'all come back anytime." She didn't look at me when she said it because she knew I never would.

Outside I put the duffel in the back seat of the rental and walked toward the art college. I saw the sign for Queen Street Antiques from across the square. I thought I might find something for Juli. An icebreaker.

When I opened the door an electric chime rang. Two men were deep in conversation behind a counter in the back. One looked to be in his fifties, the other younger but not by much. Around my age. The older man looked at me with mild interest as if I was either a potential sale or a promising new acquaintance.

"Let me know if you see something you absolutely can-*not* live without," he said.

"Thanks," I replied.

One side of the shop was festooned with sequined drag queen dresses and a rainbow of boas. Lots of '50s and '60s kitsch. Pillbox hats, beaded handbags, high shiny plastic boots, and satin evening gloves. There was a table full of African fertility carvings with genitalia of every shape and size. The furniture was either art deco or primitive like the standing ashtray made with half a lacquered coconut nailed to a stand of three palm fronds. There was a "painting" of Fats Domino made out of jelly beans glued to a piece of canvas board. I found a ceramic bobble-head figurine of Mr. Magoo and thought Juli might get a kick out of it. Something to put on the desk while she answered the inane questions of one clueless reporter after another.

"How much?" I held up Mr. Magoo and looked at the older man. He ground out his clove cigarette in the black ashtray that was shaped like a hand, palm up, with the middle finger extended upward. The younger man turned away, miffed because I had interrupted their conversation.

"Let's see." He walked over to look at the figurine. He delicately took Mr. Magoo out of my hands and turned it around several times, pulling his reading glasses up from where they hung around his neck on a silver chain. "Don't you simply love this?" The man was bald on top, and on the sides his gray hair was cropped close to the scalp. He had a little rat tail in back, gathered in a red elastic, and a small gold stud in his left ear. "Fifty dollars," he said.

"Can you do any better?" I asked.

"Well," he said, "I'm sure you'll be able to find a more affordable one down the street." He put it back where I had gotten it, straightening the Jetsons and the bobble-head Jesus that kept it company on the table as if I had disturbed the feng shui of his store.

"No, I'll take it," I said. "It just seems a little expensive."

"Whatever," he said, as if he wasn't quite sure he wanted to sell it to me anymore.

I took out my wallet and gave him my MasterCard.

"Credit?" he huffed.

"It says on the door you take MasterCard, Visa, and . . ." I had to look over my shoulder. "Diners Club."

He swiped the card violently through the machine on the desk. I could hear the muffled beeping as it dialed up the number. The younger man crossed his legs, bouncing the top one up and down. He was wearing heavy, square black shoes with thick heels.

The older man held the card between his first two fin-

gers and flipped his hand over palm up to give it back to
me. He wrapped Mr. Magoo in some tissue and put it in a
paper bag with handles. "Y'all come back," he said.

As I left Queen Street Antiques, I knew there was just
one other thing I had to do—I might need a little something
for Colt Reeves, too.

6

The day the bridges to Hilton Head Island replaced the ferries was the day the whole damn place started down the road to hell. Hilton Head is a 41-square-mile barrier island off the South Carolina coast, just north of Savannah. During the Civil War it was the base for the South Atlantic Blockading Squadron and the encampment of 40,000 Yankee troops in charge of sealing off both Savannah to the south and Charleston to the north. After the Civil War the island returned to the swampy, malarial habitat it had always been, populated by a handful of families, mostly black, who subsisted, if it could be called that, as rice planters and shrimpers. Electricity didn't come to the island until 1951 and there was no telephone service until 1960. Once Hilton Head became readily accessible, though, it was as doomed as a blue crab in boiling water. Greed was in the driver's seat.

It's never been entirely clear what drew the mob to Hilton Head, or how they managed to get in, but the "Outfit" took over several of the plantations—the real estate developments hellbent on hearkening back to the good old days of slavery—and leveraged every nickel they could out of the dirt before they threw them into bankruptcy and walked away with millions. Once Hilton Head was in the hands of the real estate privateers it became a designer destination with boutique houses on boutique golf courses. It grew so

exponentially that the plantations populating the island
spilled back onto the mainland and stacked themselves up
one on top of another until they reached thirty miles back to
I-95, like so many trailer parks for retired lawyers, ex-doc-
tors, and Internet crooks with phony books and impressive
portfolios.

I drove onto the island with my windows rolled down,
the hot wind blasting through the Lumina and Mr. Magoo
in a bag on the seat next to me. The new four-lane concrete
arch bridge that replaced the double spans that started all
the trouble offers a panoramic view across Calibogue Sound
toward the Harbour Town lighthouse in one direction and
up the Intracoastal in the other direction toward Port Royal
Sound. For decades there was one main road on Hilton Head
that ran along the middle of the island making essentially
one big sweeping right-hand turn. The "plantations" shot
off on both sides. Toward the end of the island, near Sea
Pines, were a pair of roundabouts, sources of endless confu-
sion to tourists and the cause of thousands of fender benders
every year. So overdeveloped was the island that it became
necessary to build a four-lane toll road so people headed to
Sea Pines could bypass the middle of Hilton Head altogether.
The island had gone from ferries to toll roads in fifty years.
Since I was in a hurry to get set up for Pietro, I took the
bypass.

Current magazine had made arrangements with the tour
to have credentials left for me at Will Call in the Sea Pines
registration building. I showed a lady in a blue blazer behind the counter my driver's license. She said I must have
lost a lot of weight and handed me an envelope that contained a gate pass, good for the whole week, an M lot parking tag that I was to hang from the mirror of the car, and a
badge that had my name and magazine affiliation etched
into it. I pinned the badge on the middle of my gray golf

shirt, in the thick part where the buttons are, so it wouldn't make a hole in the fabric.

The guard waved me through the gate with a military salute. It was still a ten-minute drive to Harbour Town near the tip of the island. The media lot was in a sandy field close to the marina, only a block from the golf course, underneath a stand of live oaks festooned with Spanish moss like carelessly tossed tinsel on a Christmas tree. The attendant flagged me into a spot at the end, my front tires almost in the marsh. I took my camera bag out of the back seat, stuffed Mr. Magoo in the top, and locked the car with the press of a button on the key ring. I noticed my hand was shaking.

The press center was in a tent located on the tennis courts where Sea Pines used to host a women's professional tennis tournament won by Chris Evert about a thousand times before it folded for lack of interest. There was a rent-a-cop sitting in a molded plastic chair outside the door, struggling like a Jack Russell to tear a bite off a gristly roast beef sandwich. On the side of the tent, two huge air-conditioning units were droning on, filling a two-foot-diameter plastic duct with cold air. Sweat was beginning to run down the side of my face. I stopped short of the tent and took a deep breath. I knew Juli would be inside.

The guard barely looked up when I walked past, just long enough to wipe the mustard at the corner of his mouth and to see that my badge was the right color. That was the job description, being able to distinguish between green and red. The door to the tent was a cheap metal patio door that stuck just a little so that when I pulled hard it flew open and banged against a two-by-four railing. The fluorescent lights suspended from the ceiling swayed back and forth, casting their white-green glow. Everyone at the table inside the door looked up. Everyone except Juli.

Trying hard not to look at her, I walked over to the

check-in table where two aged volunteers whose job it is to deny any request you might have, no matter how reasonable, looked at me like I was a yeti.

"May I help you?" asked one of the ancients.

"My name's Nick Oliver. I'm a photographer with *Current* magazine. I've already got my parking and my badge . . ."

"You'll have to sign this release," she said as she slapped a piece of paper down on the table in front of me with a shaky, spotted hand. I gave the form a quick look even though I already knew the gist of it. Basically, the release said I couldn't do anything with the pictures I took that week other than give them to the publication I was representing unless, of course, I had the permission of the tour. These forms were something the tour had instituted several years before, ostensibly to protect its players from having their images used in ways they didn't approve. Actually, though, it was because the tour, itself, was in the business of selling photographs to their own sponsors and various equipment manufacturers and they didn't want to have any competition from freelancers. If I didn't sign, I couldn't work, so I scribbled my name and underneath that, *Current* magazine. The hair on my neck stood up and I knew Juli was looking at me.

"Hi, there, you," she said, picking up the release. She was wearing a permanent badge that said "Juli Oliver." At least she hadn't given up on the name yet.

My stomach dropped right through the carpeted plywood floor, bounced back up to my throat, and then dove down again with what I felt certain must have been a thunderous crash. I knew she was no longer mine; I just wasn't sure I could live with the knowledge yet.

"Hi," I said. She looked great. Juli always looked great. She seemed fit and tan. Happy. Her features were etched.

Her hair was dark and shiny, cut short and laid down close to her head. It was a simple, elegant style. She was wearing black slacks that did as much to accent her figure as a pair of tight blue jeans ever could. Her simple white blouse was a little big to disguise the breasts she preferred to hide at work. She used to tell me about the writers and photographers and even players who hit on her and how hopeless they seemed. It never really sunk in before that I had once been one of them. And there I was, right back at hopeless.

"They told me you were coming," she said.

"Oh." I didn't have a clue what to say. What do you say to an ex-wife you can't get out of your mind? I bent down to give her a polite kiss. She turned her face and I brushed against her cheek. It seemed such an awkward dance.

"You look different," she said. "It's the glasses. Where are your glasses?"

"I finally had the laser surgery," I said.

"Like it?"

"It's been great. First time in years I've been able to see when I wake up in the morning."

"Do you need a photo locker? There are plenty, you know," she said, faking an East Indian accent.

"That would be great." I smiled.

Juli turned around to a filing cabinet and took a Yale combination lock out of one of the drawers. She handed it to me. Our fingers touched. It seemed to embarrass her. It withered me.

"The lockers are over there, behind the big scoreboard," she said.

"Thanks," I said. I put the camera bag up on the table in front of her. "I brought you something." I opened the top flap and pulled out the figurine, still wrapped in tissue. When she set it on the table, it looked like a pint-sized version of the bundle in *The Maltese Falcon*.

"You shouldn't have done that," she said, peeling away the outer layers.

"I saw it and thought you might like it, that's all." I could sense the press room volunteers watching us. Just a couple of crazy, middle-aged kids.

Mr. Magoo made her smile. When she saw the Queen Street Antiques label on the base, she bit her lip. Savannah had been worth it after all.

"Thanks," she said. I thought I detected a catch in her voice.

"I better stow my gear. I haven't got much time before I have to shoot Pietro, so to speak."

"He's coming in for an interview at three o'clock," she said.

"I'm supposed to work with him at five."

"That sounds about right. Maybe thirty minutes in here, then a little time to practice." She made Mr. Magoo's head sway with a gentle push. "Is there anything else you need?" Back to business.

"I don't think so. We're doing the picture at the stables. I need to touch base with the agent, what's his name?"

"Peter Hammett."

"Right. Sounded like a real sleaze when I talked to him."

"He's OK," she said, looking at Mr. Magoo. "Better than most."

"Apparently Pietro is a player on some polo club in Palm Beach in the winter." I felt like I needed to explain to her why we were taking the photograph at the stables. "They Fed Exed his uniform to the pro shop. We're doing a setup with a horse. Can't you see the headline now? 'Italian Stallion.'" I shook my head.

"What an original idea." She laughed.

"I work for idiots, I know. What can I say? It's a job." I

closed the camera bag and picked up the strap and put it across my shoulder.

"Where are you staying?" she asked.

"I'm at the Palmetto Inn, the one on the beach near Coligny Square. You?"

"I'm at the Westin. It's where most of the players are," she said.

"Is Pietro there?"

"I don't think so. He's got a condo in Sea Pines. Trying to hide out."

"Makes sense," I said. Then I surprised myself. "How about dinner?"

"I don't know," she said. "It might not be a good idea."

"Sure. I understand." I began to turn away.

"Nick," she said.

"Yeah?"

"It's good to see you."

"You, too, Juli. I mean it. You, too."

7

I put my camera bag in a metal locker, took a deep breath, closed it with a clang, and threaded the lock through the handle. The combination—two full turns right to 27, left past 27 to 5, right to 19—was printed on a card and I put it in my pocket. By the time I was finished on Wednesday, I just might be able to remember it without looking. I hated getting old.

Outside the tent I walked through the players' parking lot on my way to the pro shop. Sitting under a tree on the end of a golf bag near a white Cadillac Escalade was a caddie I recognized. The Escalade was in a space reserved for Ian Person.

"Stormy," I said.

He looked at me with all the facial expression of an Egyptian death mask. It is a tour stare common to caddies and players alike. They meet so many people in so many different towns their natural inclination is to assume anyone who approaches them is some cross-wired cretin they gave a lousy putting tip to during a torturous six-hour pro-am. Or, more likely, snubbed one night in a bar over an autograph request or a woman. If you're lucky, the blank stare transforms into a spark of recognition. I saw the pilot light go on in Stormy's eyes—not that it made his day, mind you.

"Nick," he said, not bothering to get up. "Long time no see, man. Where you been?"

Stormy's real name was Donnell Monday, hence the nickname. That and the fact that his consumption of Smirnoff vodka was sufficient to insure that Tuesday was always just as bad. I met Stormy when I first came out on the tour for *Golf Digest* and he caddied for Jerry Pate. That was at least five bags ago for Stormy and most of a career and a whole marriage ago for me. At first glance, Stormy seemed like a throwback, one of those hard-drinking, hard-living caddies from the old times. But first impressions can be mistaken. As much as anyone, Stormy was the man responsible for the new breed of techno caddie. He was the first bag man to buy a laser range finder and the first to show up with a pocket-sized optical level for measuring the exact grades in greens. Even before he got the new toy, he could read greens better than any man alive. After tournament rounds, he double-checked Person's scorecard to make certain it was filled out correctly. And he was never, ever late. He made no secret of the fact that he liked his vodka but, on work days, Stormy was in the caddie Hall of Fame.

"You carrying for Ian now?" I asked him.

"Yeah," he said. "I see Juli every once in a while when the man makes it to the press tent but I haven't seen you in, like, forever."

"We're divorced," I said.

"I heard," said Stormy. "It can be real tough out here." He was trying to say it wasn't really anybody's fault. "I always figured you two would make it."

"Like you say, it's tough out here. So, how's Ian, good gig?"

"The best. It's like bein' on Social Security. Ian can still play. Still making money. But the pressure's off. He don't worry about being No. 1 anymore. Don't fight it so much. Three, four good weeks and we've made our nut for the year.

Easy money." Stormy took a gold pack of Winstons out of his pocket and lit one.

"Where you been?" His voice was worn down, coarse from cigarettes and alcohol and years on a job that came down to being the all-weather, gentleman's gentleman of sports.

"I had a studio in Charleston for a while. Moved to Chicago. Did a little real news, mostly for *Current* magazine. Picked up some other stuff. *Travel & Leisure*, that sort of shit. Then *Current* needed someone to do golf and the art director remembered I'd done it before so here I am, back in the saddle."

"You at Augusta?" he asked.

"Yeah, in fact, I'm working with Pietro this afternoon. What do you think, Tiger choke?"

He tilted his head and looked at me. "Like a pig in a python. Tiger Woods ain't no different than anybody else even if he won't admit it. We shot 71–76, missed the cut," he said hoarsely, getting back to his player. The plural referred to Stormy and his man, Person. Every caddie and player are a "we."

"Adios, motherfucker," he waved his hand and flicked his ash at the same time. "We were hitting it pretty good but we couldn't put it in the hole at the Chicken Ranch. It hurts to watch him. Since Hawaii I've been telling him he needs to go to the belly." Stormy was talking about Person using a longer putter. "The right hand's starting to twitch bad. The man just won't listen to reason, you know what I'm saying?"

"You done for the day?" I asked.

"Yeah, his back is killing him. He's in with the commissioner then we're going to the barn. Been in with Pierce over an hour. Ask me, he spends too much time on that advisory committee and not enough time on the putting green."

"Want to make a quick hundred this afternoon, work as my assistant?" The money wouldn't mean much to Stormy. A hundred bucks to a tour caddie didn't mean what it used to. As tore up as Stormy could get on Sunday and Monday nights, he kept Count Smirnoff bottled up the rest of the week. Spending an otherwise free afternoon working for me would at least help him stay out of the beach bars. He was bound to see that as a bigger benefit than the cash, the call of the vodka and the women playing beach volley-ball being what they are. From my standpoint, I could use a hand with the heavy case of metal reflectors I used. Besides, Stormy had the dirt on everyone and was never reluctant to share it. He'd be good for at least two hot rumors a side.

Stormy saw Person striding toward us across the park-ing lot. He stubbed out his cigarette and got slowly to his feet. It was only Tuesday, after all, and he was still in the shadow of the previous night.

"I'll do it," he said to me.

"Meet me here about four o'clock then."

"Sure," he replied, standing the professional bag up-right so that the NASCAR-like array of endorsements was readable. I began to walk across the lot toward Person and the clubhouse.

"Hi, Ian," I said as I got near him.

"Hi," he said, looking straight through me the way you look through Saran Wrap at a ham sandwich. Then the gleam of recognition crossed his face, too. "Nick," he put out his hand. "How you doing? Everything OK?"

"Yeah," I said. "How about you?"

"I was real sorry to hear about you and Juli," he said. Few players had known me well but most all of them knew Juli. It was mildly surprising Ian had put the two of us to-gether. Your average, everyday, what's-in-it-for-me player wouldn't have bothered. He was one of the good guys who knew that life existed beyond the razor wire border of the golf tour. I got the feeling he really was sorry.

"Thanks, Ian. Me too." I said.

"What brings you out?" he asked, a little distracted, as if his thoughts had turned elsewhere, maybe back to his meeting with the commissioner.

"I've got an assignment with Pietro this afternoon," I said.

"Same circus, different clowns, eh?" Ian said.

"I guess," I laughed. "How's the back?"

"Like linguine," he said and began walking toward Stormy, ready to break off our little encounter. "With clam sauce," he called back over his shoulder.

The clubhouse at the Harbour Town Golf Links is surprisingly small. The back stairway is a set of cement steps made to look like South Carolina tabby, a mixture of cement and oyster shells, to give it a faux low-country feel. There were four or five pros on the putting green, none of whom I recognized and all of whom looked to be about 12 years old. They didn't shave every day but they had portfolios worth millions and agents with gel-coated hair who carried three cell phones at a time.

If the Italian didn't stiff me, the only thing that could screw up my assignment would be if the FedEx package hadn't arrived from the polo club. If that happened I'd already decided to take the usual fallback position and make a simple, clean, well-lit portrait, which would have been my preference to begin with anyway. This assignment was strictly from-the-top-down art. Some manic-depressive failed writer turned editor had started with a headline. My picture had to match it. The Italian Stallion. How could the Pulitzer Prize committee resist it?

Inside the clubhouse the pro shop was on the right and a small restaurant was on the left. The restaurant had bad oil paintings of past champions hanging on the walls and a menu that featured breakfast and lunch items named after them. The Watson Waffle with Kansas City bacon. The Langer Knocker, a bratwurst sandwich with sauerkraut on German rye. The Norman Conquest, half a cheese sandwich and a cup of egg drop soup.

The pro shop staff was decked out in Hawaiian shirts and nameplates that supposedly divulged their places of origin. I asked "Hi My Name Is Sylvia," who purportedly was from Taos, New Mexico, if they had received a FedEx package that was supposed to be held for me, Nick Oliver from Iowa, Charleston, and Chicago.

"I don't think so," she said, folding a $700 Coogi sweater that looked like acrylic cockatoo droppings on Christmas wrapping paper—a surefire big seller now that it was eighty degrees.

"Do you think you could check?" I asked.

She seemed a little put out but she finally strode off into the back room to, I was certain, make an exhaustive search that would last upward of seven seconds. Fortunately, she just about had to pole vault across what turned out to be three boxes addressed to me just to get into the store room.

"Could I see some identification?" she asked, returning with the first box.

"Have you had a lot of people in here today trying to claim packages for Nick Oliver?" I asked as I showed her my driver's license. "I know, it doesn't look a thing like me."

"I think it looks exactly like you," she said. I helped her with the other two boxes, slipped her five bucks, and we parted almost like friends.

The boxes weren't terribly heavy but they were awkward. I carried two of them stacked one on top of the other on the palm of my right hand like a couple of odd-shaped pizzas. I put the long one under my other arm and backed my way out of the tiny shop. I walked back to the M lot and set the boxes on the trunk of my car to open them. The long skinny one had a polo mallet wedged in it. The square box contained a scarred riding helmet with a protective cage on the front. Enclosed in a standard FedEx overnight box was an open-collared green jersey with a red eagle insignia I didn't recognize and a pair of riding pants. There was a note saying they didn't have any of Pietro's boots and that they were sorry. I put the gear in the back seat of the car and checked my watch. It was after three o'clock. I wanted to get back to the press tent before Pietro's interview finished. Peter Hammett, super agent, would be there, too, and we could nail down the photo shoot—meaning he'd try to tell me what I'd be allowed to do and how long I had to do it.

The press interview area was in a tiny tent that was an appendage of the larger one. There was a riser at the back with two wingback chairs separated by a coffee table. A fifteen-by-ten-foot banner hanging on the wall behind the chairs displayed the tournament logo and sponsor name repeated ad nauseam. That way if one of the local TV stations captured video of a player's interview, the sponsor—in this case Bubba Gump Shrimp—would necessarily have its name appear, too. It was standard operating procedure.

Juli was sitting in the chair on the right, Pietro was in the other chair. They each had a microphone and the Italian had apparently said something funny because everyone was laughing. Anything players say automatically gets witty after they win a major championship. There were a dozen or so writers sitting in folding chairs holding tape recorders and taking notes on pads of paper printed specifically for the Harbour Town tournament, listing each hole's par and yardage in a column down the left side. Two TV stations, one from Savannah and one from Charleston, had video cameras mounted on heavy tripods taping the interview. Off to one side, a stenographer was transcribing Pietro's every word.

"You've just won on large, fast, and very undulating greens at Augusta National. Now you're playing on small greens that don't have nearly the speed or the contours. How do you make the adjustment?" asked one of the writers sitting in the front row, crossing his thighs that were the size of country hams, wrapped in khaki. I recognized his face but couldn't remember if he worked for a paper or a web outlet.

"I hit my putts a little harder and straighter," said Pietro, whose English seemed better than my own. He flashed a thin, captivating smile. The writer dutifully wrote down the answer word for word. Holding the microphone in both hands, the Italian bounced it against his chin, waiting for the next question. With his command of English and that self-deprecating grin, he was going to turn his Masters victory into ten billion lira and Peter Hammett was on hand to help him do it.

Juli looked relaxed and comfortable sitting next to the Masters champion. She'd been conducting interviews like this one for seven years. Most of the players knew her and liked her. A few tried to date her but she was never interested. Every professional golfer is at the center of his own universe and Juli wasn't the type to orbit around a man.

"Francisco, you've won nearly twenty tournaments around the world. The Masters was your first major. Do you feel like you got the monkey off your back?" asked an elderly woman reporter who was wearing a dark green skirt and straw hat with pieces of plastic fruit attached around the brim. Local, I decided, probably the *Island Shopper*.

Pietro paused as if he was giving his answer the benefit of careful consideration when, in fact, he'd already answered the same question what seemed to him like a thousand times since Sunday night. Yet he showed no signs of impatience. This guy is good, I thought.

"There are no golfing monkeys," he said, showing his carefully rehearsed grin. A couple of writers chuckled. "No. No. I am being the most serious with you. Sometimes, it is your time. Last week, it was my time, not Tiger's. Maybe at the U.S. Open, it will be Tiger's time and not mine. This is the way of golf." I could tell he really wanted to say he beat the living snot out of Woods and he'd do it again, too, but the guy was way too smooth.

Standing in one of the back corners of the interview tent was a man I took to be Peter Hammett. He was the only person in the room in a coat and tie. He had a soft, buttery-looking black leather case under his right arm and smiled appreciatively at Pietro's answers. He reached into his pocket and pulled out a cell phone that must have just vibrated because I never heard a ring. He left the interview area and walked outside the main press tent. I followed him and waited at a respectful distance for his conversation to end.

"Mr. Hammett?"

"Yes," he said, slightly distracted as if his mind was still making calculations.

"I'm Nick Oliver." There was no sign of recognition. "From *Current* magazine." Still nothing. "I'm the photographer doing the pictures of Pietro this afternoon."

"Oh, right," he said.

"I just wanted to make sure we were still on."

"As far as I know. What was it we're doing again?" he asked.

"We've arranged for the polo club in Palm Beach to send his uniform. We're going to take the pictures at the stables."

"Right. Right. How long will this take? His schedule's really tight."

"If Pietro gets there at five o'clock, it'll take him a few

minutes to change. I'll shoot for maybe fifteen minutes. I'll work as fast as I can," I assured him.

"Five o'clock?" he asked like the very thought of it was insanity itself.

"The light should be less harsh by then, fairly low. I need good light. This won't take long." Of course, he and I both knew I'd take as much time as they would give me. It was the same old waltz. Agents, for their part, are afraid of their players. If they ask too much of a guy, an agent can be out of a job. If I ask too little of the agent, I could be out of a job. We were pulling in opposite directions on the same rope—the player.

I could see Peter Hammett's mind slip a gear. I was beginning to think Pietro had someplace else he wanted to be at five o'clock and Hammett was trying to figure out how he was going to finesse this.

"Do you know where the stables are?" I asked, figuring the best thing to do was press ahead.

"By the back entrance to Sea Pines, right?"

"Yeah. If you meet me there, I'll be set up and ready to go at five sharp. I'll get him dressed and on his way as quick as I can," I said. I was hoping the panic I was beginning to feel wasn't creeping into my voice. I couldn't even imagine what Pound would say if I had to tell him the Masters champion stiffed us.

Pietro and Juli came out of the press tent and got in the E-Z-Go golf cart with the MEDIA sign fixed to the front. It beeped as she backed up. They pulled up next to Peter Hammett. I was a nonentity as far as the Italian was concerned. Juli smiled at me.

"I'm going to the range," Pietro said coldly. You could tell there was something in his game that was troubling him, Masters champion or not. In the end, the game goes on and they just keep chasing it.

"I'll be over in a minute," said his agent, and Juli drove off before anyone had a chance to wander up, maybe ask for an autograph. Players hated being outside the ropes where they could be approached by anyone.

"How about if I give you the polo clothes? He can change here and you can drive him over," I offered.

"He's not going to walk through the locker room wearing riding pants. You've got to be kidding," Hammett said and thought for a minute. "Give me the stuff and I'll have him change at the condo."

I got the shirt and pants out of the car, came back, and gave them to Hammett.

"I'll bring the helmet and the mallet," I said.

"OK," continued Hammett, as if he was about to make a personally painful concession. "Five o'clock. You get ten minutes."

8

Stormy was a thin black man who wore comfortable old Nike cross trainers that caved inward at the ankles like a child's ice skates. He had on a red polo shirt and a pair of shorts that cost more than a round of golf at Harbour Town. Because he was Person's caddie, he got a 75 percent discount on all the preppy Ralph Lauren stuff he could stand to wear.

"Looks like shit," said Stormy, exhaling smoke on the ride over to the stables, "but at least I don't work for Jesper Parnevik."

I pulled the Lumina off the blacktop road and up next to the stable fence. A woman in blue jeans with wide hips and skin that was rough and smooth at the same time, like a gym class basketball, was walking a sorrel quarter horse wearing an English saddle to a corner of the corral near us. I'd selected the spot because it was semi-secluded but still in full sunlight late in the afternoon.

I popped the trunk from the inside and got out of the car. I pointed to a four-foot-long cylindrical black case about a foot in diameter. "That's the one I need," I told Stormy.

He grabbed the handle and began to lift it. "Sheeeit," he said. "This goddamn thing is heavy. What the hell you got in there?"

"Metal reflectors," I said.

"What did you do, melt down a fuckin' Ranger Rover?"

While Stormy alternately dragged and carried the reflector case over to the fence, I pushed around several other plastic cases containing camera equipment until I could reach the one that had the 2¼ in it. I didn't use medium format much so I wasn't one of those photographers who had expensive Hasselblads. I just had one Pentax body and a couple of lenses, one for tight portraits and one zoom that gave me a little extra flexibility. The only drawback of the Pentax was that it was a bitch to change film. I wasn't going to have much time with Pietro, though, so changing film wouldn't be a problem. I figured one roll of medium format, ten shots, and one or two rolls of 35 mm. That would have to do.

"I ain't lifting this over that damn fence," Stormy informed me, leaning on the top of the case.

"No need," I said and checked my watch. It was 4:30. Plenty of time.

I slammed the trunk, putting my camera bag over one shoulder and bringing along the small case with the Pentax in it.

"Go ahead and get on the other side and I'll pass everything through to you," I said.

Stormy climbed over the fence with the deliberateness of a man free-climbing the face of El Capitan. It occurred to me I had no idea how old he was.

"Here," I said, and handed the camera bag and then the small case between the railings. The woman with the horse came up behind Stormy, who seemed none too pleased to be so close to such a large and fragrant animal.

"This is Broadstreet Annie," she said to no one in particular.

"I don't give a shit if it's Miss July," Stormy said. "Keep that damn thing away from me."

The woman smiled the way trainers do when they come across someone who is timid around horses. There is a strange hubris to horse people, an intoxication that seems to come with exercising control over an animal so much larger than themselves, even if that control is admittedly tenuous. I had no particular feeling about horses one way or the other except that it always seemed to me when it comes right down to it, it's pretty much the horse's call. I preferred not to put my well-being at the mercy of something with a brain the size of a racquetball.

I pulled off the top of the large black reflector case and took out the three-legged stand. I unrolled the three-by-four-foot silver metal sheets, slipped the edges into the side rails, and snapped the cross bars in place. Then I passed the assembled reflectors and the stand through the fence before climbing over myself.

"I'm Nick Oliver," I said to the woman holding Broadstreet Annie's reins.

"Bernadette Austin," she said in a no-nonsense monotone.

I looked at my watch. "Bernadette, this is where I want you to position the horse, facing that way." I showed her and she began to back Broadstreet Annie's ass end around. I stroked down the horse's nose tentatively. The hair was smooth and she turned her head to get a look at me with one big, brown eyeball. Then Broadstreet Annie lifted her tail and pissed enough to float a kayak.

"Jesus," I said, moving aside to keep my feet out of splash range. "Pietro isn't going to be here for at least another fifteen minutes. When I see him, I'll wave. In the meantime"—I looked over at Stormy—"you may want to walk Broadstreet Annie around a little, keep her relaxed."

"Come on darling," said Bernadette. "Come on sweet

thing." She clicked her tongue several times and the horse began to walk away from us along the inside perimeter of the dark brown fence.

The top of the reflector stand slipped into a socket on the crossbar and I tightened the screw down. "Stormy, stand here a second." I pointed at the ground about where I thought Pietro would be. We couldn't move too far in either direction or we'd lose the sunlight. It was getting low and live oaks shadowed most of the corral. Stormy stepped gingerly around Lake Horse Piss, which was receding nicely into the loose earth. The reflector bounced the light and filled in the shadows on his face. "I'll probably have you hold that one," I said, nodding at the second reflector on the ground. "We'll have to move them around once he gets here. You know him at all?"

"Ian played with him twice last year. Westchester and PGA." Stormy was talking about the tournaments at Westchester Country Club outside New York City and the PGA Championship at Valhalla Country Club in Louisville, Kentucky. Players and caddies refer to golf tournaments by the course or, if it's a major, the name of the tournament. Westchester and Colonial. The PGA and the Open. If it's played on a bunch of courses, it's the town or the celebrity, like Vegas or the Hope, except for the old Crosby, which is just Pebble now. Sponsors' names are never used. They come and go like congressional investigations. Sometimes a player puts a tournament on his schedule because of a sponsor obligation but usually it's nothing more complicated than figuring out where he thinks he can keep his high fade or his screaming low hook in play in front thousands of people who have no clue how nervous he really is. Players come back to courses they think suit their games, figuring they'll play better. Go out twenty-five weeks, finish in the top five twice, toss in another top ten, and you've made as much as a Major League shortstop who hits .238. Of course, get lucky and win one or two and you get a license to become delusional and start thinking you're the player of the year instead of Tiger Woods. Except for Colonial, of course, which is the one tournament of the year everyone plays, if they're invited, because of the drop-dead gorgeous women with the shipped-in-fresh-from-California tits.

"He's cold, man. C-O-L-D. Cold," Stormy said of Pietro. "Plays to the crowd like Chi Chi, though. You heard he fired Donnie right after the Masters, didn't you?"

"Who, his caddie? You've got to be shitting me. He wins the Masters and fires his caddie?"

"In the parking lot at the National."

"Get out."

"Donnie was supposed to be waiting for him, after all the interviews and shit. When Pietro comes out of the clubhouse, he's not there. Gone to piss out the beers he had while he was waitin'. Most expensive leak of his whole damn life."

"That was *it*?"

"Pretty much. They'd had a couple of problems here and there but everyone who's ever worked for Pietro had some issues, you know what I mean? All I know is I heard Donnie had to walk to a gas station on Washington Road and call a cab."

"Who's got the bag now?" I asked.

"Jingles."

"Zinger's ex?"

"The same."

"He's still out here?" I figured Jingles had to be at least a thousand years old.

"Where else's he gonna go?"

Jingles, whose real name was A.J. Wisemann, had come by his nickname honestly, if breaking and entering can be considered honest. One year at the Ryder Cup, the main topic of conversation on the American side preceding the matches was the gamesmanship of Cesar Vargas. He was always jingling the change in his pocket at the most inconvenient times. While the players were at the opening ceremonies, Jingles relied on a pair of pinking shears and a bit of criminal knowledge he'd accumulated in his youth to break into Vargas's room in the Belfry and cut all the front pockets out of his pants. In the end, it didn't do much good because Vargas just developed a raspy throat that required constant clearing whenever his opponent was getting set to play.

I took my Pentax out of the case, opened the back, and put in a roll of 120 mm Astia. It was a 100 ASA film that put some life in the flesh tones without rendering the subject the color of a pomegranate. I attached the 50–100 mm zoom lens to the front. I loaded my two 35 mm Canon bodies with the same type of film and put a 35–70 zoom on one camera and a 70–210 zoom on the other. That would give me all the options I needed, even in a quick shoot. If Stormy's take on Pietro was right, I wasn't expecting much cooperation.

A gray Cadillac Escalade pulled up behind the Lumina. Francisco Pietro, dressed in his polo shirt and riding slacks, and Peter Hammett got out. The agent's face was stern, all set to be the bad cop. Pietro tossed away a cigarette. I climbed over the fence, walked up to the Italian, and introduced myself. His handshake was surprisingly delicate and soft. He looked a little odd in his riding uniform, slightly diminished even, since he was wearing Fila tennis shoes instead of tall riding boots. I thought of a hockey player in stocking feet.

"We've got five minutes," Hammett stated dutifully.

I opened the back door of the Lumina and pulled out the helmet and mallet. Pietro seemed bored and uninterested. We walked toward the fence and when we got there Pietro climbed over it with the practiced grace of a horseman. I passed the equipment to Stormy and got over the fence myself, looking a lot clumsier in the process.

"We'll do the picture over there, beside the horse." I waved to Bernadette and she turned Broadstreet Annie and began moving into position. Using Stormy as a stand-in, I trained the reflectors, both the one on the stand and the one I wanted Stormy to eventually hold. I showed him the angle he needed to kick in the light. Stormy passed the helmet and mallet to Pietro and took his spot crouched low in the dirt.

"Watch where you step," I said to Pietro, pointing out the dark circle where Broadstreet Annie had relieved herself. He looked at me as if I'd told him the sun was going to rise. The fact that horses piss was not news to him.

"This is not a proper polo pony," Pietro said as he cradled the helmet under his arm and got in close to Broadstreet Annie. "This horse has no thoroughbred in it."

"It was the best I could do." Where the hell did he think I was going to find a champion polo pony on Hilton Head Island? This wasn't exactly Argentina. And, besides, who the hell was ever going to know the difference? "You won't see much of the horse in the shot."

"Enough to know it's not a proper polo pony," he said stubbornly. Then he sighed deeply as if my ignorance was an affront to Western civilization. Great, I thought, he doesn't give a damn that he's wearing gym shoes but he's pissed about the goddamn horse. I could just imagine trying to explain this to Justin Pound. Peter Hammett looked down at his watch. This is going great, just great, I thought.

I told Pietro to take the reins of the horse from Bernadette, who moved away but was still standing in the background of the picture, watching.

"Bernadette," I said, waving her off.

"Oh, sorry," she said, jogging off quickly.

My movement made the horse back up and swing its rear end to the side, shoving Pietro and his gym shoes in the dirt where Broadstreet Annie had emptied her impressive bladder. "Bagascia," he said, pushing back against the horse.

Pietro was holding the horse's reins with one hand; in the other he held the mallet and trapped the helmet between his arm and his side. He whispered something into the horse's ear and Broadstreet Annie seemed to perk up. I quickly adjusted the freestanding reflector and repositioned Stormy. Pietro's thin, handsome smile formed on his face the way arena lighting grows from dim to full as it warms up. It was show time. I ran through the roll in the Pentax in a matter of seconds, moving slightly in one direction and then in another. I did the same thing with the first 35 mm, the one with the 35–70 zoom on it, except I was making the angles more severe, more dramatic. Then I finished with half a roll of tight face shots using the 70–210 mm lens. In all, the shoot took less than seven minutes.

"That it?" Hammett asked, when I was almost through.

"Almost," I said as I moved and shot at the same time. I wanted to end the session myself, not have it be ended by the agent. After the tight face shots, I slung the camera over my shoulder, walked over to Pietro and stuck out my hand. "Francisco, thank you very much. I really appreciate your time. Congratulations on the Masters and good luck this week." He never looked at me, just down at his shoes.

"It's all?" he asked.

"That's it. Finished," I said. I knew I had plenty for the one picture Justin Pound was going to use. The backup stuff I'd get tomorrow on the golf course. "Thanks," I said to Hammett, who seemed relieved.

"I'll leave the shirt and pants with Juli tomorrow morning in the press room," Hammett said.

"Perfect."

Pietro patted the side of Broadstreet Annie's neck and muttered "buon giorno" in her ear. I collected the polo gear and Stormy and I tore down the reflectors, then loaded the equipment in the Lumina. I could hear the Italian spitting vulgarities at Hammett from inside his Cadillac as he wiped off his shoes with a golf towel and they began to drive away.

9

I drove through an ATM and got $100 for Stormy, dropped him off at the Red Roof Inn, and continued on to the Palmetto Inn Oceanfront Resort. If you believed the brochures at the front desk you'd think you were checking into the Breakers in Palm Beach or the Ritz-Carlton at Kapalua. I took my duffel and my laptop up to a fourth-floor room. The windows were so old and scratched by blowing sand it was almost impossible to see through them. The air conditioner rattled like it was farm machinery.

The cell phone was all dotted up so I dialed Justin Pound's number at the magazine to let him know everything had gone well with Pietro. At least it was done. I was delighted when I got his voice mail instead of the man himself.

"Pound. Leave a message."

Beep.

"Justin, it's Nick Oliver. I just finished with Pietro. It went fine. I'll follow him tomorrow in the pro-am. Then I'll ship film. I'll put the Jeremy Howe shots in the same envelope." I pushed End. I knew it would be no problem getting the film out. Pietro was first off on No. 10.

I remembered a little sandwich shop in the nearby shopping plaza that had decent gyros and the coldest beer on the island. There was a high-dollar restaurant in the shopping center, too. It specialized in Cajun-seasoned alligator. Juli and I had eaten there years ago. I was still hoping I could talk her into dinner so I decided to save the good spot.

I walked around the traffic circle and crossed the street into the plaza. The Pita Sparta was about halfway down the colorful line of bathing suit and kite shops. I looked back across Marsh Street at an old, musty 1950s-style motel comprising a dozen or so dingy cinderblock cabins. It was called the Monarch of the Sea and would have been built back in the early days, when Hilton Head was just a beach. Now, the oceanfront property the motel was on had to be worth $20 million if it was worth a nickel. Before long a developer would buy it, raze it, and put up just another three-story condominium project with a gate and an old, fat security guard who sat up all night reading *Soldier of Fortune* magazine.

One of the cabins was encircled with yellow crime scene tape and there were two police cars parked outside along with a copper-colored van. A skinny woman wearing surgical gloves and a blue shower cap put several brown paper bags in the back of the van, leaving the doors open. She ducked back under the tape and disappeared into the cabin. I went into Pita Sparta and found a table near the window so I could watch what was happening across the street.

A waitress ran a damp rag across the top of the table and put down a laminated menu. She was in her thirties and didn't have a wedding ring but she was wearing a real gold Rolex and her hair was perfectly frosted. Her figure was flawless. When she turned away you could just barely see the tops of the wings of a blue Harley Davidson tattoo peeking above the waistline of her blue jeans. On the flip side, her navel had a small silver stud through it.

"What can I get for you?" she asked.

"Bud Light," I said. "What's going on over there?"

"It's awful," she said. "A woman was murdered. Rick Hightower found her." She left and came back with the beer, propped one hand against her hip, and settled in to talk. "He's one of the county marshals. Comes in for lunch almost every day. Eats a Greek salad. Dressing on the side. He really takes care of himself, you know what I mean?" The way she looked at me, it was clear she'd decided I didn't.

I nodded. I was going to order a gyro but didn't quite get the words out fast enough.

"That sort of thing just doesn't happen around here. Maybe a cocaine bust every once in a while. Like every place, I guess. And that's exactly what I said to Rick," she said. "He said there hadn't been a killing on the island since about this time last year. And they were the only ones he'd ever heard of and he's lived here like, forever. Since ninety-one or something. It was eerie, you know? You must be thirsty."

"Yeah," I said, putting the bottle down. I figured I might as well drink while she talked. "There have been murders here about this time two years in a row? During the golf tournament?"

"Is the golf tournament this week?" she asked. "No wonder we're so busy. Duh. What can I get you?"

"How about a gyro?" I said.

"Another beer?"

"Why not?"

As I ate I kept watching the woman with the rubber gloves across the street carrying paper bags, going back and forth under the tape. No way, I thought. There's no way this could have anything to do with the killing in Augusta. It was too ridiculous to contemplate.

When I got back to my hotel room I set up my G4 laptop on the desk and hooked it up to the phone line. Photographers and graphic art designers are about the only people left in the world who use Macs. I did a quick search and found the local access number in Hilton Head, selected it, and hooked up on AOL.

The first thing I did was check my e-mail. There wasn't much there. Couple of things from U.S. Airways and American Airlines offering discounts from places you aren't in to places you don't want to go. Several solicitations from Orbitz. An order confirmation from L.L. Bean for two pairs of khaki shorts. One message from Stewart McKie, a bug-eyed Scottish immigrant who was a contributing writer at *Current*. He said he was writing the lead story on Francisco Pietro and he'd be arriving on Hilton Head Wednesday afternoon. He was hoping we could get together. I remembered McKie from a couple of previous assignments. He was an OK guy if you were on his good side. A weasel if you weren't. I decided I'd try to avoid him as much as possible. I didn't seem to be on anybody's good side lately.

The next thing I did was go to the Web site for the *Augusta Dispatch*. I looked through the Monday and Tuesday issues for stories about the dead woman at the King & Queen Inn. The piece in the Monday paper identified the victim as Randi Willows, twenty-five, from Tampa, Florida. It said she had been a waitress at the Tamiami Trail Hooters for three years. Whenever there's a special event like the Kentucky Derby, the Indy 500, or the Masters, in a town that has a Hooters, the story explained, the management imports an all-star team composed of the best off-the-rack hooters in all the known universe. The picture of Randi accompanying the story was from the cover of the Hooters calendar two years before. She was gorgeous. No denying that. I thought about what Richard McPhee told me about poor Randi and it made me shiver. The story went on to say she was an aspiring fashion model who loved water sports and had two previous convictions for misdemeanor possession of marijuana. She was survived by a three-year-old son who was staying with his grandmother in a trailer park in Kissimmee, Florida, at the time of the murder. The article said the police had no suspects and there was no known motive in the killing. It didn't say whether or not she had been sexually molested but it purposely left open the possibility.

The follow-up in the Tuesday morning edition was shorter yet. It didn't add any information and quoted the Augusta chief of police, who said he didn't believe robbery was the motive and they still didn't have any suspects. He said there was no reason to believe the murder was in any way connected with the Masters other than it was the golf tournament that brought the poor girl to town in the first place. The large two-column picture accompanying the story showed Randi wearing tight orange jogging shorts, a white tank top, and an utterly superfluous push-up bra. Nothing like sex and death to sell a few newspapers—or magazines, for that matter.

I walked down the hallway and bought a Diet Coke and a bag of Planters mixed nuts. When I came back to the room I closed the door and fixed the security lock, a U-shaped bar that dropped over a ball attached to the door's molding. I went back to the main Web site for the *Augusta Dispatch* and clicked on the button for Archives.

I got a prompt saying it would cost $29. I entered my credit card number and address and, after the computer processed them, another screen appeared. I didn't know the exact date I needed so I guessed. A window came up for Tuesday of the previous year's Masters. I scrolled through the headlines but found nothing of interest. Golf, golf, and more golf. I went to Wednesday. Nothing. Tiger Woods this, Phil Mickelson that. Thursday. Changes in Augusta National. Blah. Blah. Blah. Friday. The wind blows at Augusta, scores soar. And so on. If you were in the field and had a pulse, you were featured in the *Augusta Dispatch* at some point.

Then I saw it in the Saturday edition. The headline said, "Woman Found Dead in Super 8 Motel."

The story was only a few inches, barely a hundred words. A woman who had been working for minimum wage, selling memorabilia out of a tent across Washington Road from Augusta National, was found strangled to death in her room at the Super 8 off Bobby Jones Expressway. Robbery was the implied motive. She was 22 years old, from Columbia, a senior art history major at the University of South Carolina. I looked in the Sunday paper and the murder rated only a two-paragraph update. There was no further information. The big news was Tiger Woods had won the Masters.

"I'll be damned," I said. I went back to the main search page and put in dates around the time of the Masters from two years before. There it was, on the Monday after the tournament. A woman found dead in the Best Western on Washington Road. The story suggested the death was the result of a domestic disturbance. The cause of death was strangulation. Her live-in boyfriend was being held for questioning. In the following day's edition I found a story that said the police had released the boyfriend, who had been attending a telemarketing conference in Colorado Springs at the time of the murder. There were witnesses to his alibi, including the deceased's sister, who had accompanied him there. I'd found three murders in Augusta the week of the Masters Tournament in three successive years. I couldn't believe what I was thinking.

I went back in the paper's archives one more year but found nothing. I searched back still another year. More nothing. Was it really possible they could be related? The very notion seemed unthinkable. And how could it have anything to do with the killing on Hilton Head? That would mean someone was following the tour, coming to town with the circus, picking an innocent victim, maybe at random, and killing her—the victims all were women—and then moving on. Each an isolated, unsolved crime.

Augusta wasn't a very big city, maybe 65,000 people. Killings were rare but they happened. But little Hilton Head? Designer Island? Murders two years in a row during its golf tournament seemed much too much of a coincidence. The more I thought about it the more possible it became. Everything a twisted mind could ever want or need would be right in front of him—it had to be a him, right?—served up on a platter.

I found the main Web site for the *Savannah Morning Traveler* and again went through the drill of giving my credit card number so I could search the archives. I went back two years, found the tournament dates, and scrolled through the news pages. There was nothing. No murders reported on Hilton Head.

So that was it. Five murders in the same two weeks over a three-year span. I looked at my watch. It was nearly midnight. Pietro was going off the back nine at 7:30 A.M. I shut the laptop down, stripped, and got into bed, but not before I made certain to double check the security lock.

At 7:00 A.M. I walked into the press tent with my 600 mm lens on my shoulder and my Nike running shoes squishy from the heavy dew on the thick-bladed St. Augustine grass. Juli wasn't there yet. A boy in a white shirt, black slacks, and a black clip-on bow tie was setting up coffee and bite-sized bagels on a table off to the side. The ancient volunteers were wearing cheap red windbreakers against the chill of the morning air conditioning.

I organized my equipment at the foot of the locker, setting out what I wanted to use. I'd do all my shooting with 35 mm cameras and most of it with my 600 mm lens. I wanted tight, could-have-been-taken anywhere action shots. Pound wanted all new stuff. To him, the entire take from the Masters was radioactive. I'd also carry the 70–210 mm on another body just in case I needed something wider. I was only looking for one good shot and I knew I was most likely to get it with the 600. Still, if something happened and I needed a shorter lens, I didn't want to have to pass up the picture just because I was too lazy to carry an extra camera and lens. I filled my fanny pack with film, zipped it shut, and buckled it around my waist. I planned on walking the first nine holes with Pietro. After that the sun would be too high and his face too shadowy under the brim of his Alfa Romeo cap to do much of anything worthwhile.

I spritzed myself down with a mixture of Avon Skin So Soft and water to keep the no-see-ums off me. They're among the world's most vicious bugs. Their bite releases a chemical into the skin and it feels like a piranha has taken a chunk out of you. After I washed the greasy spray off my hands, I sat down with a cup of coffee and the Savannah paper. I skipped over the sports section and pored through the news looking for something about the murder on Hilton Head Island. I found it on page six under the headline "Death Revisited."

The story identified the victim as a thirty-seven-year-old mother of two named Donna Pedrosian. She was a real estate agent who lived with her daughters, Willow and Jasmine, in the posh Wellington Plantation. She had been divorced from her husband, a Dr. Stanley Pedrosian, for three and one-half years. Her ex was a plastic surgeon at Hilton Head Mercy Hospital. I was guessing he performed liposuction on women who took tennis lessons and drove Mercedes 500 series cars while their husbands cheated on them with girls in butt-floss bikinis. The newspaper story said Mrs. Pedrosian was last seen leaving the Harbour Town Golf Links in a silver car with the golf tournament's logo on the side. Her body was discovered at the Monarch of the Sea Motel and the police were withholding the details surrounding the death. Mrs. Pedrosian had been a volunteer working on the transportation committee, shuttling players' families, sponsors, officials and a few of the more important members of the media—that meant TV—to and from the Harbour Town golf course or anywhere else they wanted to go on the island, for that matter. She had finished for the evening and was not believed to be transporting a passenger when she was last seen. Her ex-husband was cooperating fully and was not, at this time, a suspect.

At the bottom of the story it mentioned the previous year's murder, also during the week of The Heritage presented by Bubba Gump Shrimp. I looked at the byline. The story was written by a woman named Salem Washington. I didn't know whether she would be at the tournament that afternoon or not but I made a mental note to ask Juli if she knew her.

I tossed my plastic coffee cup in the garbage, folded the newspaper, and put it in my locker. I rested the padded monopod attached to the heavy 600 mm lens on my shoulder and headed out of the press tent to catch Pietro as the morning sun began heating up the air.

Some players are more easily distracted by photographers than others. Not many of the really great ones have rabbit ears but there have been a few. The best players I ever knew who were easily disturbed were Sam Snead, Gary Player, Greg Norman, and Tiger Woods. On the other side of the coin, when I'd photographed Jack Nicklaus or Tom Watson in competition, you could just about fire off a cannon next to their heads and they wouldn't hear it. Another player who could see a photographer a mile away was Jack Saxon. A photographer friend of mine from the *Miami Herald* told me about a run-in he once had with Saxon at Doral.

In the morning my friend was taking pictures at the federal courthouse in downtown Miami where John Gotti was being arraigned. In the afternoon he was working the golf tournament, sitting on a tee box taking pictures of all the players as they came through—"driving heads," we call them—just so the paper would have the shots available in its files. Saxon's caddie came up on the tee before anyone else and saw my friend sitting there. He walked over and said, "You better put that camera away. He's really pissed off." My buddy looked up at him and said, "Man, John Gotti gave me the finger this morning. What makes you think I'm worried about Jack Saxon?"

Pietro had a reputation for being every bit as edgy as Saxon, Norman, or Woods. You might think at 7:30 A.M. on a Wednesday morning in a pro-am, he wouldn't care. You would be wrong. Players who hated photographers were constitutionally unable to differentiate between the times when it mattered and the times it didn't. They were like a dog who had tangled with a porcupine. The dog remembers it hates porcupines but it can't remember why. Some players loathe photographers because of an unpleasant incident, usually accidental but nonetheless real. They can't stand the sweaty smell of photographers. Can't stand the way they move around. Can't stand the way they travel in packs like vultures or the way they stand out if they're by themselves. Added to that was the fact I was pretty sure Pietro would remember I was the guy who ruined his Filas.

I was the only photographer on the tenth hole with Pietro and his pro-am partners, a pairing that was no doubt upgraded the day after he won the Masters. In his foursome were the chairman and CEO of Bubba Gump Shrimp, a graduate of Oxford and the Harvard Business School who was a member of The Country Club in Brookline and played to a three handicap; the CFO of Bubba Gump Shrimp, also a

Harvard grad and a member at Seminole; the governor of
South Carolina, Wendell Stutts IV; and Judge Jackson
Vanmeter, who made a billion dollars in the poker machine
business before divesting himself and then helping the Supreme Court of South Carolina declare the business illegal,
a move that had the secondary effect of transforming all the
formerly legal gambling joints located on South Carolina's
state borders into strip joints almost overnight.

I hated shooting pro-ams. It's one thing to let the best
players in the world send golf balls whizzing past your head.
It's quite another when four fat guys with Great Big Berthas
do it. Neither one of the officers of Bubba Gump Shrimp
managed to dribble a ball all the way to the fairway. The
governor hooked his tee shot across the pond on the left
side of the hole and rattled it off the weatherproofed deck of
a nearby condo. Judge Vanmeter came within about seven
inches of decapitating me with a blistering drive that never
got much more than six feet off the ground. Through the
first five holes of the back nine, I tried to hide the best I could,
lining up the shots I needed of Pietro and then quickly ducking behind trees while his playing partners sent balls rock-
eting through the woods like 20-gauge buckshot.

On the 15th, one of the great par- 5 holes the tour plays
all year, I got a nice, clean, front-lit photo of Pietro laying up
with a mid-iron into the dogleg short of the green. The useful thing about the picture was that the woods in the background were so thick it would go almost completely black,
making Pietro stand out in his tan slacks and light green
shirt. After that I knew I had what I needed but I hung around
for the last few holes. Work is work. In photography a big
part of the job is showing up, sticking with it, and, on pro-
am days at least, staying alive. On the 16th the latter proved
problematic since there weren't any trees to hide behind
down the right side of the hole, the only side you could walk

on. The boys from Bubba Gump took out three spectators with two shots. By then the governor had his swing grooved and went out of bounds left again while the judge hit the side of a baby carriage, sending the startled mother into a hysterical fit.

The 17th, a par 3, didn't yield a picture but I got two more chances on the 18th, which was playing not only toward the red-striped Harbour Town lighthouse but into the morning sun as well. I got a wide photo of Pietro on the distant tee and another one after his approach shot barely cleared the marsh and landed in the bunker in front of the green. It was a good explosion shot, lots of sand and nothing whatsoever in the background except Calibogue Sound. He hit the shot about three feet from the hole but I could tell through the lens he was irate. The nine holes had taken nearly three hours. He'd been fawning all over his four amateur partners but when he looked up at them after his bunker shot I could see the pure loathing in his eyes. He despised each one of them for wasting his time. It was as if he'd suddenly hit the emotional wall. As for myself, I was ready to pack it in, too. With what I had, I knew Pound would be as happy as Pound ever got and maybe I'd be back in his good graces for a while. But I doubted it.

Since it was Wednesday, deadlines weren't going to be a problem. I could FedEx the film to *Current*. When I got to the press tent, Juli was there. She was eating a bagel and staring down at her laptop. There was a speck of cream cheese at the corner of her mouth. Her hair was combed back and stayed in place obediently.

"Good morning," I said.

"How long have you been standing there?"

"I just came in. Finished off the Italian. He's playing with the big kahunas from Bubba Gump Shrimp. Is that a contradiction?"

Juli smiled. She looked content, the way I remembered her from Charleston and Savannah. I had to admit, being away from me seemed to suit her. "Hammett left the polo outfit," she said, pointing at a small package on the desk.

"I've got to FedEx my stuff. Pietro's polo shit, too," I said. "Do you know if there's an office on the island?"

"There's one out by the airport."

"Do you mind?" I said. I carefully put the tip of my index finger near her mouth and scooped away the dot of cream cheese. "You're like a little old lady."

She blushed and ran her paper napkin over the same spot. "Thanks."

"I'm done for the day," I said, "but there's no point in leaving now. After I ship film I'll call the office. Probably go for a run on the beach. How about dinner tonight?"

"I don't know," she said.

"Come on, it's just dinner. It's Wednesday, you don't have to work late. How about we take the ferry over to Daufuskie Island? I hear there's a little hole in the wall over there that serves great catfish and has a beer-drinking pig."

I could still make her smile.

"How about Alligator Alley instead? It's closer," she said.

"Fair enough. Want me to pick you up?"

"I'll meet you there. Around seven."

"Deal." I was pleased. So much so that I almost forgot to ask her about the writer from Savannah. "Do you know a local reporter named Salem Washington?"

She looked at her media list. "Name's not on the list. Why?"

"I read a story she did," I said and changed the subject. "You haven't seen Stewart McKie, have you? He's the writer from *Current* who's working on the Pietro story."

"Not yet."

"When he comes in, tell him I left to ship film and he just missed me."

"Ducking him?"

"Not exactly. I just don't want to get trapped into dinner. I want to have you to myself."

I cleaned out the few things I left in my photo locker, some film boxes and an extra body. When I looked up I saw Juli talking with Colt Reeves, who had come in the press tent like a policeman on break to get a donut and a cup of coffee. He was wearing one of those Greg Norman–style straw cowboy hats, except his had the tour logo on the front instead of a shark insignia. He wore blue tinted Revo sunglasses that he never removed, inside or out. He twisted the volume control on the top of his handheld radio with his thumb and forefinger, back and forth, back and forth. Juli seemed uncomfortable talking to him. Was she uncomfortable because they were no longer seeing one another or because she knew I was standing there watching? Poor Bridgett Reeves, I thought, married to a slimeball like that. And poor me, too.

A part of me wanted to hit the son of a bitch over the head with my monopod but I knew I had to put that aside. Juli and I were divorced and I guess that meant the window of opportunity for a little simple assault must have closed. But love isn't always civilized and it's certainly never rational. Of course, maybe I just didn't have the guts for it. That thought depressed me, too. Maybe I wasn't trying to be reasonable and adult, maybe I was just a coward. Maybe it was as simple as that.

I busied myself at the locker until Reeves left. He never saw me. On the way out I stopped in front of Juli's desk. I stood in front of her with my equipment draped from my shoulders like great weights. I wanted to say something but I was drawing a blank. "See you tonight," I finally said. My voice sounded unfamiliar to me, anxious.

She looked up. It was the way she used to look at me when I came home from a road trip infected with some Asian bug I picked up in a plane full of kids on their way to Disney World.

"You OK?" she asked.

"Yeah," I lied. "Seven o'clock."

When I walked out of the press tent I saw Reeves digging around in the trunk of a red BMW in the players' parking lot beside the clubhouse. The car didn't have the customary Bubba Gump Shrimp decal on the side. Instead it had South Carolina tags and a Fighting Gamecocks sticker on the rear window. I knew he lived in Columbia. After the Masters, he must have flown home to see poor Bridgett and then driven his own car down. Reeves had been an All-American golfer at the University of South Carolina, where he won the NCAA individual championship. He tried to play the tour out of college but his game was wild and uncontrolled. After a couple of years knocking around the Asian circuit, he came back to the States and attempted to requalify. He might have made it, too, except the week before school started, he badly dislocated his left shoulder in a fight in a topless club, pretty much a career-ending injury for a golfer in those days. Reeves eventually found a job as a rules official, watching kids not quite half his age with—he was convinced—not quite half his talent making enormous fortunes. And he secretly despised every one of them.

After Reeves drove off in his golf cart to dawdle away the rest of the afternoon checking the markings on Harbour Town's ground under repair, I walked casually up to his BMW. In the distance I heard the small crowd by the 18th erupt, probably reacting to some orthodontist holing out from the greenside bunker for a 12. There were people milling about the clubhouse but no one was paying attention to me. I opened the car door. Reeves hadn't even bothered to lock it. He must have thought it would be safe in the players' lot. They were serving jumbo teriyaki shrimp in the press dining tent. I thought a couple down each defroster vent might do the trick. I put my cameras down. A malicious prank was just what the doctor ordered. I deserved at least that small measure of revenge, I told myself. He deserved a helluva lot worse. But something was getting in the way. I couldn't bring myself to do it. So, I slammed the car door shut hard.

"Shit," I said. As I gathered up my stuff, I saw Juli watching me from across the lot and my shame returned.

10

The bar at Alligator Alley was curved and trendy, the kind of place where men wear black T-shirts under sport coats and the women have rings on their index fingers and their middle toes. It had metal stools and a surface of burnished steel. Tiny halogen lights with royal blue shades about the size of the palm of your hand were suspended from the ceiling by dangling curlicue wires. Bottles of backlit wine reclined at just the right temperature behind a glass door. The mini-bottles of liquor mandated by the state of South Carolina were hidden underneath the bar, too pedestrian for display. The bartender was wearing a blue micro-fiber shirt with an open collar. His waxed mustache was carefully twisted with a thumb and forefinger.

"Another beer?" he asked me, almost out of boredom. The dinner crowd on Hilton Head was only beginning to trickle in.

I looked at my watch and passed my hand over my balding head. It was already 7:20. I'd had two beers at the beach bar at the Palmetto Inn before I walked over, washing the taste of the misadventure at Reeves's car out of my mouth and watching the waves roll up on the smooth beach. I didn't want to drink too much before Juli got there but I was getting pissed she was late. It was Wednesday. Pro-am day.

What the hell could be keeping her? I knew it wasn't really about her. My nerves weren't so good.

"Sure," I said to him. The bartender used the bottle opener fixed to the back of the bar to pop off the cap, saving the skin on his hands. He put a fresh napkin underneath the new bottle. He knew I didn't need a glass.

The bottle felt cold. I took a long sip. At least it had been a productive afternoon. After I took care of my FedEx chores, I went for a run on the beach near the hotel. The tide was out and the sand was firm. It was hot, too hot to go very far, but it felt good because I had so much to run off. The Masters. Pound. Teriyaki shrimp. Reeves. The dead women. The Italian. Juli. I had five miles in before I realized it. Back in the room I showered, lowering the water temperature in increments to lower my body temperature. In the end it was refreshing and cold. With just a towel around my waist, I booted up the laptop.

As I nursed the beer, I tried to put some of the pieces together. Searching Augusta and Hilton Head was easy compared to the other cities I tried. From here the tour was moving on to major metropolitan centers. New Orleans, Dallas, D.C., and New York. Even if I found comparable homicides in those places the same week as past tournaments, it could be nothing more than coincidence. I did find a similar death in the New Orleans *Times-Picayune* two years ago, a young white woman, twenty-six, found in a hotel in the French Quarter, raped and strangled. But there was nothing from last year.

I shook my head when I thought about searching the *New York Times* database. It was a labyrinthine undertaking. The Web site must have been designed by the same techno-wizard who wrote the software for *Dungeons and Dragons*. The *Dallas Morning News* wasn't much better. I did manage to find a couple of possibles there and three in New York, all during last year's tournaments. Each city also had killings during the same week the year before that. And before that. And before that. And that didn't even include the suburbs. None of the newspaper accounts gave much detail and the ones that did didn't seem to fit the pattern. I checked Columbus, Ohio, and drew a blank. Every paper was charging about the same for access to their archives. I was hoping I'd be able to charge some of it back to *Current* somehow. Hide it in the expenses somewhere. Red Cap tips was always a good dodge.

I took another sip of beer and set the bottle back on the cocktail napkin with the little abstract alligator logo in the corner. I was keeping an eye on the door. Still no Juli. Maybe these murders weren't related after all, I thought. Maybe I was making too much out of a couple of sad, unfortunate deaths. Maybe they were just women who were in the wrong place at the wrong time. It happens. There had to be some way to link the killings in Augusta and Hilton Head. If I found that, then I might be able to sift through the information in the larger cities. A dead body just wasn't enough. There had to be some common thread. Then, I'd know if it was a story or a coincidence.

"I'm sorry I'm late," said Juli. I looked up from my thoughts.

"It's OK," I said, standing and pulling out a stool for her. "You look great." And she did, too. She'd just gotten out of the shower. Her wet hair was swept back with a thick-toothed comb and her gray blue eyes seemed even brighter than usual against her tan face. She was wearing a pastel print shift made out of a soft fabric that rested on her curves like mist on a lake.

"Let's get a table," she said.

When we were seated I ordered a bottle of Grgich Hills

chardonnay. Juli said she had heard I was doing a lot of work for *Current* again.

"I thought you hated Pound," she said.

"It's a living," I replied.

We ordered tomato and mozzarella salads. She asked for the seared mahi mahi. I got the Cajun alligator tail for old times and I wondered if she noticed.

"Are you seeing anyone?" she asked me.

"No," I replied. "You?" Sitting across the table from Juli, I felt like nothing could ever really be right again. I wanted to ask her if it was too late for us but I couldn't because I already knew it was. It was like being in the front row at a hockey game when a player gets checked into the boards in front of you and they're all smashed up against the glass and you feel like you're right there, part of it, but you're not. You're walled off.

She hesitated. "No, not really," she said. Well, that's better than an out and out "yes," I thought. I didn't know if I could take *that* at the moment.

"What were you doing at Colt's car?" she asked, looking down at her hands.

"Nothing," I said but I knew she wouldn't believe me. "I was going to play a practical joke on him. I decided not to."

"Good," she said as the waiter put down the salads. "I guess my boy is growing up." She smiled and took a sip of wine.

I thought about telling Juli my suspicions about the deaths of the women in Augusta and Hilton Head. I wondered if anyone else had put it together. Jesus, what would it do to the tour if word got out that a stalker was following it from town to town? And what if it wasn't just anyone, what if it was someone connected to the tour? A caddie. An official. A newspaper guy. Someone with the Golf Channel.

The weatherman. A trainer. One of the guys who puts up and takes down the scoreboards. A swing coach. A psychologist. God, even a player. It could be anyone.

"Juli," I said, resting my forearms on the table, "is there a psychiatrist who travels with the tour?"

"There are dozens of them out here all the time," she said.

"No, I don't mean those guys who tell everyone to stay in the present and not get ahead of themselves and trust their ability," I said. "I mean a real clinical psychiatrist. Someone who would recognize a serious mental disorder."

"I don't think so. It's not a bad idea, though. There are some players who could use one," she joked. The waiter came by, took the chardonnay out of the ice bucket, wiped it down with a white cloth and refilled both glasses, holding the bottle with his thumb in the indentation at the bottom, twisting the pouring motion off at the end with a flourish.

"Is everything all right?" he asked, looking at another table altogether.

"Fine," I said. When the waiter had gone away, I leaned across the table toward Juli. She lost her smile when she realized I was being serious. "Can you think of anyone out here who has been behaving strangely over the last year or two?"

"Besides me?"

"You know what I mean."

"Out here?" she sighed. "You know what it's like. The clown car is full."

She was right. Obsessive behavior was the norm.

"Anybody violent? Any rumors of guys beating their wives or girlfriends, getting in fights in bars or with other players, anything like that? Can you think of anyone everyone is scared of?"

Juli switched into her press officer persona. I had officially become someone she was wary of. Was I looking for
dirt for some hatchet job, maybe a player who had been ar-
rested for slapping around his wife? "Even if I knew someone like that, I couldn't discuss it. Wouldn't discuss it," she
said.

I wondered if Juli already knew something. I was going
to tell her about the dead girl in the motel room in Augusta,
the women who died during the Masters the two previous
years, and the two women who had been murdered on
Hilton Head Island when in walked Colt Reeves with Stewart
McKie, the writer from *Current* I thought I'd managed to
avoid. "Damn," I said.

The maitre d' seated them across the room but Juli and
I could see them and they could see us. McKie walked over
to our table. Reeves remained at theirs, looked the other way,
and ordered a drink.

"Oliver," said McKie. "I was looking for you."

"Stewart," I stood up. "This is Juli Oliver. She's the press
officer for the tour."

"We've already met," he said, shaking her hand and
holding on to it a little too long. "Colt tells me you and Nick
were married once," he continued slowly, as if he wasn't
quite sure where he was going just yet. "I never knew that
about you, Nick. You never should have let her go."

I didn't answer.

"Isn't it nice that you're so amicable. So many divorced
couples aren't. I, for one, would greatly prefer to see my ex-
wives, of which there are several, pilloried in the town
square. And, bless their hearts, they all feel exactly the same
about me," said McKie, who was enjoying the sound of his
voice. "Sit down, Nick. Sit. Divorce can be such an unpleasant and nasty thing, can't it? Mistakes were made, am I right?

Why dwell on them? Move on. That's what I say. Move on. You two certainly have." I watched him put his hand gently on Juli's shoulder. "Any children?"

"No," I said.

"No harm done then. Am I right?" He transferred his hand to my shoulder like some uncle you grow up despising and I wanted to move out from underneath it.

McKie was a pudgy man with a comb-over and a face ravaged by acne and yet he considered himself irresistible to women. It was good that his taste was none too particular. He didn't believe in setting his sights too high when it came to the opposite sex. He preferred to pick off what he called the "low-flying ducks."

"How was Pietro?" I tried to change the subject. I knew he had had a one-on-one with the Italian that afternoon.

"Couldn't have gone better," he said. "What a grand fellow. He's going to be a huge star in America. With my help, of course." He smiled, only half-joking.

The last thing I wanted was for McKie and Reeves to pull up a couple of chairs so I decided to beat him to the idea. "I'd ask you to join us," I said, "but we're almost finished."

"Nonsense," said McKie, peering down at Juli, "we'd be delighted to join you. You can have a glass of port while we order. Let *Current* pick this up, shall we? Old times are overrated. A little new blood is just what you two need." He motioned to Reeves, who seemed every bit as enchanted with the idea as I was. He muttered to himself the entire way across the restaurant.

"Colt," said McKie, "I know you know Juli Oliver but I'm guessing you've never met her ex-husband, Nick, who is an outstanding photographer for *Current* magazine." He motioned to me. I didn't put out my hand and neither did

Reeves. We nodded. I wanted to jump over the table after him.

"I remember Nick," said Reeves. "He hasn't been around much lately, though."

It was difficult to tell exactly how much McKie knew but he clearly knew enough to engage in his favorite pastime—stirring the pot. It was what he did to entertain himself. He considered it high sport. Just the right impertinent question here, the perfect embarrassing fact there. Nothing amused him more than other people's discomfort, particularly after he'd had a few drinks. Nothing like lancing a boil to make the evening a raging success.

"Well," said McKie, pulling up a chair for himself and another one for Reeves. "Isn't it lucky we ran into one another?"

"Actually," I said, "I really have to be going. I still have to pack my equipment. I'm leaving early in the morning."

"Come on, Nick. Just one glass of port. How about a nice twenty-year-old tawny? I need to ask you some questions for the piece." McKie ordered the drinks and turned to Reeves, "What do you make of Pietro?"

"I think he's one of the really good guys on the tour. A real asset," said Reeves, taking the toothpick out of his glass and sliding it between his clenched teeth, scraping the olives off into his mouth.

"Very good with the media," chimed in Juli, who was looking at the door.

"Yeah," I said, "he's such a great humanitarian he fired his caddie in the parking lot of Augusta National the night he won the Masters."

"Really?" McKie dropped his chin and looked at me over his reading glasses and his embossed menu.

"It's just something I heard," I said. "You'll have to check with the caddie. He might not talk but I'm sure someone will know what happened. It's not the kind of thing that gets forgotten—or that the other caddies are reluctant to talk about, if you don't use their names, that is."

The waiter delivered two glasses of port and a second round for Reeves and McKie.

"Could I have some coffee?" I asked. "Regular."

"Perhaps I ought to have a cup, too," said McKie. "With a bit of cream. Foam the runway, you know."

"Tea for me," said Juli.

"So," continued McKie, "there's a dark side to the great Pietro. I thought he played the media game a bit too smoothly. Good stuff." He looked down at the menu.

"That's what I heard." I took a sip from the small glass. The wine was strong and sweet. The table fell silent. Juli gave me a worried look. Everything seemed on the verge of spinning out of control. A strange and unpleasant feeling swept over me, one that I knew I would regret but couldn't help. I tried to focus on something else but it kept coming back.

"Colt, how's the family? How's your wife, Bridgett, isn't it?" I asked. McKie watched me with rapt interest, no doubt hoping for the worst.

"Fine," he said. His eyes were brown and they seemed to darken as he spoke. "Thanks for asking."

The words just kept spilling out of my mouth. I couldn't have stopped if I had wanted to. "You are still married, aren't you?"

Reeves kind of grunted. Something about 15 years.

"Juli," I said, "have you ever met Mrs. Reeves?"

She kicked me under the table. "No."

"Why did you do that?" I looked at her, then back at

Reeves. "I was just curious. I think everyone ought to know everyone else. Perhaps we could all have dinner together one night. Wouldn't that be civilized?"

Juli took a deep breath. McKie's eyes were going around the table from one person to the next like he was following a reckless round of betting in a high-stakes game of poker.

"I just thought you might have spoken with her," I said to Juli. "I mean, she had my phone number. I just assumed she must have yours, too."

"That was a long time ago, Nick." She sighed. I wondered, was she talking about me or him?

"Funny," I said, "it seems like just yesterday to me. What about you, Colt? Does it seem like yesterday to you? Or maybe it seems like today."

Reeves was staring coldly at me. He didn't know what was going to happen. Neither did I.

"Thank you very much for the dinner," said Juli, tossing her napkin down as she got up from the table.

"Wait," I said, "I'll walk you to your car."

She turned on me. "Good idea."

"Here." I passed my check to McKie, who seemed extremely pleased with himself. "Dinner's on you."

Juli almost ran out of the restaurant. When she got to her car she whirled on me like I was a mugger. "What the hell was that all about?"

"What do you think?" I said.

"Nick, we're divorced. Get it through your head."

"And that's the asshole who caused it," I said.

Then she said, "No. You're the asshole who caused it." She unlocked her courtesy car, slammed the door with the Bubba Gump Shrimp insignia on it, started the engine, threw the car into reverse, and flew out of the parking lot like a NASCAR driver.

"Dammit," I said out loud to myself. I felt like such a fool.

I knew I shouldn't have gone back inside the restaurant. Colt looked surprised when he saw me come through the door. All I could see was his crooked grin. My hands were trembling when I sat back down at the table. I took a deep breath and picked up my glass of port. There was a roaring sound in my ears.

"To Pietro," I said and raised my glass.

"Hear, hear," said McKie. "Is Juli all right, then?"

"Yes," I said. "Just a little upset."

"It's a bit awkward," said Reeves, speaking to McKie but looking at me. "Nick hasn't shown his face for, what, two years? Or is it three? Then all of a sudden, there he is. Shows up out of nowhere." He snapped his fingers. "Isn't that so, Nick?"

"I'm working," I said. "It's my job." I could feel the blood rush to my face.

"You see, Stewart, some men hang around when they're not wanted," Reeves said. "Not Nick. He just took off. Disappeared like a cat. He went away." His voice was echoing in my head. *Isn't that so, Nick?*

Even McKie thought it might be going too far. "Shall we order?" he asked.

"You can't blame him, for coming back, I mean. She is a lovely piece," Reeves said.

I was on my feet.

"For God sakes, sit down, Oliver," McKie said. "Don't be an ass."

"Yes, Nick, by all means, don't be an ass," Reeves said. "Don't you see that you're *still* not wanted here? Why don't you just go away?"

I tossed what was left of my glass of port in Reeves's face. He didn't move. He wiped himself off with his napkin and laughed out loud. "How very Bette Davis of you," he said.

I don't remember lunging at him. I know I tried to wrap both my hands around his neck but he grabbed my left wrist with his right hand. His grip was strong. Much stronger than I expected. Reeves went over backward but on the way to the ground we twisted over in the air and I was the one who hit the floor first. The back of my head made a hollow thud against the tile. I remember thinking on the way down I should have paid more attention to how much bigger he was than me but it was a little late for all that now. He landed on top of me and all the air in my lungs left my body with a deep wheeze. I couldn't breathe but I tried to jam the palm of my right hand up against his chin. I wanted to snap his head back but I could barely move under his weight.

Other people's voices were mere background noise. From out of nowhere, the bartender was trying to pull Reeves off me. I could see McKie off to the side holding his drink and watching with wide eyes. Then the left side of my face exploded. I saw the second blow coming and turned my head. I didn't understand why neither punch seemed to hurt.

"Don't bother," I heard Reeves say.

I was looking up at him though I didn't really have the sensation of lying on the ground. It was more like being on a raft in a pool. How he got up there, I couldn't say. I looked at the exposed duct work in the ceiling. It was painted a deep purple. Very geometric chic, I thought. The bartender had one hand on Reeves's upper arm. "I'm leaving. I'm leaving," Reeves said, jerking his arm free of the man's grip.

"Hey, Colt," I said, leaning up on my elbow. I spit at him with all the force I could muster. A glob of blood landed near his feet.

"You son of a bitch." He was going to kick me in the head but the bartender rode him off toward the door.

"Asshole," I said and dropped back down. For a split second, I couldn't resist smiling. At least I'd finally done something.

The next thing I knew, I was sitting in the back of a police car.

11

I was holding a bag of ice against my left cheekbone. I had a throbbing headache that arrived fast once the adrenaline in my blood wore off. Through the window of the cruiser I could see Stewart McKie standing outside the door of the restaurant talking to a policeman, the bartender with the carefully waxed mustache, and the maitre d', who turned out to be the manager of Alligator Alley. I suddenly felt very old, way too old to act so stupidly. When they were finished McKie walked back inside with his arm around the manager's shoulder. The policeman came back to the cruiser and got in the driver's seat.

"Your friend there says the man y'all assaulted used to date your ex-wife," he said into the rearview mirror, pulling his seat belt across his chest.

"You taking me to jail?" My voice sounded muffled. "And he's not my friend."

"Your friend," he emphasized, "has offered to pay any damages and buy a round of drinks for everyone in the restaurant. The manager says he won't press charges. Don't guess there's any reason to go to jail, as long as y'all goin' to behave yourself."

"I think I've had enough," I said.

"I'd have to agree with that," the policeman said. "Where you staying?"

"Right over there," I motioned toward the Palmetto Inn with my head, making it throb even more.

"Here's what we're gonna do," he said. "I'm going to take you over to your hotel and see you get in your room. If I find you out anywhere else tonight, or if I hear of you causing a problem any place at all, I'm gonna throw your ass in the Beaufort county jail and you'll be sportin' an orange jumpsuit and picking up beer cans on the side of the road for thirty days. OK?"

"OK."

"Then," he said, putting his car in gear, "you're going to wake up tomorrow morning and you're going to pack up your things and leave Hilton Head. We understand one another?"

"Yes, sir, officer."

The policeman picked up his car radio. He told the dispatcher he was going to the Palmetto Inn and they'd be able to reach him on his remote. He turned the car, pulled out of the parking lot, whipped around the traffic circle, and stopped in front of the hotel. He opened the rear door for me, helped me out of the back seat, and locked the cruiser.

As I was getting out of the car I noticed his nameplate said "Hightower." He was the officer who discovered the dead woman in the room at the Monarch of the Sea.

"Thanks," I said as we walked past the lobby doors toward the elevators in the adjacent building. I wondered if anyone could see he was holding on to my elbow, escorting me. It was embarrassing but I didn't dare say anything. Besides, I needed the help. "I'm not much of a fighter," I offered.

"I pretty much figured that one out already," he said. "Sometimes in these domestic situations, folks act kinda strange. I see it a lot. Take my word for it, fighting doesn't solve anything. Just makes things worse."

"Yeah," I said. I knew I felt worse. We were both looking at the numbers above the two elevator doors, waiting for one of them to come down. Officer Hightower was a little shorter than I was but thick through the chest and strong. "Weren't you the guy who found the body over in that motel, the woman who was killed?"

"I was," he said, still looking at the numbers.

"I read in the paper there was a murder here about a year ago, too," I said.

"There was."

"Similar?"

"Seem to be."

"So, you think it was the same person, I mean, who killed both women?"

"I do. And I'll bet you we find GHB this time, too," he said. The elevator door on the left opened and two laughing college girls and their boyfriends fell silent when they noticed the policeman standing in front of them next to a man with blood all over his shirt. They watched as Officer Hightower steered me into the elevator.

"GHB, what's that?" I asked as the doors shut.

"Georgia Home Boy. It's a date rape drug. We found it in the victim a year ago and I bet we'll find it in that poor woman we found yesterday, too," he said. "Ladies need to be careful who they accept a drink from. Which floor?"

"Four." He punched the number. "Is that what killed her, the drug?"

"No. Drugged, then murdered. Probably never knew what happened." The elevator stopped at the fourth floor. "What room?" he asked.

"I'm in four seventeen," I said. "How was she killed?"

"That's not really any of your concern. The SBI's got the case now," he said. The officer steered me down the hallway. "Let me have your key." He put out his hand. "Anyone else in there?" I shook my head no.

I reached into my pocket and took out the old-fashioned plastic Ving key with holes punched in one end. He slid it into the lock and pushed the handle, then maneuvered me into the room. I took an immediate right into the bathroom and turned on the light. It seemed bright. Brighter than I could stand. The exhaust fan came on automatically when the light was switched on and I remember thinking it was terribly loud. I took the ice bag away from my face and looked in the mirror. My left eye was nearly swollen shut and my cheekbone was so bruised it looked black. The rest of that side of my face was red from the ice. There was a trickle of blood behind my ear where the second blow landed and Reeves's NCAA championship ring cut my scalp. My nose had bled all over my shirt.

"Do you think my cheek's broken?" I asked the officer. "Maybe I need to go to the hospital."

He stepped in the bathroom. "Let me see," he said as he looked at my face. "Naw. It ain't nothing. I see worse most Saturday nights."

I got three extra-strength aspirins out of my kit bag and swallowed them as the officer walked around the room, poking in cases and looking in drawers, satisfying himself that I wasn't armed and dangerous.

"Photographer, huh? Here for the golf tournament?"

"Sort of," I said. My words were thick. "I was doing an assignment with one of the players, you know, the guy who just won the Masters."

"Don't know much about golf. Never cared for it," he said.

"Yeah, sometimes I don't care much for it, either. Look, Officer, I appreciate your bringing me back to the hotel and believe me, there's nothing I'd like better than to get out of here first thing tomorrow morning but I left some things in my locker in the press room," I lied. "I've got to pick the stuff up. Then, I'll leave. Promise."

The officer looked at me. He glanced around the room one more time, took another look at my face, and decided I wasn't much of a threat to anyone or anything. "OK, but I want you off the island by noon. You hear?"

"Noon," I repeated.

"What kind of car you drivin'?"

"It's a rental car. There are the keys." I pointed to the desk, where there was a lamp, a phone, my laptop, a small pile of coins, and a set of car keys with the telltale plastic Avis tag. Hightower picked the keys up, turned them over, and took a notebook and pen out of his breast pocket. He wrote down the Georgia tag number for the Lumina. "Noon."

"Thanks, Officer," I said, closing the door behind him.

I sat down heavily on the bed and took the Hilton Head phone book out of the desk drawer. It listed a number for the *Savannah Morning Traveler*. I picked up the phone, punched in the number, and asked for Salem Washington.

"Newsroom."

"Ms. Washington?" I asked. My jaw didn't feel like it was working too well. The lights in the room seemed to get alternately brighter and dimmer.

"Yes. What can I do for you?"

"My name is Stewart McKie," I said, trying to affect a bit of a Scottish lilt despite the facial swelling. "I'm a writer for *Current* magazine."

"What can I do for you?" she repeated, more interested now. I could tell she was impressed to be talking to someone from a publication with a national reputation, even if it wasn't always a good one. And a foreigner, to boot.

"I'm in Hilton Head on assignment and I read a story you wrote about a murder here on the island," I continued.

"Yes?"

"I thought *Current* might be interested," I said. "Not for me to write, you understand. I thought it might be something you could contribute on a freelance basis."

"Really?" She was hooked. I could tell Salem Washington was a woman with ambition.

"That angle of yours about two unsolved murders a year apart on a quiet little island," I said, "it sounds like something the magazine might be very interested in. Of course, I don't know what they pay . . ." I also knew money wouldn't matter to Salem Washington. This would be a career move, a step on the road out of Savannah and all the way to New York City. She would pay *Current* out of her own pocket if she had to.

"You think so?"

"I feel certain of it," I said. "It's just that I need a few more specifics so I can recommend it to my editor."

"Sure," she said. "What do you want to know?" Poor thing.

I didn't want to mention the GHB because I didn't know if she knew about that. I wanted the information to flow strictly in one direction, from her to me.

"When your story ran the other day," I said, "it was too late in the news cycle to have much detail. Understand, I'm not faulting you. I was just wondering what you've heard from the police since then. Have they established any connection between the two deaths? Your piece certainly suggested there was." I was disgusted at how feeble my Scottish accent was. It sounded more like Ocala than Edinburgh.

"There are some similarities," she said. "The police and the SBI seem convinced they're related."

"They called in the SBI?" I acted like this was new information even though calling the State Bureau of Investigation would be routine.

"Immediately."

"What about the cause of death?" I asked.

"That's where all the bells are going off." She lowered her voice as if someone might overhear her. "They asked me to keep it out of the paper."

"Really?"

"Both strangled with bare hands. Well, gloved hands, they think."

"Anything else?"

"Not that I know of. Seemed like a firm connection to me, though."

Of course, she was right. But Washington probably didn't know about the GHB or, if she did, she wasn't sharing that tidbit. The victims would have been in a drugged stupor. Killing them would have been easy. Between the drug and the cause of death, related crimes ought to be pretty easy to identify, even in a big city like New Orleans. I wondered about the woman in Augusta, though. According to Richard McPhee her death had been a violent one. Maybe none of this was related after all. Maybe it was just a depressing set of circumstances on a resort island in South Carolina. The killer could be strictly local.

"Let me call my editor tomorrow morning," I said. "Is there a number where you can be reached during the day?"

She gave me a cell phone number. I wrote it down just in case I needed to speak with her again. "Thanks, Salem, and good luck with this," I said. "I think it could be a good move for you. Oh, and here's my cell phone." I gave her Stewart McKie's number. Fuck him, I thought.

"Thanks," she said and hung up.

I knew I had to apologize to Juli in the morning. I couldn't live with myself if I didn't. After that, I was going to drive back to Augusta and find Richard McPhee. I looked around the room. The lamps and cases, the chairs and desk all seemed to fade into black shapes, transform into shadows. I laid back, swung my legs up on the bed and passed dead out.

12

God.
      I looked at the clock on the night stand. It said 9:36 in big red numerals.

I tried to get up but my head felt as heavy as a medicine ball and I flopped back down. When I finally got upright, the pounding started again. Each heartbeat was a shot from a carpenter's nail gun. Looking out of my left eye was like staring through a straw.

I shed pieces of my clothes on the way to the bathroom, showered, shaved, and took basic inventory of the damage. Teeth, check. Jaw, OK, I guess. I had a lump behind my left ear topped by a small crusted-over cut. My cheekbone was bruised but, as Officer Hightower had noted, not broken. My left eye wasn't quite shut but blood had drained into the white of the eyeball, making it look much worse than it actually was. The discoloration around the eye had begun in earnest. The nose had only received a glancing blow, but enough to make it bleed like an open faucet.

With a towel wrapped around my waist, I sat down at my laptop and logged on to the Internet and did a Google search for GHB. I found the *Idiot's Recipe for Making GHB*. The chemical formula was $C_4H_8O_3$. I scribbled down the ingredients and the equipment required to make it. When I was finished, I packed up my cases and called the desk for a bellman. He arrived with a luggage cart and a curious look on his face when he saw me. I gave him $5, let him load everything up, and told him I'd meet him out front as soon as I checked out. My wing-shaped Oakleys didn't do much to cover the damage but at least they hid the crimson eyeball.

The woman working behind the front desk had a nameplate that said "Gladiola" and that she was from Sun Valley, Idaho. It seemed everybody on Hilton Head was supposedly from someplace nicer than where they were. They were never from McClellanville or Aiken. I had to tip the sunglasses up to check the bill. Her eyes got wide when she saw what I looked like.

"That's fine," I said, pushing the bill back across the counter. "Sun Valley's a beautiful place. What ever possessed you to leave it?"

"Huh?" she said, staring vacantly at my face. "Keep it on the credit card?"

"Please."

I let the bellman put everything into the Lumina. I took my M lot sticker out of the glove box, hung it back on the rearview mirror, and headed out to Harbour Town. It was going to be awkward, seeing Juli, but I knew I couldn't leave until I did.

The press tent was almost empty when I got there because the lunch spread had been laid out next door and most of the media had descended on it like turkey buzzards. One of the few still in the main tent was Jeremy Howe, the TV commentator with the bushy sideburns. He was loitering around the table of tournament clippings and tour releases, picking up stories he planned to read before his afternoon rehearsal. Howe was still a player at heart. He preferred to walk up and down the practice tee and ask golfers what they were working on and how their families were doing but he had grown to like a few of the writers, too. He enjoyed giving information and getting it back. Value for value.

"Good God in heaven, Oliver," he said when he saw me. "What on earth happened to you?"

"Wrong place at the wrong time," I said. I could tell he'd already heard about it from someone but he wanted my version.

"Apparently," he said, shaking his head and picking up a clipping from the Charleston *Post and Courier,* a newspaper so old Thomas Jefferson was president when it started publishing. "How did it go with Pietro yesterday?"

"He showed up," I said.

"Did he have anything to say about the Masters?" he asked.

"Not really," I replied. "I think he was more concerned about the gym shoes he ruined when he stepped in a puddle of horse piss."

"That so?" said Howe, who laughed. "I'll have to ask him about it. Clumsy beasts, those Italians."

I knew the little tidbit would be a good icebreaker for him the next time he saw Pietro. It would be a chance to share a joke at my expense. It could be the opening in a conversation that might just lead to something he could use on the air. Frank Deford said interviewing was like flirting on a high school date and he wasn't far wrong.

"I better be going," I said.

"Where to next?" Howe asked.

"I'm not sure," I said, though I knew it was back to Augusta.

"Perhaps I'll see you in Pinehurst, at the U.S. Open," he offered, careful to distinguish it from "The" Open—theirs.

"Perhaps," I said. I walked across the tent to Juli's desk.

"Oh, Nick," she said, looking up at me, keeping her

voice low. "What the hell is wrong with you?" Obviously, she'd heard all about it, too. It was probably the talk of the tour staff.

"I just wanted to tell you I was sorry," I said.

"Why did you go back in there?"

"I don't know," I said. "It was dumb."

"You get that awful look in your eyes," she said, as if she was picking up a conversation we'd left hanging years before. "This is where I work. If you can't behave when you're out here I'll make sure you're not allowed back. I'll have the tour call Justin Pound. I mean it."

There wasn't much I could say. She was right. I had screwed up, again. "I'm sorry. I just . . . I don't know. It won't happen again. I promise."

"Not that it's any of your business," she said, "but there isn't anything between Colt and me." She paused. "Or you and me."

The phone in front of her rang. She picked it up and talked for a minute. It was the office in Ponte Vedra. Someone wanted something with Pietro and she was going to have to try to arrange it. She knew he wouldn't want to co-operate. As far as Pietro was concerned, he'd feel like he'd done his media duty for the week. Now he was preparing to play golf.

"Let me see your eye," she said after she hung up.

I took off the glasses. She made a low whistling sound. I put the glasses back on.

"It looks worse than it is," I said.

"Head hurt?"

"Like a bastard."

"Well," she said, folding her hands in front of her, "what have we learned from this experience?"

"Give me a break, will you? I feel like enough of an asshole as it is."

"I think you should apologize to Colt," she said.

"Fuck him," I said. "I was wrong. Let's leave it at that. Besides, what the hell am I going to apologize to him for, scraping his knuckles on my face?"

"I guess you're right."

"*Current* wants me to do something next week in New Orleans," I lied. "Would you leave a parking pass and credentials at Will Call for me?" I needed the credentials in case the trail led to New Orleans after my return trip to Augusta. I thought about the woman who had been killed in the King & Queen Inn.

"I guess I can do that."

We were quiet a moment, like we'd run out of all the little things to say. "I miss you," I said.

"You better get going," said Juli. "I heard you got run out of town, too."

"Yeah, like in *High Noon*. Guess there aren't many secrets out here, are there?"

"No." Her look softened. "I don't guess there are."

"I better go," I said.

"I miss you, too, Nick," she said it quickly, looking around. "I'm sorry about . . . everything. I know you probably don't believe it but I am. I wish it had all turned out differently."

"Wouldn't it be great if it had?" I said.

"Too bad we can't unring the bell." She got up, walked around from behind her desk, and gave me a little kiss underneath my bruised cheekbone.

"Easy," I said.

"See you in Nawlins."

"Bourbon Street, here I come." I knew that if I didn't show up, it wouldn't matter. I'd just call and say the magazine had canceled.

When I walked out of the press center I saw Stormy standing by the bag drop waiting for Ian Person. He was smoking a cigarette and had a white towel slung over his left shoulder.

"Man, what the hell happened to you?" He tossed the cigarette on the sidewalk and snuffed it out with the toe of his dirty cross trainers.

"Accident," I said.

"Accident's name wouldn't be Colt Reeves, would it?"

"News travels fast, huh?"

"We're better than the Internet, man. You oughta be careful. He's a bad guy," Stormy said. "Should have asked me first. I'd a told you not to fuck with that bastard. He's as flinty as they come."

"It was my own fault," I said.

"Whatever," laughed Stormy.

"Who you playing with today?" I asked him.

"Shit." He took another Winston out of the pack and lit it. "We got David Duval, which is OK. That ain't too bad. But then we got Justus Litchard, too. That guy scares the living shit outta me."

"How come?"

"You don't know Justus Litchard?" He leaned back and looked hard at me in mock disbelief.

"Never heard of him. He any good?"

"Naw. Can't hit it out of his own shadow. And the son of a bitch cheats. He cheats and there's nothin' in the world you can do about it," Stormy said.

"Don't sign his scorecard," I said.

Stormy snorted at me. "Right. The last guy told Justus Litchard he wouldn't sign his card, Litchard broke the man's hand with a ball peen hammer."

"Oh, come on."

"The next week. Tell me I'm not serious. Guy grew up

in Philly. The word is, he's connected. They say he used to do favors for his friends, you know what I mean. Sometimes still does."

"What kind of favors?"

"He'd talk to people, understand?"

"Collections?"

"You ever see the guy? He's six feet four inches and there ain't enough fat on him to grease a pan of brownies."

"And he cheats?"

"Yeah. There are just too many stories from too many guys. Lost balls that get found all of a sudden. Bad lies in the rough that turn out to be real decent by the time he plays the shot," Stormy said.

"What about the rules officials? Can't they do anything?"

"Shit. They don't want to see nothin'. *Nobody* wants to see nothin'. They're as scared of him as everybody else. Besides, he's still gonna shoot seveny-three–seventy-five most weeks and miss the cut. No harm, no foul. Bottom line is, it's not worth getting hurt over. When you draw Justus Litchard you keep your mouth shut, that's what you do. He says he gets a drop, he gets a drop. He says he found his ball, he found his ball. He says it's a ball mark and not a spike mark, it's a ball mark and not a spike mark. That's just the way it's going to be that day. There he is now."

Justus Litchard pulled his courtesy car into the players' lot and parked in a spot marked for the defending champions because it was the closest one to the clubhouse. It didn't matter to him that he'd never even made the cut there. Stormy said Litchard enjoyed doing it just to see if they would say anything to him. No one ever did. His neck and shoulders were broad and thick and his golf shirt was stretched across his chest like the yellow jersey in the Tour de France. His waist was small and his legs were long. As he walked toward the locker room he said, "It's us today, Stormy." Litchard liked the caddies. He liked to think they came up hard, like he did. And he really did love his golf. He loved being on tour. He thought it gave him some class.

"Yes, sir," Stormy replied.

"Ian inside?" Litchard only looked at Stormy. I was standing there but I might as well have been invisible.

"No, sir. He's not here yet. His back's so bad right now he just spends a few minutes in the trailer getting worked on, then hit two, three balls and go play," Stormy said. "Can't do much more than that."

"That's too bad," said Litchard, turning for the clubhouse and the locker room entrance. "He should have taken better care of himself."

"Yes, sir," Stormy said.

When he was gone, Stormy nervously scanned the parking lot looking for Person. "Lord, that man scares the life out of me."

13

The house was on Buccaneer Lane off Forest Beach Road. It was a simple house, one story raised a few feet off the ground to protect it from storm surges off the Atlantic. The shake shingles had gone gray from the salt air. There was a small porch with pots of yellow marigolds and small fuchsia petunias and a bleached Pawleys Island hammock hanging in the corner, more for decoration than use. It was mostly too hot to lounge around outside.

He didn't like it, coming to a house, even one hidden way back in the live oaks and the palmettos, even if she did live alone, which is what she said. He didn't like it but he couldn't help himself. This was something different and because it was different it was just a little bit dangerous and because it was a little bit dangerous he could feel the jazz in his blood again. He'd started to lose that feeling but now it was back. This was the first time he'd ever done it this way. The other times they came to him. It happened in a place of his choosing. He was careful, not reckless like this. Not stupid like the ones on the TV news or in books or on those idiotic videotaped cop shows. No one even knew he existed. Imagine. They only saw his best work, never him. Now he was taking chances and it made his palms sweat. What if someone saw him? What if someone saw his car? No one did, he told himself. No one saw anything. The car is behind the house. Parked behind three huge plumes of pampas grass.

There was a photo in a cheap frame on the dresser in her bedroom. She was younger then. There was another woman in the picture with her. A sister maybe. It was something in the eyes. She was on the bed. There was a piece of duct tape across her mouth, though he probably didn't need it. Sometimes they cried out. The one in Augusta had been too loud. He put the tape over her mouth so no one would hear her but then she drowned in her own vomit before he could do it. He was still surprised how angry it made him. Hadn't he done everything the way he was supposed to? And then she did that. Disgusting. The thought of it still made him mad. Made him feel cheated. He'd gotten even with that bitch, though.

This one was different. She talked a lot while they were sitting in the car until the salty liquid in her Smirnoff Ice began to take her legs away and roll her eyes back in her head. She wanted to take him back to her house. It had been her idea. The thought of it made him laugh now. It was always their idea. No one is home, she said. I live alone, she said. My boyfriend travels, she said. He's in Atlanta. It will be fine.

It was after midnight when he pulled in the driveway. He parked the car, put on his rubber gloves, and entered the house through the back door, scouting it out before he carried her in. No dogs. Just a tabby cat that ran out when he went in. His eyes adjusted quickly to the darkness. There were dishes in the kitchen sink and an open box of Wheat Thins on the counter.

There were candles in the living room. He lit two, carried one with him, and left one behind. There was a guest room with a teddy bear on the bed. Maybe the sister in the photograph had a kid. Visit her auntie. Go to the beach. There

were scented candles in the bedroom and around the bath-
tub. He lit one in each place. He needed to piss but knew it
would be too risky so he breathed deeply and held it in.

Lean and fit, she had been easy to lift. He banged her
head getting her out of the car but it didn't matter. A little
cut. He needed to remember to clean the spot off the car.
Inside, he put her on the bed, took her sandals off. He unbuttoned and unzipped her blue jeans, then rolled her over
to pull them down. He saw her thong bikinis. Pink. She had
a Harley Davidson tattoo just above the crack in her ass. He
pulled the underwear off and rolled her back over.

She was wearing a red tank top and he pulled it up and
over her head. Her breasts were real. They fell slightly off to
each side. She had a silver stud in her navel. When she
moaned quietly, he put the duct tape across her mouth just
in case. Then he rolled a condom on.

He climbed on the bed on top of her and began to slide
up and down along her body. She barely moved. Her eyes
opened for a moment but they didn't see anything. He
moved again, slowly, up and down. Up and down. He was
excited now. And then it happened like it always did.

He jumped off the bed, walked to the window. He could
see his own reflection, lit dimly by the candle. This was the
hardest part. He didn't always like doing this. Who could
understand how difficult it was? Did he really have to? No.
No, he didn't. He could say no. Sometimes he was the stronger one. Sometimes. He walked out of the bedroom into the
kitchen. He was still wearing his gloves. Inside his pants,
the rubber stayed in place. He looked in a couple of cabinets
until he found some glasses. There was a water and ice dis-
penser in the door of the refrigerator. He got some ice cubes
and filled the glass with cold water but he didn't dare sip it.
He put the glass against his forehead and rolled it back and
forth.

The refrigerator was decorated with pictures of the woman he'd seen in the photo in the bedroom. There was a little girl with her in some of the shots. No man. There was a magnet that said "Give the Dangerous Bitch Her Chocolate" and another one that had an orange-and-purple Clemson University tiger paw insignia. Underneath that one was a telephone bill, due yesterday. There were tiny magnetic words scattered at random all over the refrigerator. He began to rearrange them.

lust will cry to sleep beneath the
hot honey goddess ugly beauty dream of death
moon time moan symphony heave sweet breath
whisper pant & fiddle in the sordid worship scream
help me

He put the glass in the sink and walked back into the bedroom. It would be easy. Then he could go. The other one told him to get on with it.

"Do it now. Don't waste any more time, you fool."

"I won't," he said out loud.

"Now. DO IT NOW. It is the only way."

"Not this time," he said and covered his ears. "She won't remember anything. Why do I have to hurt her?"

"Stop being gutless. Do it. You've done it before. There's nothing to it. They never struggle. Just enough pressure to cut off the blood to the brain, that's all it takes. You don't even have to squeeze hard. She'll thank you."

"I won't," he said. "It's too dangerous. Someone might have seen me."

The voice laughed.

"No one saw anything you fool. There was nothing to see. It's just another one of your excuses. An excuse to get out of doing what you know you have to do to be great. Don't be a coward. Have some balls. Do this one for me."

He left the room, walked through the kitchen and into the living room. He paced quickly back and forth. There was a *TV Guide* on the coffee table next to the remote. He could feel the rubber starting to slip.

"Not tonight." He walked back into the bedroom. "Not tonight." The woman hadn't moved. Carefully with his gloved fingers, he peeled back the duct tape from her mouth. There was a tiny bit of spittle in the corner of her lips. He pulled back the bedspread and sheets and rolled her underneath them and pulled them up to her chin. He leaned over her and gave her a kiss on the forehead, then he patted her frosted hair. He thought she was very pretty.

"I'll be back," he said. "Next year."

He blew out the candles and left.

PART TWO

June

14

The U.S. Open paralyzed Pinehurst.

The old village with its white clapboard buildings and tidy flower beds was clogged with people and cars going exactly nowhere. The town's four hotels were overflowing. Bellmen were scurrying about in front of the Carolina, with its old creaky floors and copper-colored roofs. Cars were backed up in the semicircular brick drive at the Holly Inn, blocking traffic in the middle of the village. At the Manor, people were parking illegally in front of the firehouse while they checked in. The other hotel in the little town, the Pine Crest, was once owned by Donald Ross, the architect of the No. 2 Course the USGA had come to play. It was the only hotel not under the umbrella of CPA Resorts, the corporation that liked to lay claim to everything inside the city limits. Even though it was independent, the Pine Crest was joined to CPA Resorts at the hip, accepting overflows and kicking back 20 percent of the rack rate in return for a few tee times in the high seasons of fall and spring.

Stewart McKie and *Current*'s top crime reporter, Gavin Webster, were staying in the Carolina with most of the players, at least the ones who hadn't rented their own houses for the week. Not wanting to spend that kind of money on mere photographers, the magazine had booked Jenny Killets and me into the Aberdeen Inn Bed & Breakfast, a little Victorian house with no air conditioning two blocks from the village sundry. The location was great but the heat was bound to be monstrous.

On the way into the village I passed through a checkpoint at the traffic circle on the outskirts of town. I showed the state trooper the green media card the USGA had issued me. He stared at it as if it was printed in Mandarin Chinese and asked to see my driver's license. After he checked the picture on the license against my face, he handed everything back and grunted me on my way.

I parked my standard issue rented Lumina—this time it was white—in one of the three spaces in the gravel drive in front of the Aberdeen Inn. Jenny Killets was already there, sitting sideways in a wicker chair on the porch. She was dangling her thin legs back and forth and curling her stringy blonde hair around the index finger of her right hand. Her face was tan and weathered and had her usual lost-in-space look.

"Do you realize this dump doesn't have air-conditioning?" she yelled at me before I was even out of the car.

"That's what I heard," I said as I crawled out and hung my laptop case from my shoulder. I opened the trunk and pulled out my clothes duffel and the small carry-on bag I used for film. I figured I'd leave everything else there for the time being.

"June in North Carolina and no air-conditioning. What's up with that? And the woman who runs this place is one cold bitch," said Jenny when I got up on the porch. "It's hotter than hell in my room. All I did was ask for a couple of fans and she gets this attitude, like, there's already a fan in the room, which there is, but it's one of those ceiling things that doesn't do diddly squat and I thought at least she could get me one of those big industrial window fans or something. So anyway . . ."

I tried to put the brakes on her. "Where do you check in?" I asked.

"There's a desk right inside the door. It's got a little bell on it. You hit the bell and she comes in like an hour and a half and then it takes like another hour to fill out this little three-by-five index card she keeps for godonlyknows what reason. You think they've heard of computers in North Carolina? Forget about it. What's your phone number? What's your address? What's your social security number? I told her to stuff it. She couldn't have my social security number. I give it to her, anyone could get it. Hasn't she ever heard of identity theft? That's all it takes. They can get a driver's license and credit cards and everything. Go on-line and get a goddamn mortgage."

Inside the door I put my duffel down next to the desk and tapped the bell with my index finger. Killets's ogre turned out to be a slender five-foot-two inch lady in a red print dress with gray hair neatly coiled on top of her head. Her face was smooth and she looked at least ten years younger than she must have actually been.

"May I help you?" she said.

"Yes. I have a reservation for the week," I said, producing my room confirmation.

"Mr. Oliver? We've been expecting you."

"Yes, ma'am."

"Welcome to Pinehurst. This y'all's first time?" She copied a couple of things off the sheet onto a file card.

"No, ma'am," I said. "I was here in ninety-nine when Payne Stewart won."

"Really? Well, welcome back. What credit card would you prefer to use?"

I handed her my MasterCard. She slid it through the machine and punched in a few numbers. After a couple of seconds she copied down the authorization number on the index card.

"You'll be in room seven. That's the Loblolly Suite," she said and handed me a key attached to a metal disc about the size of a silver dollar with a big 7 etched into it. "There's a Continental breakfast served every morning from seven o'clock until nine in the sitting room, over there." She pointed with the end of her pen.

"I'll probably be out at the golf," I said.

"Well, bless your heart. Just the same, it'll be there if you want it." She smiled. "There's cheese and crackers and sherry every evening from six thirty to seven thirty. Your room is up one flight of stairs and then to the left. It's got a very nice view of the village and a good breeze that you'll be grateful for."

I thanked her and started up the stairs with Jenny Killets crowding right behind me.

"See what I mean?" whispered Killets.

"What are you talking about?" I said. "She seemed perfectly delightful." I opened the door and dropped my bag on the bed with a bounce. Killets followed right after it. It was a double bed with a canopy and lace trim. The room was done in flowered wallpaper, mostly yellow. There was a little clump of potpourri in a blue Wedgwood dish on the bureau. The windows were open. A breeze was moving the thin white curtains. A ceiling fan was twisting around and wobbling back and forth like someone rubbing their stomach and tapping their head simultaneously.

"She seems nice at first but she's a raving Nazi," continued Killets.

I hadn't seen Killets since the Masters. As far as she was concerned, nothing had changed. The tournament was on like normal. The fact that the world was now looking for a murderer who might be following the golf tour didn't seem to interest her. To Jenny, it was just another week. I was the freelancer, she was the staffer. She was in charge. It was common knowledge Killets had come by her status at the magazine the old-fashioned way. *Current* and twelve other magazines including *Men's Muscle* and *Assets* are owned by Iron Mask Publications, a wholly owned subsidiary of iBytes, Inc. Killets was the live-in mistress of Dudley Sommers, who had moved over from *Current* to become the managing editor of *Amped*, Iron Mask's hot startup that had been kicking *Rolling Stone*'s ass on the newsstands for three years, only losing $12 million a year, which was $7 million less than it was projected to lose. In the magazine business that made it an industry darling and, corporately, Sommers was bulletproof. His girlfriend, Killets, fancied herself a photographer so Sommers arranged for her to work for Justin Pound, who was only too happy to have her since, in a way, it made him bulletproof, too. Pound was careful never to send Killets out on an assignment by herself because—although she would come up with the occasional picture—her work was uneven. The irony was that because Pound couldn't count on her, he only assigned her to big events where there would be several photographers working for *Current* at the same time. In short, all the best assignments. She shot the Super Bowl, the Olympics, even political conventions. In golf, it was the Masters and the U.S. Open, and I was the one who was supposed to cover her back. We all knew what the drill was when Jenny Killets was your partner. She was ambitious but she wasn't all bad, either.

"Have you talked to Justin today?" asked Killets.

"No," I said, opening my duffel and stuffing underwear in a drawer. I hung my shaving kit on the towel rack in the bathroom. Killets was still talking but I had pretty much quit listening. I put the titanium laptop on the desk and plugged it in but decided I'd wait to check e-mail until after Killets was gone.

"I'm supposed to follow Tiger." She looked at me like I was going to object except I couldn't have cared less, particularly with everything else that was going on. Killets would grab whatever assignment she thought would be best. That meant Tiger Woods. In the past, other photographers had complained to Pound about the way Killets sucked up assignments. Once, when one of his "stars" complained, he actually took a job away from her but Jenny just called up Dudley Sommers, who called up Pound and she was back where she wanted to be in forty-five minutes. And I certainly was no "star." Even with all that, I didn't dislike Killets. She had a certain straightforward charm about her. She never hid what she was doing, never did it behind your back. The only way to work with her, though, was to let her do whatever she wanted to do and try to fill in the blanks. She was like a lucky deer bounding through a mine field and never touching anything. You had to follow along and hope like hell you didn't step in the wrong place. I got blown up at the Masters.

"Have you been out to the course?" I asked.

"Yeah. And I tried to get two lockers but they'd only give me one. The media parking is, like, way, way out in the middle of nowhere. We have to take this shuttle from, like, some school for the deaf or something that's like half an hour from the course. I complained but they wouldn't give me anything closer," she said. "The players are right next to the clubhouse, too. I told those fucking USGA assholes I had a lot of heavy stuff to carry but they didn't care."

"Jenny, the golf course is only a five-minute walk from here."

"I know. But I have all those lenses and cameras and

rain gear and shit. An umbrella. I couldn't walk with all that."
Killets always brought three times as much stuff as she actually needed. It was her nature. At every golf tournament
she hired a high school kid to work as her assistant, carrying her equipment and obediently following her around the
golf course, and I'd never yet seen one make it all the way
through the week. She had at least a two-assistant-per-week
habit, sometimes three if she was really spiraling out of control.

"I think I'll walk over," I said.

"Now? It's only Tuesday."

"I'll get checked in. Get a big locker before they're all
gone," I said as I dropped my extra pair of running shoes,
the ones I packed in case of rain, in the closet. Truthfully,
though, I just wanted to see Juli. She was going to be the
tour media rep helping the USGA press room types because
she knew the players better than they did. And she was there
because the commissioner, Jacob Pierce, was going to have
a big press conference on Wednesday to talk about the status of the "situation," as they were referring to it corporately.
I was hoping Juli wasn't still angry with me. Maybe disappointed would be closer to the truth. More and more it
seemed that all I had ever done was disappoint her.

"I'll go, too," said Killets, who was afraid she might miss
something.

"Grab the film, would you?" I nodded at the bag that
held a week's worth of various speeds of film. "I'll get the
600 mm out of the car. That way I won't have to carry everything over tomorrow."

She let out a troubled sigh and picked up the bag. I was
about the only *Current* photographer who worked with
Killets without complaining to Justin Pound. Jenny knew it,
too, so I suppose she thought of me as a friend, in her own
fashion. And, like it or not, she *did* work her ass off, even if a

lot of it was just busy work. So she got her break by screwing a managing editor. A lot of guys had gotten their chance
by fucking somebody over, one way or another. What the
hell difference did it make? Personally, I was just glad to be
working. It was good to be paying my bills again.

"When are you going to finally switch to digital?" she
asked, as if, had I done that, she wouldn't have to carry the
film.

"I know I need to," I said. "I still like film. Stubborn, I
guess. Besides, you can't do a proper portrait with digital.
There's too much depth of field. Everything's in focus."

Killets and I came out of the Aberdeen Inn and I got the
600 mm lens out of the trunk. I screwed in the monopod, set
the crook of the L on my shoulder, and began walking toward the golf course. It was only a few blocks away and the
press room was set up near the clubhouse on the tennis
courts.

At the gate Killets showed the guards her USGA photo
badge and I showed them my gate pass. I'd never seen security like this at a golf tournament, not even after the collapse
of the Twin Towers. There were policemen with dogs and
policemen with Kevlar vests. And no one seemed to have
any idea what they were looking for or guarding against.
The USGA apparently figured that if there was a sufficient
show of force, no one would dare try anything.

The press tent was the size of a field house. They could
have put six tents the size of the one at Hilton Head inside
it. The media was turning out in force to cover the Open
and the murders, a twofer that would move the TV ratings
and sell out the newsstands. The USGA could barely handle
the requests. Not even Tiger Woods at his zenith packed
them in like this. A lot of publications were sending both
sportswriters and news reporters. The ESPNs of the world
were there but so were *Ten Most Wanted, 20/20,* and *60 Min-*

utes. The first two people I saw when I walked into the press tent were Morley fucking Safer and Jeremy Howe.

The check-in lines were alphabetized according to publication and I got in the A–G queue. A short man who was clearly retired military took my credential card and looked at me suspiciously. He dug around in a cardboard box until he found an eight-by-eleven envelope with Nick Oliver and *Current* printed on it. It was stamped with big red letters NEED ID. He dumped the contents out in front of me. One parking sticker—remote lot—which meant it was even more useless than Killets's media lot. One armband that would give me access inside the ropes, a huge improvement over the Masters. One invitation to the USGA party at the Carolina Hotel that night. One combination lock with locker assignment. I'd be in No. 15. 32 right, 14 left, 27 right.

"Is this a large locker?" I asked. The USGA only had a few big enough to accommodate a 600 mm lens. The others were the size of a basketball for the radio guys to store their tape recorders. A small locker would barely hold my film.

"Yes, sir. The large lockers are numbers one through thirty-five," he said. He told me I'd have to sit for a picture to make a photo ID badge. Usually that was done in advance but apparently Pound didn't have a picture of me to submit to the USGA. He showed me where to sit behind a curtain, and the whole process of taking the digital picture and printing it on the photographer's badge only took a minute.

"Thanks," I said as he handed me the badge. "Do you know if Juli Oliver is here yet?"

"I don't believe so. The woman from the tour, right? I think she's coming in tomorrow."

"Good." I wondered if I looked as disappointed as I felt.

The photo lockers were hidden behind the big scoreboard that dominated the front of the tent. Once the championship began, rows and rows of writers and reporters would be seated facing it. The photographers are hidden away behind it.

To the left was a separate tent for interviews and to the right was yet another tent for food. Knots of media people in comfortable old shoes and wrinkled shorts wandered in importantly now and then as the transportation vans from the remote lots unloaded outside. It was mostly the same people who had been at the Masters, with the exception of all the talking heads with the fifty-dollar haircuts on site to do thirty-second spots on the killings. There were a few who did the weekly golf grind but the columnists from the big metropolitan papers and the writers from the national magazines only showed up for the majors and, now, the murders. The European writers were there in force, particularly since Francisco Pietro had a chance to win back-to-back majors, and the Japanese contingent was as big as ever.

With Killets scampering along in my wake, I walked behind the big scoreboard to put my film and the 600 in the locker. I saw David Hailey, the Brit who had gotten Pietro at the Masters, stuffing his gear into a locker down at the far end. After I put my lens away I walked down.

"Hey, laddie," I said. "Over to trounce us again are you?"

He laughed as we shook hands. "Thought I'd give it a go."

"How did you make out with the stuff of Pietro?"

"Smashing. It was the best month I ever had. Everyone on the continent wanted it," he said as he looked Jenny up and down.

"Killets," I said, "you remember David Hailey. *The Sunday Times*. He's the chap who kicked our ass at the Masters. The only one who got Pietro at the fourteenth. Made a bloody fortune." I thought, damn, just talk like an American for God sakes.

Hailey and Killets shook hands. "Pleasure," said Hailey. Killets didn't remember him but she was impressed now.

"Sure," she lied, "I saw you at Augusta."

"When did you get in?" I asked him.

"Yesterday afternoon," he said. "Already got a good night's sleep under the belt. Feel right as rain."

"Where are you staying?" asked Killets.

"I'm at the Pine Crest," he said. "A rowdy crowd there, if I do say so. Don't quite know how I got in. The office must have used its influence with the USGA. It's convenient. I'll give it that. Where are you?"

"We're at the Aberdeen Inn," Killets said.

"The B&B in the village," I said.

"Near the drug store, the one that makes the old-fashioned what-do-you-call-them, milkshakes?" he asked.

"Yeah. The Victorian house up the block," I said.

"That's bloody perfect," he said. "Oh, excuse me." He looked at Killets to see if the slang had bothered her. Killets couldn't have cared less. "Of course you know Victorian means something quite different to us." He grinned.

"We'll have to do dinner one night," she said, "since we're practically neighbors."

"Can't think of anything I'd enjoy more," said Hailey.

I began to feel like the chauffeur of a limo with a couple making out in the back.

"I'm going to wander around a bit and have a look at the golf course," I said to Killets.

"You go ahead," she said. "I think I'll hang around here for a while. Talk to the office. I'll see you back at the Inn."

"Later." I shook hands with Hailey again. Good luck and God save the Queen, I thought.

15

I came out of the press center and started walking toward the golf course. There was a makeshift path of gardening bark. It was like walking on fudge so I cut over to the grass and found a shortcut up behind the first tee, near the putting green the players use just before they tee off.

The first hole of No. 2 is one of the easiest on the course. There is out of bounds on the left where the course borders a road leading to the traffic circle, but there is so much room on the right that actually hitting it out of bounds almost never happens. A chain link fence covered with a green curtain had been put up all along the left side of the hole to keep people from sneaking in. This time it had the additional benefit of keeping the grounds more secure, too.

Phil Mickelson was getting ready to begin a practice round. His caddie, Bones, was emptying sleeves of golf balls into his large, thin hands, marking all three, putting them back in the sleeve, and returning them to the big pocket in the bag right below Phil's name. Typically, Mickelson would use a new ball on every hole, giving it away to a kid at the green after he finished putting to what he believed would be the various pin positions on the four days, paying particular attention to what he guessed would be the Sunday placement. By the end of the day, Bones would have gone through exactly a dozen and a half golf balls.

"Let's go," said Mickelson, who was taking his preparations seriously, having finished second in the Open the last time it was in Pinehurst when Payne Stewart grabbed him by the face with both hands and told him how lucky he was because he was going to be a father. I thought about Stewart and it made me shiver—death had already visited this place once and now it might very well be coming again, in a very different form. I passed the little putting green and walked behind the 18th toward the big putting complex next to the clubhouse. Looking back down the hole, the big scoreboard was on the left, by the starter's shack. It looked empty without Woods and Mickelson and Stewart. At least it was a proper scoreboard, not one of those electronic boards the tour hauled around from week to week—the ones the players had begun calling "stiffy boards" because of the erectile dysfunction drugs advertised on them.

Heartbreak Hill, the practice ground, was behind the giant grandstand along the 18th to the players' left, and I decided to see who was beating balls, getting ready for Thursday. On my way around the stands, I saw Stormy walking up the hole and I went down to meet him. With all the sweat rolling off him it looked like he might have had a rough couple of days wrestling the Count.

"Hey, Stormy, you out measuring the golf course for Ian?"

"Hell, no," said the caddie, who was wiping his face with a white towel, the kind caddies carry around the way normal people carry Kleenex. "The game's on, man. Jimmy Wildheart and Billy Ray Toomey. The Lubbock boys are coming up eighteen all square. Wouldn't miss this for the world."

Stormy had his laser distance finder and he looked back down the 18th. Though it was against the rules to carry it during the tournament, early in the week he'd walk the entire course, double-checking the distances in his yardage book from the marked sprinkler heads to different parts of the green. A bad yardage, particularly at Pinehurst, could be costly. Even a yard off and a well-struck shot would roll down the shaved collars of any green into deep collection areas and almost surely lead to a bogey or worse. The reason Stormy had it with him now, however, had nothing to do with yardages. Not only did it measure distance but it worked like a spyglass, too. Stormy was carefully eyeballing Billy Ray Toomey, Jimmy Wildheart, and the respective wives, Sandi and Soozi, the surgically enhanced sisters from Bovina, Texas, who had been fully engaged in the art of motivating their men, one way or another, since they were all Red Raiders at Texas Tech.

"Look, over there, coming up the hill," Stormy said. "The wives." He handed me the laser. The woman on the left had long, straight, blonde hair. The other one had that dyed L.A. redhead look. I remembered them from the back of the 18th green at Augusta. There was something in the thin noses and the thick eyebrows that tipped off the family relation or, if nothing else, the fact that they'd been loyal to the same plastic surgeon. They were each packing a Texas-sized shirt-full, with no intention of disguising it, and carrying shooting sticks and bottles of pure drinking water. Jimmy had driven it right onto a waste area and the girls set up their leather-seated folding sticks—what the players called "bitch seats"—a few feet away to watch.

Billy Ray was easily the bigger hitter and he'd driven it a mile, dead down the middle. According to Stormy, he only had 173 yards to the pin. Jimmy Wildheart had a good, clean lie on a bit of hardpan but Stormy said there was a lump of grass close to the back of the ball.

"It might catch the club on the way back," said Stormy. "He's going to have to take it a little outside."

Stormy peered through his range finder. "He's got to

have at least a five-iron. Maybe more," he said. Then he turned to look at Billy Ray Toomey. "Can't be more than a seven-iron from there. Eight maybe."

I could see Jimmy bending over to look closely at the lie. His caddie glanced over at the women and smiled. Jimmy stood back up, took the towel off the golf bag, and carefully wiped the sweat off his hands.

Stormy was watching them closely. "Damn," he said. "Jimmy winked at them."

By almost any measure, Billy Ray Toomey was a better player than Jimmy Wildheart. You can look it up. He'd won a tournament every year he'd been on the tour. Top 10 in greens in regulation. Top 15 in driving distance. Jimmy Wildheart, on the other hand, had won a piss pot full of money but he'd never won a tournament, finishing second eleven times.

"He's going to cut it in there," said Stormy, studying Jimmy Wildheart. "Back left. Impossible pin for a cut. Looks like . . . yeah, it's the five. He's going to hit it high, see if he can set it down in that corner, put some pressure on ol' Billy Ray. But if that ball doesn't cut, he's screwed." Stormy turned to look at Toomey through his laser. Billy Ray was leaning on his bag, smoking a cigarette, looking fidgety. Even his caddie seemed nervous.

"I swear that guy's about to piss down his leg," Stormy said. He passed over the laser.

I looked through it. Billy Ray Toomey looked like he'd already lost.

Jimmy Wildheart tugged at the left shoulder of his sweat-soaked golf shirt, pulling it up so it wouldn't restrict his movement. The caddie picked the bag up and moved out of his player's peripheral vision. Sandi and Soozi unscrewed the plastic caps on their water bottles and drank in unison.

Wildheart took a practice swing off to the side, finding a spot where he could approximate the lump of grass behind his ball. When he finally seemed comfortable, he stood behind the ball and sighted down the intended line of flight like a matador taking the measure of his bull. He took his stance, gripping the club firmly but not too hard, the way a baby squeezes a grown man's finger. His swing was short and compact. When the head of the 5-iron cut through the hardpan it produced a puff of dust like smoke from a cherry bomb. With a crack that echoed off the pine trees, the ball started right on the flagstick and kind of fell out of the air to the right, landing like a marshmallow dropping off the end of a stick into a campfire. It stopped ten feet to the right of the hole.

"Shot," said his caddie.

Jimmy handed him the club, looked at the women, and tipped his cap. Billy Ray Toomey flicked his cigarette away. "Fuck," he said, clearly enough I could read his lips. I handed the range finder back to Stormy.

"He's trying to decide whether to hit an easy seven or hard eight," Stormy said, watching the conversation between caddie and player.

Toomey flipped several iron heads out of the way and finally pulled one. "Wrong," Stormy said. "He took the eight-iron. He's going to try to hit it hard. Should have gone with the easy seven. Bet he overcooks this."

Billy Ray Toomey's caddie said something to him and then backed away, dragging the bag along the grass.

I took Stormy's laser and watched Toomey. He was doing everything too fast. A quick practice swing. Up to the ball. Laid off at the top. He turned it over and hooked it into the bunker left of the green. He angrily buried the club toe down in the fairway and trudged forward. The caddie ran to catch up with him, bouncing along with the bag over his shoulder, wiping the dirt off the face of the 8-iron.

"Easy up and down," the caddie said when they were just about in front of us. "He can't make that putt."

"That sumbitch," Billy Ray Toomey said, then spit tobacco juice.

Stormy and I walked the rest of the way up the hill to the green. There were a half dozen players standing on the clubhouse porch behind the 18th. Two applauded. Jimmy Wildheart tipped his cap just like he'd done for Sandi and Soozi and marked his ball. It was just inside 10 feet with a little left-to-right break.

Billy Ray dug his feet deep into the sand. The bunker wasn't the deepest one on the golf course but the pin was in a tough spot. If he was short or left, the ball would run off the green to that side; if he was just a few feet beyond the hole, it would run off the back. He hit a high bunker shot with a lot of spin that landed three feet right of the hole and checked immediately. At least he'd force Wildheart to make the putt. Billy Ray tapped the sand off his shoes with his wedge and accepted his putter from the caddie, who began to rake over his footprints.

With Sandi and Soozi standing near the big scoreboard, Jimmy walked all around his putt. He looked at it from every angle. Two players were waiting behind them in the fairway but they didn't mind. Once word of the game reached the caddie pen that morning, the news cut through the entire field like swine flu.

If Wildheart's golf game had a weakness, it was his putting. He was ranked 141st on the tour and just that week had turned to the claw. It improved his stroke but he still wasn't completely comfortable with it. When he hit the putt, it looked dead center but it lost its speed as it neared the cup, caught the right edge, and spun out. Toomey looked his three-footer over every which way and finally twitched it in, the ball just barely making it to the front edge. The ex-roommates took their hats off and shook hands. Billy Ray was smiling like he'd just hit all five numbers and the Powerball.

"It's a push," said Stormy.

"What were they playing for?" I asked.

"The way I heard it, the boys went deep on a bottle of blue agave tequila last night before the wives got to town. Story is Billy Ray put up Sandi against Jimmy's brand new Hummer."

"She know about it?"

"I'm guessin' not," Stormy said. "From everything I ever heard, if Billy Ray told her what he done, she'd cut off his dick and make a corndog out of it."

When it came to pure fear, Sandi Toomey didn't have anything to worry about. She was a carrier.

16

When I got back to the Aberdeen Inn I decided to lie down and relax before the USGA party that night. The room was hot but not unbearable. The innkeeper had been right about the breeze. It was peaceful. Killets was nowhere to be seen. Through the window I could hear people's conversations as they walked in the village, though I couldn't make out the words exactly. I had some reading to catch up on and put the most recent issue of *Current* plus a couple of back issues of *Golf World* on the nightstand. I'd get through what I could.

Ever since the cover story about the murders in *Current*, the tour seemed a different, more dangerous place. It wasn't just Tiger Woods's personal traveling show anymore, it brought death with it everywhere it went. The players and officials were determined to say all the right things. "You can't go through life being afraid." "We're not going to let one lunatic change the way we live." So on and so on. But the fact was, most everyone was scared. The shadows seemed darker, more foreboding. One lunatic had changed the way people lived their lives. In some cases, he'd taken that life away.

One of the issues of *Golf World* was their U.S. Open preview with an account of the week-by-week developments as the story of the murders unfolded. I let the magazine drop down on my chest, closed my eyes, and listened to the fan wobbling uncertainly above me.

After Hilton Head, it all seemed to fall apart. I drove back to Augusta to find the photographer I'd seen after the Masters at the King & Queen Inn. It was easy to track down Richard McPhee. I went into the main offices of the *Augusta Dispatch* on Broad Street a little after 5 P.M. McPhee was gone for the day but someone in the photo department told me I'd find him at Fitzgerald's Pub on Twelfth. "It's where they all go," said the photo librarian, her voice thick with disapproval.

The pub had a hand-carved bar imported from the Irish coastal town of Kinsale. Guinness and Harp were on tap. I ordered a pint of Harp and asked the woman bartender with the stretched-tight Georgia Bulldog T-shirt and the big blonde hair if she'd seen McPhee.

"He's in the back playin' darts," she drawled.

I recognized McPhee immediately.

"Sure, I remember you," he said. "If you don't mind my asking, what the hell happened to you?" He pointed at the bruises from my one-rounder with Colt Reeves.

"Accident," I lied.

He shrugged slightly. Obviously, he didn't believe me.

I asked him if we could talk and he motioned to a booth in the front.

"Start me a pint, Katie," he said to the bartender as we sat down. "What can I do for you?"

"I was wondering what else you've learned about the woman who was murdered at the King & Queen," I said.

"You have some personal interest?" he asked, watching the bartender out of the corner of his eye.

"Maybe. I have a feeling her death may be connected to something else but it's only a guess," I said.

"I'm probably not the guy to talk to. Russ Chalmers is the police beat guy. He'd know a lot more about it than I would. He's back there playing pool." He nodded over his shoulder.

"I'd rather we kept this between us," I said. I was turning a cardboard coaster around and around with my fingertips. I didn't want to get a reporter involved. I didn't want someone to jump the story, if there was one. Looking back, I guess I was an idiot. I ended up getting jumped by my own guy anyway.

"I don't want too many people involved," I continued. McPhee understood the shorthand. He knew I wanted to keep the story to myself. I knew he'd relay our conversation to the reporter at the pool table as soon as I was gone. It's the nature of the beast. Everyone wants to be one up on everyone else.

"I'm just curious about a few details," I said.

"I'll tell you what I can." His eyes seemed sad and tired with the memory of it.

"That night you told me the victim was badly cut up. Was that the cause of death?" I asked. "I looked at a couple of the followup stories but I never saw any official cause of death."

"As a matter of fact, no, it wasn't," he said. "In a manner of speaking, it was drowning."

"Drowning?"

"Yeah, she had a piece of duct tape over her mouth. Apparently she vomited and inhaled the vomit. She drowned." He looked at my hands fidgeting with the coaster. Katie put a pint of Guinness down in front of him. "Thanks, darlin'," he said.

"What about all the blood?" I asked.

"Post-mortem. She never felt a thing. Guy cut up the body bad, though. Real bad." He took a sip. A line of light brown foam stuck to his top lip and he wiped it away with the back of his hand. "It was on the walls and everything. Like a Franz Kline painting, except in blood."

"Was she drugged?" I asked.

"Not cocaine or anything like that. Not even marijuana. But someone had slipped her one of those date rape drugs— GHB. The cops here call it Georgia Home Boy."

I nodded. That was good enough for me. The two deaths on Hilton Head had to be tied in to this one. There was a chance I could be wrong—there hadn't been the same level of postmortem violence in the murders on Hilton Head— but I was convinced it all fit together somehow. And it was all so very unthinkable.

Sooner or later, I was going to have to tell the police what I knew. It wasn't just a story anymore. Lives might be in danger. What if no one had put it together except me? Scarier yet, what if the tour knew and wasn't telling? I thought about asking McPhee if he was aware of any other murders in Augusta the same week as the Masters but I didn't want to serve the story to him on a platter. I didn't want to give the *Augusta Dispatch* a chance to solve the riddle first. It was selfish but this was going to be a big story, the kind that makes careers or, in my case, remakes them. I could do the right thing and still break the story with the right help and the right timing. But what if someone was hurt in the meantime? I wanted the story but I didn't want blood on my hands either. The thought made me a little sick to my stomach.

When I walked out of Fitzgerald's I knew what I needed to do. It was a Thursday. I flew from Augusta back to Chicago, and got home to my North Side apartment late. I checked my e-mail and messages and tried to sleep. I spent the next day entering everything I'd learned into my laptop and in the afternoon taking a long run in the park along

Lake Michigan. It was chilly and the wind was blowing hard. The run tired me out and helped ease my mind. On Saturday I went to see the Cubs play the Mets. After the game I stopped at Bleachers, a bar across the street from Wrigley Field, then walked home on Waveland with my hands stuck in my pockets. I didn't even know who won the game. I couldn't shake the feeling that somewhere, something bad was going to happen to someone. Maybe even someone I knew.

On Sunday morning I called Justin Pound.

"Pound."

"Justin, it's Nick Oliver."

I hadn't talked to Pound since he'd gotten the Hilton Head pictures.

"Well?" he said. "What do you want, Oliver, a pat on the back? An attaboy? You fucked up the Masters. So, you did a decent job with the polo pony, so what?"

"Justin, I think I'm on to a story."

"You're a photographer, Oliver, not a writer. You're on to a story when I tell you you're on a story." I could hear Pound dragging his computer mouse and double clicking, working while he was talking, probably sizing a paparazzi shot of Julia Roberts to fit a hole in "Kiss & Tell," the expanded and reformatted gossip section of the magazine.

"I can't tell you what it is . . ."

"You're wasting my time, Oliver."

"Eventually I'm going to give the story to McKie but I'm going to ask him to hold it. I don't know how long yet. With what I've got to tell him, we'll be able to put something together for a cover piece. I'll send you an e-mail just before I give McKie the details."

"Spare me the *Seven Days of the Condor* bullshit. You expect me to tear apart an issue and redo it on your say-so? Not likely," he said, but he had stopped clicking his mouse.

"I want a credit on the story and a bonus, too, Justin. My e-mail is going to be copied to Art Hurley," I said. Arthur Peabody Hurley II was the publisher of *Current* and the son of the founder of the company. Hurley the Younger was a five-foot-one silver-haired man in his early fifties who drove a red Viper and changed top editors the way professional golfers change gloves on a hot day. Pound had managed to survive longer than almost anyone on the masthead but he lived in fear of the day he would open the *New York Times* and read he'd been replaced by the deputy art director of *Vanity Fair*.

I knew this could make Pound look good. So did he, if I wasn't bullshitting him.

"Just be ready," I said. Then I hung up.

On Sunday night, I sent my e-mails and then phoned McKie. He was still busy doing a rewrite on his profile of Francisco Pietro. His editor at *Current* had told him it lacked depth and Stewart was in a foul mood.

"I'm busy here, Nick," he sounded exasperated.

"I think the profile is going to be able to wait," I told him.

"Are you daft?" he said. "I'm on deadline."

I told him about the murder at the hotel in Augusta, the two killings in Hilton Head, and the GHB. I gave him the names of the photographer at the *Augusta Dispatch* and the reporter in Savannah. I spelled out my suspicions and I asked him to hold the story until I gave him the OK to go with it. There was someone I needed to speak to first, I explained.

"Let me make a couple of phone calls," he said. I could hear the excitement in his voice. Just that quickly, I realized I wouldn't hear from him again after he hung up. Shit, I thought, I just gave away the biggest story I ever had. I knew McKie would cut me out.

"Stewart," I said. "I expect credit on this."

"Certainly," he said. "Wouldn't think of doing otherwise." The line went dead.

I needed to see Juli, warn her the shit was going to hit the fan. I knew McKie wouldn't talk to anyone at the tour until the very end, just before he closed the story. He'd call the commissioner, Jacob Pierce, and ask for a comment. That would be it. He would try to surprise him, trick him into giving up a good quote, an honest answer, not some canned response. I decided I'd fly from Chicago to New Orleans in the morning and talk to Juli as soon as she got there. She deserved to know the tour was about to be turned upside down and she deserved to hear it from me face to face. Besides, I was now officially worried about her.

The next day I flew to New Orleans and checked into the Chateau St. Marie on Toulouse Street. It was one of the more affordable hotels in the French Quarter with wrought iron balconies and its own parking. The location was perfect, just a leisurely stroll to the shops on Royal, the restaurants on Chartres, and the bars on Bourbon.

I was booked on a flight back to Chicago the following afternoon. When I called the press room, they said Juli wasn't scheduled to arrive until the next morning so I visited my favorite photography gallery on Chartres. While I was looking at a disappointing collection of Walker Evans prints I was thinking about what must be going on at *Current*. Researchers would be checking facts, calling police departments. Picture editors would be chasing down photographs of the victims, both when they were alive and at the crime scenes. The bloodier the better. Pound would demand at least one photo of a body being taken out on a gurney. News adrenaline would be flowing like white water in Colorado. Later, I ate a light dinner at the Napoleon House with its conspiratorially dingy bar, in a building built in the late 18th century for an emperor on the lam.

In the morning I drove south and west of the city to the Crescent City Club, the brand new course that hosts the New Orleans tournament. Just as I'd asked, Juli had arranged for credentials to be left at Will Call. When it came to remembering details, she was the best. The press tent was off to the side of the antebellum-style clubhouse. As soon as I walked in I could see she already knew what I had come all this way to tell her.

"Why didn't you say something? Why didn't you tell someone?" she said. She looked at me with contempt.

"I couldn't," I said. "You know that."

She nodded, her lips clenched. "Look at this." Juli passed over a copy of the *Times-Picayune*. She had it folded back on itself. The item was small. At 3 A.M. a transvestite had been found murdered in the French Quarter. There had been complaints about noise in the room. Complaints about noise in the French Quarter don't exactly get a quick response. The night manager eventually called the room but there was no answer. When he investigated he found "Jasmine" duct-taped to the towel rack and disemboweled. There was a plastic beer cup on the nightstand that had traces of GHB in it.

That week the cover of *Current* featured the 48-point headline:

Death Tour

The cover picture was of a body being wheeled out of a motel room on Hilton Head Island. The subhead said, "Murder Haunts World of Golf." The story was written by Stewart McKie. At the end of the piece I was credited along with nine others as "research provided by" even though most of the story was a rehashing of details from newspaper accounts I'd found and quotes from the people I suggested McKie speak to. People like Salem Washington, Richard McPhee and the officer on Hilton Head, Rick Hightower. It was sensational because no one had pulled it all together before. Not until I showed him how it all fit. McKie had done a good job with the writing, straightforward and emotionless. I was pissed but, in the end, my feelings seemed so unimportant.

I picked the *Golf World* up off my chest and read a few more paragraphs. I couldn't shake the memory of Juli's look of disgust that day in the press center in New Orleans.

After that, the tour moved to Texas. At the Colonial a few volunteers began quitting, or just not showing up, but there weren't many outward signs of crisis. Justin Leonard won by four shots. The tour's damage control people were in place for the Fort Worth tournament but nothing happened there. In Charlotte the week after, though, another victim was discovered strangled, with GHB in her bloodstream. Jack Nicklaus himself called a press conference to confirm that the Memorial would be held as scheduled in May. The United States Golf Association also remained undeterred. As Jacob Lambeth, the president of the USGA and an investment banker from Kansas City, said, "We refuse to be intimidated by the evildoers."

By June, it wasn't just volunteers who were being scared away. Some players' wives had stopped traveling with their husbands, particularly with the children. On the Sunday night of Westchester, the week before the U.S. Open, a twenty-six-year-old courtesy car driver washed up on the west bank of the Hudson River near Nyack. She'd been strangled after being drugged with GHB. Commissioner Jacob Pierce appeared on *Nightline*. He confirmed the tour had been cooperating with the FBI for over a year.

I wondered exactly how long they had known. Maybe

from the very beginning. They must have thought they could keep it quiet, rely on their own security. I rested the magazine on my chest and drifted into an uneasy sleep. The last meandering thought I had was of Jimmy Wildheart's 5-iron.

17

The USGA party was in the Marlboro Ballroom of the Carolina hotel. All the members of the executive committee were there as well as all the permanent staffers, the people who actually run the USGA's championships. Every member of the media in attendance at the Open received an invitation and a lot of them came because the alcohol was free and the buffet was easier than trying to pass through six different highway patrol roadblocks without getting a DUI.

The executive committee is made up of volunteers—bankers and lawyers, CEOs and CFOs—who think they know more about running a golf tournament than the permanent USGA staffers who do it all year long. Actually being on the staff at the USGA means constantly having to fend off the bad ideas of people who, in every other walk of life, are used to being obeyed implicitly. It's a job that requires being half court jester and half kingmaker and no one does it long without winding up either on the junk heap of administrative history or hopelessly enamored of their own political skills.

Judge Winfield Thomas, the executive director of the USGA, was an example of the latter. Undergrad: Brown. Major: psychology with a minor in sailing. After that,

Dartmouth Law. Memberships: Pine Valley and Newport Golf and Yacht. Thomas once served as a three-strikes-and-you're-out Superior Court judge in Newport County, Rhode Island, before resigning to accept the position of executive director of the United States Golf Association. Thin and properly weather-beaten, he had a wardrobe consisting of bow ties and seersucker. He preferred that the staff address him as "Judge" and he traveled with his own King James Bible. He was a man who had successfully negotiated the pitfalls of the executive committee, largely because the head of that committee, Toby Winter, was his former roommate at Brown who had become a managing partner of the largest accounting firm in Manhattan.

Judge Thomas was holding a scotch and soda, standing in front of a large framed print of 18th-century golfers on the Old Course in St. Andrews, and expounding on the brilliance of Donald Ross's No. 2 Course to Jenny Killets, who was showing enough cleavage in her red dress for her chest to qualify as a wee burn.

"The brilliance is in the green design," he offered without being able to lift his eyes above her chin. "The putting surfaces accommodate only the best shots. Anything less requires a high degree of imagination and perfect execution in order to save par. There are lots of, uh, humps. And swales. Ben Crenshaw once called this course the greatest test of the short game in all of golf." He didn't mention that the inverted saucer shape of the greens had been arrived at willy nilly by decades of top-dressing with sand and that Ross, himself, would likely have been appalled at them now.

"Don't you think there should be bathrooms for the photographers out on the course?" Killets asked, acting as if her question was somehow a logical extension of their conversation. "I mean, we're out there all day and it's not healthy. It can lead to all kinds of bladder problems. Urinary tract infections. We could use fruit stands, too." She paused to take a sip of an indifferent champagne.

Judge Thomas had the puffy-eyed look of someone who'd been adrift at sea. A few minutes trapped alone in Killets's train of thought could do that to you. I decided to show some pity on the USGA. I introduced myself to the judge, and, before Jenny could say anything else, I took her by the elbow and began to steer her away. I apologized to the judge over my shoulder. "Will you forgive us a moment?"

"By all means," he replied, followed by a deep swallow of his Glenmorangie Single Malt.

"Did you ever find McKie?" I whispered to her.

"Who?"

"Stewart McKie. You remember. Our writer. You were going to look for him this afternoon," I said, suspecting full well that the only thing Jenny Killets had found that afternoon was a cozy place for her and David Hailey to exchange bodily fluids. Even though Killets owed her job to Dudley Sommers and *Amped* she didn't feel any greater need to be faithful to her managing editor than he felt to be true to her when it came to diddling middle-aged rock stars with pierced tongues and face lifts. They preferred to give each other their "space."

"No. I talked to Justin though. He wants you to be sure to shoot the commissioner's press conference tomorrow, you know, what's his name."

"Pierce."

"Yeah, him." She hid her face behind a raised champagne glass.

The thought of receiving my assignments from Jenny Killets pissed me off but I also knew it was, in fact, coming from Pound. The commissioner was going to have a 10 A.M. press conference to try to deflect as much bad publicity as he could. Murder was definitely bad for business. Pound would need pictures, particularly since *Current* had broken the story. Virtually any development had become a matter of proprietary interest to us. On the plus side, Juli would be there, too.

"OK," I said to Jenny, "what's your plan?"

"I thought I'd follow Tiger."

"Jenny, it's a practice round."

"I still might get something," she said. That was Killets for you. She was a seven-frames-per-second barracuda. Or maybe she'd arranged a nooner with Hailey. Either way, I was doing the press conference at 10 A.M.

On the other side of the large banquet room from the buffet table, I saw Stewart McKie. He and Gavin Webster had cornered the commissioner. Juli was with them, too.

"There he is," I said to Killets. "I've got a bone to pick with Mr. McKie." I headed in their direction, knowing Killets would follow sooner or later. Probably sooner.

Juli was wearing a dark pantsuit, gray with stripes, perfectly tailored, very flattering with her slicked-back short hair and comfortable curves. I tapped her on the shoulder.

"Hi," I said.

"Hello," she said. I kissed her cheek. She didn't pull away.

"Mr. Pierce," she said to the commissioner, "this is Nick Oliver."

"The fellow who started all this," he said. We shook hands.

"You wouldn't know it by reading *Current*," I said, making a point to look at McKie when I said it. Pierce was a short man, starched, with an Ivy League house tie. He'd done his undergrad at Yale and had a law degree from George-town. He'd worked in two Republican administrations as an executive assistant to cabinet-level secretaries and ran five miles a day, rain or shine. He stretched before and after and made certain to check his pulse. It looked like the salt was beginning to overtake the pepper in his hair. His face was waxy and his eyes weary as if he hadn't slept in weeks. I suspected he probably hadn't.

"I suppose in some way we owe you a measure of gratitude," he said, but didn't mean it. His world was in disarray and it was beyond his ability to do anything about it. Not what an Ivy League power broker was accustomed to.

"Good to see you, Oliver," said McKie, who clearly thought I was getting in the way of his ad hoc interview. This was an opportunity for him to ambush the tour commissioner. I was a sorry and unwelcome diversion. I couldn't have cared less, though. Screw Stewart McKie. I'd asked him to sit on the story until I could talk to Juli but instead he went with it. "You're looking rather better than the last time I saw you. You know Webster, I presume?" he said.

"We've met," I said. I'd met Webster once at an editorial meeting in New York. We shook hands. Webster was wearing a white polo shirt, tight around his biceps, and black Nike warm-up pants, even though every other man in the room had on a coat and tie. He seemed not to notice or care. He hated golf and held most golfers in complete disdain. To him, it wasn't even a sport. He liked being in on the action, though, and murder is as good as it gets. Webster was terrifically fit with his right forearm noticeably more muscular than the left. His forearms were covered with a dusty crop of sun-bleached hair, the same sandy color as his carefully cropped mustache.

"The last time I saw this lad," McKie said to the commissioner while nodding in my direction, "he was lying on his back with blood coming out his ears."

"I'm sure I don't have to tell you that writers lie," I said to Pierce. "They also don't keep their promises."

McKie grinned into his vodka.

"Juli, have you got a second?" I asked.

"Will you excuse us for a minute?" she said to the commissioner, looking guilty for abandoning him.

"Right," said McKie. "It'll give me a chance to ask the commissioner a few questions concerning my investigation."

"Your investigation?" I asked. McKie smiled that superior smile of his.

"Don't be long," said Pierce, adding, "I've got a meeting with Judge Thomas." It was a lie but he was relying on Juli to navigate him through the evening, and Webster and McKie were two of the rocky shoals he particularly wanted to avoid.

We moved away near a window that looked out on the dark rocking porch. Several people were swaying back and forth in white chairs, enjoying a drink and a cigarette on a hot, soupy night.

"Can't this wait?" she said quickly.

"I know, you're working." I glanced back at the commissioner, who was shifting his weight from one foot to the other as he talked to McKie. "I just wanted to let you know how sorry I am and I hope you understand. About the story. I tried to slow it down but it got away from me." I put my hand up to stop her from speaking. "Maybe I should have gone to the police right away. I don't know. I'm not going to argue about that. But you can't blame me for what some lunatic is doing. I'm not responsible for that."

"No," she said, taking a deep breath. "I'm not blaming you. That was unfair."

We watched the rocking chairs.

"Pierce knew," I said. "He knew all along. Way before I did. The tour tried to hush it up." I could tell by her silence she knew the truth, too.

"Friends again?" I asked.

"Not hardly." She patted my arm and walked back toward the commissioner. She looked so beautiful. I watched the cigarettes on the porch light up strangers' faces and then fade back into the darkness.

"What did you find out?" It was Killets, at my elbow.

"I found out it's going to be a long week."

18

I couldn't face going back to my empty room after the USGA dinner so I decided to stop in the Pine Crest for a drink. The evening was still warm and the air was thick, like you could grab a handful of it. Sweat started to pop out on my temples almost as soon as I came out of the Carolina. I walked past the spa, through the old, whitewashed brick gates and into the village. There were a few people walking around, not many. I recognized one or two. The shop owners could have stayed open late but fear of an unknown danger caused them to close early instead. Couples pressed their faces against the windows, peering inside at autographed golf memorabilia and empty jewelry cases. I passed the Aberdeen Inn and continued down the brick sidewalk toward the Gentleman's Gentleman, an overpriced clothing store. The Pinehurst Sundry was the only business on the block still open. Two schoolgirls were making milkshakes while a half dozen people waited in line.

I wandered in to look around. There were cheap Pinehurst T-shirts on the shelves and a sparse collection of deodorants and tubes of toothpaste. The business survived mostly on the sale of milkshakes, hot dogs with chili and slaw, and bad picture postcards. On the shelf next to the Sudafed was a box of Sharpies. I thought I might need a couple to mark film so I picked out two black ones, took them up to the counter, paid one of the girls, and put them in the inside pocket of my blazer.

As I came out of the store a Pinehurst policeman passed by in his cruiser. The car was barely moving. He was shining his searchlight on the paths between the old buildings that connected Chinquapin Road with Market Square. When I got to the corner at the Holly Inn, I turned left down Dogwood Road. The Pine Crest was less than a block down on the right and I could see the party had spilled out of the bar, off the porch, and into the street.

It was like a bizarre funhouse festival. We were all captives for the week, medieval villagers brought together inside the castle walls for their own protection. The state troopers had pulled up the drawbridge at the traffic circle and no one was going to harm us here in the village. For the next five days we would all try to forget someone might be stalking us and enjoy our little fiesta.

I threaded my way through the crowd and squeezed up onto the porch. Francisco Pietro was wedged into a corner talking with three women who were laughing too much and brushing back their unruly summer hair. One seemed drunker than the others and she kept touching Pietro's arm below the sleeve of his $150 golf shirt. Even though tomorrow was just a practice round, all he had in his hand was a bottle of Perrier.

Inside I recognized Billy Cheeks, the golf swing guru of the moment. Built like Ichabod Crane, he was wearing a boldly striped golf shirt that bore his own personal logo adapted from his long neck, protruding chin, and roostertail cowlick, all done up in profile. He was talking to three on-air reporters from the Golf Channel, who nodded their heads knowingly.

At the fireplace a rowdy group of men were pitching golf balls at a board with a hole in it that hung across the

mantel. They were yelling obscenities at each other and exchanging five-dollar bills with every miss. I pushed past the
piano player, who was smoking cigarettes and singing
Sinatra tunes, and squeezed into a small section of the bar.
The bartender was an older woman with cheap white crowns
a size too large for her mouth and hair the color of cordovan
shoe polish. I ordered a Bud Light and paid for it. I tried to
look around the room but it was hard to see the people for
the crowd.

Beyond the piano, near the old-fashioned pay telephone
and the bathrooms, I saw Killets talking to David Hailey.
Well, actually, it was the six-foot-four Hailey's head above
the sea of golf caps that caught my eye. Killets seemed to be
doing most of the talking. What a surprise, I thought. I decided to leave well enough alone and cut back through the
chippers and drinkers and onto the porch again. As I was
coming out, Juli was coming in.

"Hey," I said.

"Oh, hi," she said.

"What brings you out into the heat of the night?"

"I just didn't feel like going to bed."

"Me neither. Besides, no air conditioning."

"Excuse me, puleez," said a voice. Juli and I were blocking the door.

"Sorry," I said and we backed into the room. I pulled
her in like I was pulling her onto a life raft. "Can I get you a
drink?"

"I could use one."

"Cosmo?"

"You think they make a good one here?" She thought
about it. "Better not. I'll just have one of those." She pointed
at my beer. I made my way back into the bar and got two
more Bud Lights. I found her again out on the porch.

A horse-drawn carriage with two couples in it clomped

by and the people in the street split apart to make a path.

"You get the commissioner out of there in one piece?" I asked.

"Barely. I thought I was going to have to pry McKie and what's-his-name off him for a minute," she said.

"Webster," I said.

"Yeah, Webster. What an asshole that guy is," she said.

"Tough day tomorrow," I offered.

"I hope not." She took a sip of beer. "He's really not looking forward to it. I mean, what do you say? You're doing everything you can, you know? I actually feel sorry for the guy."

"When did you find out," I asked. "That he knew, I mean."

Juli sighed. "Memorial."

I nodded. The commissioner would be in for a grilling the next day. McKie would jump at the chance to write a cover-up story.

"You look great," I said.

"Thanks." She seemed genuinely pleased. "You're looking better yourself."

"Time heals. Cheers."

"Cheers."

We talked about everything that had happened since I'd seen her in New Orleans. "You can't believe it," she said. "In a way, it's completely irrational but in a way it's not. Not many wives around. No children at all. It's been hell trying to get enough volunteers to run the tournaments properly. It's eerie. Sometimes I swear the players are even looking at each other funny. It's like we used to be one big dysfunctional family and now everyone is looking sideways at everyone else. It's just so, so odd."

"Have you thought about taking some time yourself, getting away?" I asked.

"I couldn't do that. Not now," said Juli. "Besides, I'm fine. My God, I'm surrounded by people all day long."

"It's not the days I'm worried about," I said, then hoped she wouldn't think I was talking about her and Colt Reeves. I had no right. Not any more.

She sighed. "I just refuse to be scared," she said. "End of story."

I nodded. Our bottles were empty.

"You're not so fearless that you wouldn't mind letting me walk you home, would you?" I asked, setting the empties down in a forest of bottles on the porch.

"Want to know the truth?"

"What can it hurt now?" I asked.

"I'd appreciate it."

"Good."

We made our way back through the village, turning down Market Square. The windows at Old Sport, a gallery and gift shop, were lit up and I stopped to look at the bright Russian nesting dolls and the pictures of Payne Stewart punching the air on the last hole of the 1999 U.S. Open. I had stuff someplace in a drawer that looked a lot like it. We strolled past Poogan's Pub. Through the open window I could see Justus Litchard seated at the mahogany bar. He had a pint of Guinness in front of him and was talking in his low, deep voice to a middle-aged woman in a pink golf shirt who was wearing some kind of volunteer badge. She had on a ring with a yellow diamond the size of a cashew, thin, stylish glasses, and a body I was guessing spent time with a personal trainer five days a week. Litchard had an old scar on his cheekbone and it crinkled up when something amused him. He bent over and whispered in the woman's ear and they smiled at each other. He didn't look so scary to me and I wondered what Stormy had been talking about that day on Hilton Head.

Juli and I walked slowly. She was wearing a small leather backpack with straps across the shoulders, the kind that doubled as a purse and hung perfectly on her lower back. I wanted to hold her hand. We'd spent so many evenings strolling just that way in Charleston and Savannah.

"I know I have no right to ask . . . ," I started to say.

"That's right, you don't," she said.

We walked on. I took her hand and she didn't pull it away.

"I miss you," I said.

"I miss you, too."

We walked.

"Is there any chance at all?" I asked.

She stopped underneath the streetlight outside the Gentleman's Gentleman and turned to look at me.

"I know about Ashley Huddleston," she said.

The words were like a sucker punch to my stomach. Ashley Huddleston was a woman in Charleston, old family, old money, who lived in a grand house near our tiny carriage apartment. We went to a blues club together one night when I was in town and Juli wasn't and I'd made a mistake. That was all it was, a mistake.

At first I couldn't say anything. Juli stayed quiet, waiting for me. "How long have you known?" I finally asked her.

"I knew right away. You're not the only one who can see things, you know," she said.

"Why didn't you say something?"

"I thought it would go away. And, later, I didn't want you to think that's why Colt and I . . . I didn't want you to think it was to get even."

"No. I . . . was it?"

"It's not that simple, Nick."

We began walking again.

"I never meant to hurt you," I said. But it sounded so weak and foolish, so out of context, for something that happened so long ago. "I never wanted you to find out."

"Of course not."

"That's not what I meant. I, I just meant I didn't want to hurt you," I said.

We turned the corner.

"How did you find out?"

"What does it matter?" she said.

"It didn't mean anything," I said. "God, that sounds like such a cliché."

"You're right. It does," she said. "Besides, it did mean something, you just didn't know it."

I couldn't say anything. I had been so hurt by what Juli had done that I had managed to erase from my mind my own mistakes. As long as she didn't know, I could tell myself, what she had done and what I had done weren't the same thing. I was sparing her the pain. I could pretend it hadn't happened at all. She, on the other hand, went out looking for somebody better. Colt Reeves was entirely her doing and I was the injured party. All this time I felt so betrayed, so hurt, and she'd felt just the same. What an idiot I was.

"I thought I could get past it," she said. "I thought if we ever had this conversation, it would be the end of us."

I nodded. She was right.

"I didn't think it would happen again," she said.

"It didn't."

"Yes, it did," she said. "Only it was me."

Neither one of us could find the right words and we were both afraid of the wrong ones. At the Carolina, I pulled her aside in the nighttime shadow of a broad-leafed magnolia.

"I'm so very sorry," I said, "for everything."

"Me, too," she said. She turned away and I watched her go up the steps. One of the bellmen in plus fours opened the door and she disappeared into the bright light of the crowded lobby.

19

David Hailey had fallen into a deep sleep but Jenny Killets took her work seriously. She slid out of bed and dressed in the dark. He'd been good fun, she thought, trim and attentive. The hotel clock said 12:03. She wanted to get to the golf course early. Tiger liked to play his practice rounds at dawn to avoid as many people as possible. She didn't want to miss him. She kissed the tips of two fingers and touched it to Hailey's shock of hair, then shut the door carefully as she left.

The lobby of the Pine Crest was still full of people drinking beer and hitting pitch shots at the fireplace. Somewhere along the line, the piano player had started to sound good to them and some were singing along to a Billy Joel song he was pounding out with both hands. The crowd had cleared out of the street. Only a few people were sitting in the chairs on the porch. Even though it was after midnight the air was still heavy with the approach of summertime.

Killets began walking up Dogwood toward the Holly Inn. Just as she reached the shadows away from the street-light in front of the Pine Crest, a car pulled up beside her.

"A little late to be out for a walk," the driver said through his open window. Killets thought she recognized the voice but couldn't see the face in the dark. She walked up to the car.

"Oh, hi," she said.

"Need a ride?"

"I can walk," she said. "It's a nice night. A little muggy maybe."

"I'm not sure being on the streets alone is the smartest thing to do just at the moment," he said.

"You're probably right," she replied, thinking he looked cute and it was sweet of him to stop.

"Get in," he said as he checked the rearview mirror. There was no one coming. He put his hand on his thigh. He could feel the pair of gloves wadded up in a ball in his pocket. "It'll only take a minute."

"Thanks," Killets said. She walked around the car and climbed inside. No one on the porch even noticed.

20

Press conferences for tour commissioners are usually as well attended as preseason football games and generate an equal amount of excitement. This one was different.

I was still a bit groggy when I got to the media center. The Loblolly Suite had been like a sauna and I couldn't get Juli out of my mind. I got to the media center in time to have a cup of black coffee with two sugars and a crusty Danish before I took out my equipment to get ready for the 10 A.M. press conference. I put some color negative film in one camera body and slide film in another. I'd use my 300 mm lens from the back of the room with the color neg film to get some tight facial expressions. The neg film, because of its latitude, could handle any kind of exposure or light temperature problems I might have from shooting inside a tent. I intended to use my on-camera strobe with a 28–70 mm zoom on the other camera. I didn't want to rely solely on that, though, because the Canon strobe was such rubbish. When you used it, you hit the button and prayed. Thankfully, computer programs like Photoshop were so good even horrendously bad exposures could often be salvaged. Still, I didn't want to run the risk of ending up with a bunch of useless clear plastic because I was saddled with a strobe that didn't know its own strength. It was infuriating. Somewhere in that autofocus camera was a computer chip that knew exactly how far the subject was and somewhere in the strobe was another computer chip that knew exactly how much light it was putting out. Why couldn't the two chips to talk to one another? I knew the day was coming when I'd have to switch to digital like everyone else and then I wouldn't have these problems. But I hated the thought of it. I liked being a dinosaur, doing things my own way. The fact that I still used film had even become something of a trademark. It made me different.

I took up a spot in the back of the media interview tent and watched the writers, other photographers, and the TV guys file in. There was a platform built in the back of the room for the TV videographers to set up their thick tripods and cameras. It was two rows deep with guys with large belts filled with heavy batteries strapped around their midsections, pressing against one another. The talking heads were either young women with swept-down hair of unnatural shades of auburn or men with square jaws wearing coats and ties and stonewashed jeans. The network had one cameraman on the platform and another who was set to roam around the room with a handheld camera followed by a guy with a red bandanna tied around his head who let out cable and gathered it up again, scrambling around stooped over like a trained monkey. Jeremy Howe was there to listen in.

"Hello, mate," he said. "You look a bit done in."

"Didn't get much sleep," I said. "It was hotter than hell in the room all night. No A/C."

"Pity. What do you make of this, then?"

"I don't know. I'm glad I'm not him though."

By the time the commissioner was announced over the P.A. system, all the folding chairs in the interview area were occupied and people were standing in the back. Several USGA staffers were wearing their disapproving looks like priest's collars. I half expected Killets to push her way in. I hadn't seen her yet. I figured she was still out with Tiger even though the sun was too high to do any good. But Killets being Killets, she'd probably dog him to the bitter end.

"Jacob Pierce in the interview room. Jacob Pierce in the interview room," announced a hollow, amplified voice. Pierce entered from the back of the room with Juli and a man I didn't recognize. The three of them walked quickly to the podium and sat behind a table with two microphones. Behind them was a background done up in red, white, and blue USGA logos. Juli took one microphone and explained that the commissioner had a brief statement to make and he would take a few questions afterward, keeping in mind that he would be unable to comment directly on any active investigations. She introduced the other man on the podium as Special Agent Trent Long of the FBI. It was hard to tell how big a man Long was because the commissioner seemed small and deflated sitting next to him. He looked strong, though. Long's upper arms stretched the fabric of his jacket. His hair was receding and somehow he'd managed to sunburn the top of his head.

The commissioner put on his reading glasses and pulled a paper from his jacket pocket. His gray suit had sharp, pressed edges and his red tie looked crisp and joined his collar at perfect angles. When he began to speak his voice was wavering and the veins in his neck throbbed. After a few words he stopped to take a drink of water from a plastic bottle Long offered and it smoothed out. The statement was no more or less than anyone expected. The tour deeply regretted . . . Everyone involved in any way with the tour had been instructed to cooperate with the authorities in any way possible . . . At this time there were to the best of his knowledge no known leads or suspects in the series of murders which appeared to be linked to the tour though not necessarily with anyone personally connected to the tour . . . The tour wished to express its condolences to the families . . . He wanted to thank the USGA . . . and so on and so on.

When he finished, he took his glasses off and put them back in his inner pocket with slow, unsteady hands. His eyes had dark circles beneath them. He looked around the room, his jaw set, not seeing anyone in particular. Juli drew one of the microphones near her.

"The commissioner will take a few questions. Please use the portable microphones available to you," she said, indicating the mikes that could be passed around in the audience, mostly for the benefit of the stenographers who were tapping out a transcript and for the viewers taking the live feed from the Golf Channel.

Juli pointed. "Over there, Section A," she said.

"Mr. Pierce," said a man wearing a bow tie and a blue shirt, "Collie Brown, *Washington Sentinel*. Has anyone been able to establish a definitive number of known victims?"

"Not to my knowledge," replied Pierce.

"Well, sir," continued the reporter, "*Current* magazine originally reported three. Is that number correct?"

"We simply don't know," he said.

"Is it greater than three?" pressed the reporter.

"Maybe I can help," interrupted the FBI agent who leaned over, getting his mouth too close to the commissioner's microphone and causing a screech of feedback to knife through the room. He backed off and the noise stopped. "There are indications that as many as eight homicides may be related. Whether or not these eight are connected to the golf tour in some way is unknown, but there are seven women and one man who we believe were murdered by the same person. Of course, there could be more victims we simply don't know about." The writers jotted down the number and looked at one another.

"Section C, in the back," Juli said, pointing.

"Agent Long, correct? Exactly what is it that convinces you someone with the tour is directly involved?" asked a heavyset woman with dark hair who was the golf writer from San Diego.

"We don't know that the tour or anyone affiliated with the tour *is* directly involved," replied Long. "All we know is, in these eight cases the tour was known to be in town when the murders took place and in several of the cases the victims were working or volunteering at the tournament. Beyond that we have no reason to suspect any person or persons connected with the golf tour."

"Section B, up front," said Juli.

"Are there any suspects or promising leads at the moment?" asked a writer from the *London Daily Mail*.

"No. But if there were it wouldn't be appropriate to divulge them here," replied Long curtly.

"Section A, front again," said Juli. While the questioner asked the commissioner what precautions had been put in place by the tour to protect players, fans, and volunteers, Juli surveyed the crowd. I was focusing on the commissioner with my 300 mm lens. His face filled the frame. I could feel his isolation, his overwhelming sadness. After a couple of photos I panned the camera over to Juli. When she saw me, she stared into the lens. I knew she wanted to speak to me. I lowered the lens to let her see I was looking at her and she gave me an almost imperceptible nod.

The commissioner and the FBI agent answered questions for over 30 minutes. They said as little as possible but emphasized they were doing everything they could and cooperating in every way they could while being equally careful not to give any details about just about anything. Some of the reporters, particularly the ones who didn't cover golf, became angry and mumbled derisively under their breath about a cover-up. When the questioning began to wind down, Juli leaned into the microphone.

"Thank you very much," she said. The three people on the dais rose in unison.

"Commissioner," yelled Gavin Webster, who was standing in the back near the door. "You've already stated publicly that you've been cooperating with FBI for more than a year now. Exactly how long have you, personally, known that people were being murdered at your tournaments?"

"Thank you, no more questions," Juli said as she leaned down to the microphone, her face flushed with anger.

Knots of reporters wandered forward trying to sneak in another question or two, trying to get something extra. The post-interview interview is a gambit that works sometimes at small tournaments, particularly if the person being interviewed is someone the writer has a history with—good or bad. But at the majors, forget it. And in this situation, it was about as likely to succeed as yelling at the president of the United States as he walks toward his helicopter on the lawn of the White House.

Juli saw the small cadre of reporters coming and wasted no time herding Commissioner Pierce and Special Agent Long out the same way they had come in. One or two writers tossed off questions in Pierce's direction but they bounced off him like golf balls hitting a railroad tie.

I emptied the film out of my cameras and put everything back in my locker behind the big scoreboard. David Hailey was putting his gear away after coming in from the course. He had no interest in photographing the commissioner but he did want to shoot Tiger Woods and any of the big European stars who were out playing early practice rounds. He was wiping sweat off his head with a white towel that said Pine Crest Hotel on it.

"Tiger finished?" I asked him.

"Finished about half an hour ago," he said as he stuffed his long lenses into the metal locker. "I stayed out with Sergio. Sun's a bit too high now. Time for a cake and some tea."

"See Killets out there?" I asked.

"As a matter of fact, no. I was going to ask if you'd seen her. She told me last night she intended to shadow Tiger's every move," he said. "Bit of a surprise not to see her about. I hope she's not ill."

I thought perhaps they'd had some kind of falling out after I left the bar. Certainly wasn't any of my business. What Killets did, thankfully, was out of my control. Way out of my control.

"That's what I thought, too," I said, dropping the subject. You never knew with Killets. There may have been a last-minute request from Pound for something and, if the assignment was juicy enough, Killets would have jumped on it instead of passing it on to me. She'd show up sooner or later.

I was pushing around cameras and lenses and boxes of film trying to make everything fit when I felt a hand on my shoulder.

"Got a minute?" It was Juli.

"Sure," I said, clanging the metal locker shut, threading the lock through the handle and turning the combination dial. I gave it one last tug to make certain it was secure.

Juli leaned in closer. "The commissioner would like to speak with you," she whispered.

"What about?" I asked.

"He'll explain." She walked briskly back through the media tent and I followed.

Outside it was as hot as an Alabama steel plant. We'd barely started up the little hill toward the clubhouse when I broke out in a heavy sweat. Five of Pinehurst's courses play out of the main clubhouse. The original wooden clubhouse had burned to the ground eons ago. The oldest part of the existing structure had a lovely pillared portico that looked out over the large putting complex. Unfortunately, the newest part of the clubhouse was the section directly behind the 18th green of the No. 2 course and was done in the architectural equivalent of early Holiday Inn. Had the portico been behind the 18th, it would be one of the prettiest pictures in golf. Instead, shots of the 18th ranged from mundane to boring. Juli led me inside the newer section, ordinarily reserved for club members only. No spectators or tourists allowed. We walked upstairs and turned left toward a conference room. She knocked on the door and pushed it open. Inside were the commissioner and the FBI agent, Long.

"Thanks for coming, Nick. Have a seat," said the commissioner, who indicated a chair across the table from him. The room smelled as if someone had tried to spray away old cigar smoke. The carpet was a spongy 1950s green and the heavy drapes were drawn against the heat and the sun.

"Care for something to drink?" asked Pierce.

"I could use an iced tea," I said. The commissioner looked at Juli and she left the room.

"Nick, I'm not going to waste your time. I want you to do a job for me, for the tour." An elderly black man wearing a tuxedo shirt and black trousers appeared out of nowhere with a sweating glass of tea on a silver serving tray. He put it on the table in front of me and disappeared as Juli came back in.

"I will if I can," I said and took a sip.

The commissioner nodded. "Good. Of course, you know the basics of our . . . situation."

I nodded.

"We know a good deal about your background," said the commissioner, looking down at his hands resting on the

table. "We know many of the details surrounding a pair of
deaths that occurred when you lived in Charleston. And we
know that you were able to be of some assistance to the police there."

"Very little," I said, shifting around in my seat, aware
of Juli watching me. Ashley Huddleston had been involved.
Another friend of ours, Porter Bancroft, had been, too. It was
after the divorce, when I had my ill-fated studio there.

The commissioner took a sip from a bottle of water on
the table in front of him. He put it down, holding it carefully
in both hands.

"You do have a . . . gift, let's say," Pierce said.

"Not really," I said.

The commissioner leaned in closer and grew quiet. He
folded his hands on the table in front of him. "I know you
see things, Nick. Maybe a better way to put it is, you get a
feel for things. He doesn't believe it," he said, nodding toward Long, "but I do. That's why I've asked you here. Juli
believes you do, too."

"Someone at Langley thinks you might be of some use.
Because you know the golf tour," interrupted Long. "Personally, I think it's all bullshit."

I could feel my face get hot but my fingers felt cold
wrapped around the glass. I was becoming lightheaded. It
seemed preposterous to me, too. It always had. Sometimes
though, when I looked through the camera, I did see things.
I never knew when it would happen or why. I could look
one minute and see a face, just a face, with light falling across
it, carving out the features like a sculptor working in clay.
Or I might look and see something deeper, something that
came right up out of a person's soul, something that the film
never seemed to be able to capture but was there, nonetheless. That's what happened to me in Charleston. I saw the

guilt and the rage. The commissioner was right about that. I'd seen it then but I wasn't able to do anything about it. I had no reason to believe I'd do any better this time, either.

"Will you help us?" asked the commissioner.

"I'll try," I said. "What do you want me to do?"

"Here's what we know," Pierce continued. "The killer drugs his victims to make them docile. The victims show signs of bruising around the neck. He kills them face to face, with his hands. Would you say that's correct, Agent Long?"

"He gets off on watching them die," Long said simply, clinically.

"In two of the cases, the bodies have been cut up badly. Post mortem. One of those was a man who dressed as a woman," Pierce said.

"New Orleans?"

The commissioner nodded. "On those two occasions the killer seems to have lost control. We don't know why. The other victims' bodies have been treated almost gently. Kind of arranged to his liking."

"And there's this." Agent Long put a plastic Ziploc bag on the table in front of me. The bag had a white space on one side for identification, and someone had carefully printed a series of numbers on it with a black marking pen. Inside the bag was a wadded-up piece of tissue, the special kind used to clean lenses without scratching the glass. "This was found under the desk in the motel room at the crime scene on Hilton Head."

So that was why Long had agreed to my help. "You think it's a photographer?" I looked at Juli but she wouldn't look at me.

"Possibly," Long said.

"He may be taking pictures of them, as sort of a souvenir," Pierce added. "That's one theory."

There was a knock at the door. "Come," said the commissioner. It was a state trooper, who first apologized for interrupting and then whispered something to Agent Long, whose face became gray and set.

"They just found another one," said the FBI man. "Woman's ID is a Jennifer Killets."

Juli and I were in the Lumina, driving toward the Forgotten City. It was a heavily forested section of the town of Dunbar, five miles from Pinehurst. It was surprisingly near the center of town and yet few people knew it was there. The houses were no better than shacks, most of them, with shake shingles that needed painting and pots of flowers that needed watering. Most of the roads were dirt and seemed to twist back on themselves like a convoluted board game. It was easy to get turned around. Even the local police didn't like to go into the Forgotten City.

The body had been dumped behind a nightclub with no name. It was a square, whitewashed, cinderblock building looking lonely and neglected in the daylight. There was no sign outside but everyone called it Eli's Inside Club. Eli was an old black man, an ex-caddie at the Hot Springs Golf and Country Club just outside town, who opened up his joint in the early sixties. It wasn't until 1995 that he even bothered to get a liquor license.

Jennifer Killets's body was discovered behind the Inside Club near where Eli dumped his grease buckets on the ground. It wasn't even in a makeshift grave. She'd just been covered over with leaves and a couple of old, bald tires the killer found lying in the woods. Eli saw a hand sticking up from inside one of the tires and called the cops himself. The area was taped off with yellow plastic tape strung from one tree trunk to another. Agent Long was already there when Juli and I drove up.

I had my camera with the 28–70 zoom and took a wide shot of the scene.

"Put that away," Long said.

I put the camera strap over my shoulder.

"You sure you want to see this?" he asked.

I took a deep breath. "Yeah, I'm sure," I said. Juli and I followed him toward the yellow tape and ducked underneath. I hadn't realized what a big man Long was. He was only a little bit taller than me but his chest was thick like a weightlifter, and his thighs bulged as he bent his legs to get under the tape.

"Can you identify her?" asked Long as he gently pulled back a large sheet of opaque plastic with his big hands.

Juli got close enough to recognize Jenny's face, stopped, and turned away. I walked closer.

"Jennifer Killets," I said. I was looking down at the naked body. She seemed sickeningly peaceful. I had expected worse. I thought back to the woman in Augusta and what Richard McPhee must have seen. Nothing like that had been done to Killets. It almost looked like she'd died in her sleep except for the bruises around her throat where the murderer had choked her life away.

"It doesn't look like anyone arranged this body," I said to Long.

"No," said the FBI agent. "We think he was interrupted. Someone might have seen him."

I put the camera up to my face and took a couple of pictures of poor Jenny. Her thin face. Her long, scraggly hair. Her eyes were looking back at me, bloodshot. For some reason, they didn't seem lifeless. They seemed to be saying something. I thought about the last person they had seen.

"Put the goddamn camera down," Long said angrily. "This is a human being, you know."

"This is how I see," I said.

"Yeah, well figure out some other way. Someone's going to take pictures here but it'll be for a reason, for a court of law. All you're doing is making me sick to my stomach."

21

He was lying in bed naked. His hands were folded behind his head. The television was on in the hotel room. Barely audible. The curtains were drawn against the morning light. He was watching one of the movies on the pay channel. It was something about young college girls. It was soft porn and didn't show any of the nasty bits.

What was the point? That sweet tea is amazing. She never tasted a thing. Have a sip, darlin'. What a joke. Dammit, at least you did that much right. You're taking too many chances. You have to be smarter. Mistakes. You're making too many mistakes. You have to be more careful. If you're not careful, you'll be sorry. Sorry. Sorry.

He slid his right hand down along his thigh and felt himself. He was getting hard as he looked at the blonde coed cheerleaders gone wild.

She went so quietly. Not even a whimper. Not even a tear. I thought you liked the ones that cried when they finally got it. You do, don't you? But you couldn't let me enjoy this one because of your foolish mistakes. You thought you were in the middle of the woods. The middle of nowhere. A good place for us to meet, you told her. You couldn't believe it when you saw that black man.

Shit, it's just an old crackhead. You careless bastard. If you aren't smart enough to do this properly you don't deserve to do it at all. Do you understand me?

He took himself in his hand and squeezed.

You don't deserve it. Next time you will make certain no one sees you. You can't just dump them and run away like a little boy. I have my needs, too. Without me, you're nothing. An idiot. Do I make myself clear?

He rolled over and moaned. "Perfectly."

The one who saw you? You have to take care of him, too. Can you handle that?

"Yes, yes, of course."

22

It was quiet in the car on the way back to the Carolina. Killets and I hadn't been exactly close, that's for sure, but that didn't matter now. We had been friends, after a fashion. She was decent and harmless, really, and her life had been snuffed out. We had our differences but we were a team. Seeing her lying there, discarded like rotten meat—nobody deserved that. It made the distant prospect of death seem very close. I thought about Dudley Sommers, the managing editor who loved her enough to stick Justin Pound with her, and I actually felt sorry for him. I wondered if he'd been told. Juli had known Killets almost as long as I had. They had a peculiar bond, two women working in the old boys' world of golf. They understood one another.

I pulled up to the front of the Carolina. Bunting was hanging from the portico in honor of the United States Open. The USGA's flag was flying on the flagpole next to the hotel, just below the American flag, and an attendant was lowering them carefully. It was dusk at the end of a long, hot day. One of the bellmen dressed in plus fours opened the car door for Juli. I got out, too.

"I'm just going to leave it here for a minute," I said. "See the lady to her room."

The valet ripped a stub in half and gave me part. "I'll

bring the car 'round the moment you need it, sir," he drawled
and drove off, screeching the tires.

"You don't have to come in," said Juli.

"I want to," I said. "I'll feel better once I know you're
OK."

The lobby was bright and cool. My shoes clicked against
the polished hardwood floors and then sank into the expensive carpets that were soft and spongy like Scottish links
land. A desk was set up next to the concierge with a big sign
that read TRANSPORTATION. There were a dozen or so volunteers loitering about in their tournament-issue shirts and
slacks or skirts, all color coordinated. I wondered if they realized they were targets. Their clothes might as well have
been bull's-eyes. Other people were standing in groups of
three or four trying to decide what to do for dinner, how
crowded everything was going to be and how long everything was going to take. Occasionally a player walked briskly
through the lobby, ignoring the looks of recognition. The
rule was, if you don't make eye contact, you don't have to
stop. The people didn't exist. Tiger Woods's entourage came
in. His tall Swedish wife. His short, Thai mother with her
wide-brimmed red hat. Two people from the Tiger Woods
Foundation. Tiger was nowhere to be seen. He came and
went through the kitchen with three beefy bodyguards.

"Can I buy you a drink?" I asked Juli.

"One."

We walked into the Old Dornoch Room, the little bar
off the lobby. The tables were all taken but there was a stool
at the bar. I motioned to Juli and she sat down. I stood behind her.

"A pint of Harp and a Cosmopolitan," I told the bartender.

When she picked up her glass, I lifted mine and said,
"To Killets."

"To Killets."

I took a big gulp and tried to wash away the memory of the deserted garbage dump behind the Inside Club and Killets's eyes. I couldn't seem to get her eyes out of my mind. I knew she was talking to me.

"Poor Jenny," said Juli. "Do you think she suffered?"

"No. I don't know," I said. "God, I hope not."

We drank in silence. There was laughter and joking in the bar but it seemed very disconnected from us. "Mickelson finished second here last time," said a voice a few barstools away. "He's the man to beat. Ever since he won that major last year, the pressure's off." No one had heard there'd been another killing. No one knew we had lost a friend. I wondered how many of those volunteers in the lobby would be there the next day after they read the morning papers.

"One thing," I said to Juli. "She knew him."

"How do you know?" she asked.

"I don't know how I know," I said. "I just do."

I looked across the room and saw Jimmy Wildheart sitting with Justus Litchard at a table in the corner. Litchard had his head dipped down slightly, partially hiding the scar on his left cheekbone. Jimmy Wildheart seemed pale and angry. Litchard's hands were thick and meaty. He had them resting in front of him, holding the plated silver bowl crammed full of packets of artificial sweetener and white and brown sugar. As he talked to Jimmy, he looked back and forth, from the silver bowl to Jimmy's colorless face, slowly turning the bowl in his fingertips. After a few moments they seemed to stop talking altogether but Justus Litchard never stopped looking at Jimmy Wildheart. He just sat there with his head bowed slightly, like a fighter tucking his chin. Eventually Wildheart nodded. Litchard got up from the table, patted Jimmy on the back, peeled a bill off a roll of cash, and tossed it down on the table. When he had left,

Jimmy leaned his elbows on the table and put his face in his hands.

"It's a funny thing," Juli said. "I don't want to scare you or anything, it's just that I've been having this feeling that someone has been watching me. Not following me exactly. More like watching me, if you get the difference. I'm sure it's just, you know, everything that's been going on."

"Have you seen anyone?" I asked.

"No," she said, taking a sip from the martini glass. "That's the point. It's just this weird feeling I've got. I'm sure it's nothing. I'm just jumpy, that's all."

"Have you told anybody?" I asked.

"Just you. It's like, if I work late in the press room or go jogging early in the morning," she said. "I can't explain it. It's just a feeling I have. There's never anyone actually there. At least, I'm pretty sure there isn't."

"No more jogging," I said. "I don't think you should be alone."

"How alone can I be? I'm surrounded all day by two hundred writers who snort Viagra."

I laughed. "Have you got someone to room with on the road?"

"I'm not sure I should answer that question."

"It's not personal," I said. "You heard the commissioner, I'm on the case."

"I suppose I could arrange to room with Polly Swift. She manages the website for the tour but she's not here this week. The USGA does it themselves. You remember Polly," said Juli. "She snores like a plow horse, though."

"I think it would be a good idea. For both of you," I said. "Get her some Breathe-Rites. What about this week?"

"Is that a proposition?"

"Always," I said.

"Probably not such a great idea," Juli polished off the last sip of her Cosmo. She looked at the lime sitting in the bottom of the martini glass.

We both knew she was right.

Gavin Webster squeezed in next to us at the bar, fresh from the tennis court, from the smell of him. He reached a hand across Juli's body to pinch a couple of pretzels from the glass bowl in front of her. He was holding a racquet with a cover on it emblazoned with a gigantic P, and his sweaty shirt was untucked and drooped from his shoulders like a used dishtowel.

"Seen McKie anywhere?" he asked, munching on a pretzel. "Water," he said to the bartender, "with a lemon."

"No," I replied.

"Sorry," he looked down at himself. "Haven't had a chance to shower yet. I told Stewart I'd meet him down here but the last set went to a tie break. I won thirteen-eleven. Played with the local pro, what's his name, at the country club."

"Good old what's his name," I said. Obviously, Webster hadn't heard about Killets yet, either.

"Doesn't matter," he said. "Guy double faulted to lose. Guess that's how he got all the way from Wimbledon to right here in the middle of nowhere." He gulped down half the glass of water. "If Stewart shows up, tell him I'll be right back. You two have dinner plans?"

"Yes," I said quickly.

"Maybe tomorrow then." Webster slipped through the crowd and out the door as people recoiled to avoid touching any part of his body.

Juli looked at me.

"He'll find out soon enough," I said. "I just didn't feel like talking about it. Besides, he didn't even know Killets.

All he would want would be the pictures. Guys like him, they love the pictures. The more blood the better. It's worth an extra five hundred words in the story."

"I better get up to the room," Juli said.

"Let me walk you," I said.

"OK." Juli put her arm through mine and we headed for the bank of elevators across the hallway from the newsstand.

She was in a room on the sixth floor. The hallway creaked under our feet. It was a muffled, comfortable sound, like the old house you grew up in. When we got to 619 she pulled the key card out of her pocketbook.

"Thanks, Nick," she said, opening the door.

I stuck my head in the room. "Just having a quick look," I told her as I came in. She smiled and tossed the key on the desk. The room already smelled like her.

After I peeked in the closet, I closed the heavy, louvered doors and looked at Juli. Her clothes were neatly pressed and hung carefully. Not one hanger physically touching another.

"All clear?" she asked.

"All clear," I said. I took a deep breath.

"Thanks." She patted my cheek with her hand. A tear welled up in her eyes. For me. For Killets. For everything.

"I'm sorry," I said.

"I know. It just went wrong," she said. "We made mistakes. We both made mistakes." At least we could still talk. It was a small thing to hang on to but it was all we had.

"See you tomorrow," I said and closed the door behind me. I retraced my steps to the elevator and pushed the down arrow. I knew when it went bad. It went bad the moment I forgot what I had and what I had promised. Some things can't ever be put right, like a car in a bad accident. You can straighten the bent frame, replace the fractured glass and plastic with factory new parts, pound out the dents, repaint the scratches. But no matter what, it will never be quite the same and you're kidding yourself if you think it will. Every time Juli looks at me and every time I look at her, we see the broken parts, the damage—at least for now. But, maybe, not forever.

23

On the way down, the elevator stopped at the third floor and a man and a woman I recognized from the USGA party got on without a word. He immediately pushed the CLOSE button three times impatiently. When we reached the lobby and the doors slid apart, Justus Litchard was standing in front of us, filling up the doorway with his large body, waiting to get on. The couple squeezed past as Litchard pushed his way inside. He blocked my exit when he extended his muscular arm to hit the button for the fifth floor. As he stood back, the elevator doors started to close. I jumped forward and put my arm between them and the doors jerked open again. Litchard looked at me like I was annoying him.

"I'm getting off here," I said, stepping into the hallway. He just grunted, reached over and hit the 5 firmly again, staring at me as the doors shut.

On my way out of the hotel, I stuck my head back inside the Old Dornoch Room and was surprised to see Stormy seated at the dark mahogany bar next to Jeremy Howe, whose oddly shaped body drooped on all sides of the barstool like a mushroom cap. He had a half-finished martini in front of him.

"Ah, the Yousuf Karsh of golf," said Howe, waving to me. "Come join us."

"And that would make you, what, Henry Longhurst?"
I replied.

"Touché," said Howe.

"When did you two get here?" I asked.

"Just now arrived," said Howe. He stirred his martini
with the olive that was impaled on a clear plastic toothpick.
"Would you care for a drink? The barman here makes a very
serviceable martini." He summoned the bartender with the
crook of his index finger.

"I think I'll pass," I said.

"Suit yourself. I'll have another, my friend," he said to
the bartender. "The man is a magician."

"Stormy," I said, leaning back to talk around Howe.
"What are you doing here?"

Howe jumped in before Stormy could answer. "He's
my bloody bodyguard," said Howe. "Isn't that right, Stormy,
old fellow?" Howe drained the remainder of his drink, holding the stem of the glass between his plump thumb and forefinger.

"Yes, sir," said Stormy. "If you say so."

"It's Juli's idea," said Howe. "She's such a mother hen,
that one. It's appalling, really. Apparently, she doesn't think
I should be running amok in a strange land."

Stormy pushed back from the bar to speak around the
famous British announcer. "Mrs. Oliver thinks it would be a
good idea for Mr. Howe to have someone to drive him
around in the evenings," he said and winked at me.

"I can see how that might be wise," I offered.

"Wouldn't do anyone any good if something was to happen," said Stormy, who was drinking a Diet Coke but, I assumed, lusting after a vodka of his own.

"What about Ian?" I asked.

"We play in the morning but it's not early," said Stormy.

"I'll be able to get Mr. Howe home and get to the course in plenty of time. I've already lasered it."

"You do this kind of thing often?" I asked Stormy.

"Every once in a while when Juli asks me to look after someone. She pays pretty good, too," Stormy said. "I'm not going to be a caddie forever, you know. One of these days Ian is going to retire and I figure maybe I can catch on doing some work for the tour, you know? Doesn't hurt to make yourself useful."

"Well done," Howe said to the bartender, taking a sip of his fresh drink. "Excellent work."

"I suppose I ought to be going," I said. "Long day tomorrow."

"Not just yet," Howe said. "Stormy has kindly offered to take me to—what was the name of it—that private club."

"Eli's Inside Club," Stormy replied.

"Exactly," Howe said, slapping the bar with his hand. "The Inside Club. Stormy says it's an after-hours establishment patronized by the locals. He's going to lead me there as if he was taking Stanley to Lake Tanganyika." Howe took a gulp of the martini, slid off the lead olive with his fingers, and put it in his mouth. "You must come with us," he said as he chewed. "I absolutely insist."

I hated the idea of going back to the place where Killets's body had been found only a few hours before. On the other hand, I thought I might get a chance to ask a few questions, maybe find out if anyone had seen anything. "I don't know," I said.

"I don't think we're going to be there too long," Stormy offered, nodding at Howe, who was already draining his martini.

"I guess it can't hurt," I said, even though I didn't necessarily share Stormy's confidence that it was going to be a short night. Howe's capacity was legendary. One year during the old Players Championship, he walked into a bar in Jacksonville Beach and saw a sign on the wall offering free martinis to anyone who could drink five. He sat down at the bar and ordered five martinis. The bartender explained to him that the sign simply meant if he was able to drink five martinis, they would be on the house. Howe looked at him and said, "My dear fellow. I'd like five martinis and I'd like them lined up here." He wet his index finger and drew a line on the bar in front of him, took his own bottle of garlic-stuffed olives out of his coat pocket, and proceeded to drink all five martinis right down. He put ten dollars down for the bartender and left. Besides, when the great British voice got in one of his moods to explore the countryside, there was no stopping him.

After Howe signed his tab in the Old Dornoch Room, Stormy got the courtesy car Juli loaned him and picked us up at the front entrance of the Carolina. The drive to Dunbar only took a few minutes. Finding Eli's Inside Club, however, was quite another matter.

The town of Dunbar grew up out of nowhere in the late 1800s, nothing more than a railroad stop to service Pinehurst. The buildings had changed remarkably little in the last century. The Forgotten City was an angular turn off one of the main roads but those were the only directions Stormy had gotten in advance. Even though I'd been there that very afternoon, I couldn't find my way back. There were no street lights in the Forgotten City, in fact, few public services at all. No city sewer. No garbage pickup. Only a couple paved roads. It was dark and hot, and, for Killets, it had been fatal.

We drove around aimlessly, turning here, turning there. Backtracking. Circling. Stopping, backing up, turning around. We wound up back in the main part of Dunbar twice and started all over again until, at last, we saw a black couple walking beside the road. He was wearing dark glasses. She had on a tight, white pair of shorts and a tube top.

Stormy stopped and lowered his window. "Inside Club?" he asked. The man looked at the three of us, smiled in a bemused kind of way, and told Stormy the sequence of turns and switchbacks.

The Inside Club was a square building with one door and no windows. It didn't even open until 9 P.M. That was when Eli heated up his fryer and began to bread his chicken and dip it in the hot oil, serving the steaming, greasy breasts on pieces of white bread as late-night snacks. Before he got his liquor license and became legal, the cops would show up every Sunday morning about 3 A.M., purportedly to close Eli down. Of course, per their usual arrangement, the cops never showed up without calling first. When Eli got the call, he'd drop a two-by-six across the door and let the police pound away until they'd made a reasonable show of doing their civic duty, usually leaving before first light. It was early enough, at any rate, for the customers locked inside to make it to a 10 A.M. service at the AME Church.

The dirt parking lot in front of the Inside Club was almost empty. The clientele had been pretty much driven off by a Dunbar police cruiser parked next to the building. A deputy was sitting inside the car, reading a magazine with the map light on. I figured he must have been assigned to protect the crime scene behind the club.

The door to the Inside Club was solid metal. With a heave, Stormy pushed it open and we walked in, turning to the left down a hallway. The two-by-six was standing upright in the corner. The bar was straight ahead, all along one side of the building. The floor was cracked linoleum tile of no discernible design, a motley collection of construction job overruns. The tables were mostly old formica kitchen tables from the 1950s. To the right was Eli's kitchen. A single bare light bulb hung down from the ceiling on a frayed wire. The fryers were behind him and next to them was a pile of bloody chicken breasts from the counter top almost to the ceiling. Eli was smoking a cigarette and periodically he'd turn around and shake the baskets sizzling in the oil. Across the room was a jukebox. Ella Fitzgerald was singing "Cotton Tail."

I was pretty certain I wasn't going to learn much at the Inside Club. There were only two customers in the place, a couple of Pinehurst caddies sitting at the far end of the bar playing a dice game for drinks, shaking a cracked leather cup with seven dice in it and slamming it upside down on the bar.

The bartender was a middle-aged white woman and she didn't seem to be in any hurry to get to us.

"Looks like the cops outside are having a bad effect on business," I said when she came over.

"You can say that again," she wiped the bar in front of us with a rag. She looked at Stormy because he was black and said, "How'd you find us?"

Stormy took a business card out of his pocket. I couldn't tell whose it was. He turned it over and showed the woman the writing on the back. After she read it she looked at us and said, "What can I get you?"

"Can you make a martini?" asked Howe.

"What you need is what I make," she said. "I'm Eli's wife, Hazel." She wiped off her hands and put one out, cold and wet.

"Jeremy Howe," said the announcer, shaking her hand. "Very dry. As dry as the Serengeti."

Hazel looked at Stormy, who shook his head. "Diet Coke," he said. "I'm the driver." She looked over at me. "Same," I said.

When she came back with the drinks she yelled toward the kitchen. "Eli, come on over here when you get a minute. Somebody here you need to meet."

I wandered over to the jukebox. It had Keb' Mo'. P. Diddy. Sarah Vaughan. Lena Horne. Miles Davis. B.B. King. I fed a dollar into it and picked two songs by Keb' Mo'. When I got back to the bar, Eli was standing there talking to Jeremy Howe, whose toupee was slightly askew.

"You must be joking," Howe said.

"No, sir. How old you think I am?" he asked him.

"No clue," said Howe. "Mid-fifties?"

"Closer to seventy," Eli said proudly. "Show him the picture, Haze."

The woman reached under the bar and brought out a framed black-and-white photograph. She laid it down on the bar in front of Jeremy Howe as gently as if she was dipping a baby's head in bath water.

"That's me," Eli said. "Me and Hogan."

"You caddied for Ben Hogan?" I asked.

"Yes, sir. In the Ryder Cup right here in Pinehurst," he said. "It was fifty-one. 'Course, I was just a boy then. Still in my teens. And I'll tell you something about Hogan—I never saw a man who could smoke so much and play so slow in my whole goddamn life. And he wasn't near as bad a putter as they say, either. Nobody wins like he did, they can't putt. Maybe at the end he lost it but not when he was going good. No, sir."

Howe asked Eli who else he'd caddied for and the names astounded him. Sam Snead. Jimmy Demaret. Ken Venturi. Harvie Ward.

"By the time Nicklaus and them started coming around, I was pretty much finished with it," Eli said. "But a lot of 'em used to come to the club. The caddies would bring 'em. I got pictures at home."

Even Howe was mesmerized by Eli's stories of the golfers he'd watched up close. Howe tried to quiz him on their
games. He wanted to know what their swings looked like.
How did they act when they were under pressure? Jeremy
Howe couldn't resist telling Eli his own stories of the champions he'd known. Palmer. Player. Trevino. Stormy told Eli
what a good amateur player Jeremy Howe had been. Howe
and Eli swapped tales the way kids used to swap baseball
cards, laughing as they tried to out-funny one another.

As the hours wore on, a few more of the Inside Club's
regulars decided to ignore the police cruiser parked outside.
The little cinderblock building began to fill up with folks
looking for Eli's fried chicken.

I was listening to a Muddy Waters song when Hazel
leaned partway across the bar in front of me.

"Somebody asking for you," she said.

"Really?" I looked down the bar.

"That one, over at the jukebox. The black T-shirt and
black jeans."

I turned around. The man had on black tennis shoes
with the laces undone and a Detroit Tigers baseball cap
turned backwards and set askew over an orange head rag.
"You know him?" I asked.

"Yeah," she replied.

"Trust him?"

"He's cash only," she said.

I walked over to the jukebox. "I understand you want
to talk to me," I said to the man. "My name's Nick Oliver."

"That's cool," he said. "I see you here this afternoon
when they come for that girl?"

"I was here," I said.

"I might maybe can help you."

"How so?"

"I might know something. But it's expensive, you know."

"How much?"

"A hundred."

"I'll give you twenty."

"Sheeit," he said.

I turned and started to walk back to the bar.

"Hey," he said. "Where you goin'?"

"I thought you didn't . . ."

"Better than nothin'."

I took out my money clip and pulled off a twenty.

"So?"

"I seen the dude."

"Could you recognize him?"

"I didn't get that close, you know what I mean? It was dark. You seen what it's like around here in the night."

It suddenly dawned on me. "You watched him kill the girl?"

"What do you take me for, man? I saw him kind of start to hide her, you know. Kind of standing over her like. She already dead." He pulled some coins out of his pocket, thought about putting them in the jukebox and then put the money back in his pants pocket. I reached in my pocket, took out a dollar bill and fed the machine. He pushed a couple of numbers and looked around to make certain no one else was coming up. P. Diddy started to play.

"What kind of build did he have? Was he a big man?"

"At least your size," he said. "Bigger maybe. Hard to tell."

"What about the car? What kind of car was he driving?"

"Never saw no car. I was out in back. Doin' my business, you know what I mean?"

What a waste of twenty bucks, I thought. Even if the

FBI questioned this guy under hypnosis, all he'd remember was where he bought his last rock.

"I can tell you one thing, though," he said.

"Yeah?"

"Dude was white."

24

I decided to watch the first ball struck in the National Open. I didn't want a picture of it, I just wanted to be there. In the morning, there was a police cruiser parked outside the Aberdeen Inn Bed & Breakfast. Two officers were searching Jenny Killets's room. It gave me a sinking feeling, knowing they were systematically going through her stuff as if they were sifting the ashes of a cold fire. I didn't know what to do, so I went back to work. I walked down Magnolia to Cherokee to Carolina Vista, crossed the road, and passed through the gate onto the grounds using my photographer's badge. It was barely past sunrise and it was already humid.

I ducked into the dining tent for a cup of coffee. The only other person in there was Colt Reeves. His straw hat was on the table in front of him. He was reading the *New York Times* sports section and eating a bowl of bran flakes with a banana. He looked up, saw me, and looked away again.

A black woman with a small waist and her hair strung in lines of multicolored beads came out of a makeshift kitchen with a basket of fruit and bagels.

"Can I help you?" she asked.

"I'm just getting coffee," I said. She quickly went back to transferring oranges and bananas onto a tray.

"Oliver." Colt Reeves had come up behind me. "I just wanted to say I'm sorry about Killets."

"Thanks," I said.

"She was a pain in the ass," he continued in his South Carolina accent. "I don't think a day ever went by I didn't get some kind of complaint from some player about her being out of position or taking pictures when she wasn't supposed to or . . ."

"Look," I said. "I appreciate the sentiment. Why don't you just leave it at that?"

"Yeah," he said. "Anyway, I'm sorry."

Reeves went back to his *New York Times*. I went as far in the other direction as I could and found a table with a *Raleigh Daily News* picked apart and scattered around like carrion. Travel. Business. Want ads. I rummaged around until I found the sports section. I read the U.S. Open preview story. It wasn't bad. They had a regular golf writer who spent time covering tour events and it showed. It wasn't the usual drivel.

As I was reading, a handful of other photographers walked in, carrying their heavy lenses, getting ready to take advantage of the early morning light. I recognized their faces but didn't know all their names. A woman from the Associated Press, a guy from *USA Today*, a photographer from *Golf*, and another one who worked regularly for the USGA. They were sticking plastic bottles of water in their packs to guard against the day's heat. I found it incomprehensible that any of them, or any of the other shooters I knew, could have left that lens tissue in the motel on Hilton Head.

After I finished my coffee I walked up by the clubhouse and took a seat in the small stands to the left of the first tee. The first player to tee off in the U.S. Open was Jack Savage, a one-time pro from Louisiana who had played the tour for three years, hardly ever made a cut and never made a nickel to speak of, took a job working in the West Texas oil fields, got reinstated as an amateur, and made it to the semifinals of the USGA's Mid-Amateur Championship the year before. The Mid-Amateur was the exclusive province of insurance salesmen, stockbrokers, and failed tour pros. Savage could play, though. He just couldn't play with the Tiger Woods and Ernie Elses of the world, or the Francisco Pietros, for that matter. With the hazy sun just beginning to filter through the longleaf pines, the drilling foreman, probably the only man in the tournament with coarse hands from honest labor, drove it wide right. His ball hit on the sandy cart path and skittered deep into the woods. He wouldn't have any trouble finding it but he probably wouldn't have a clear shot at the green either. He'd have to punch out into the fairway and hope to get it up and down from 60 or 70 yards for par. It was the same at every U.S. Open. It was a brawl. Savage seemed like a particularly good pick to start the fight with Pinehurst No. 2.

When I came down from the stands I decided to walk up toward the practice range. Ahead on the cement cart path, I saw Stormy standing beside Ian Person's Ford bag with the huge blue letters. Ian was from Detroit and he had sponsorship deals with Ford, NAPA Auto Parts, FRAM oil filters, and Thee Doll House.

"Stormy," I said. He just stared at me, almost catatonic. "Something wrong?"

"Something wrong all right," he said, flicking his half-smoked cigarette somewhere up the cart path, accidentally landing it in front of an oncoming group of Boy Scouts from Mebane, North Carolina, who were patrolling the grounds with plastic garbage bags and sticks with prongs on the end, spearing trash.

"Howe and I keep you out too late last night?" I asked.

"Naw," he said. "Maybe I shouldn't say nothin'. You being a journalist and all." He just about spit out the word.

"Photographer," I said.

"You broke the story about the murders, didn't you?"

"I guess," I said.

Stormy unzipped one of the pockets of the oversized golf bag and pulled out his pack of cigarettes. He lit another one and put the pack away. "Ian doesn't let me smoke on the golf course," he explained.

I nodded. "So, what's the problem?"

"We're playing with Jimmy Wildheart today," he said.

"What's wrong with that?" I asked. There were some players that no one liked to play with, usually because they were too slow, had an obnoxious habit, or were known cheaters, but I had the impression everyone pretty much liked Jimmy Wildheart.

"Nothing. Jimmy's good people. I can't say I mind having Soozi tagging along, either," he said.

"Then what's the problem?"

Stormy looked to his left and right, then swiveled around to look behind him. "Justus Litchard."

"And?"

Stormy took a deep drag on his cigarette. "You didn't hear this from me."

"OK," I said.

"You ever bet on the computer, on-line?" He flicked the ash off his cigarette, bent down, and wiped his sweaty brow with the golf towel hanging on Person's clubs.

"Offshore casinos?"

"Right. They're in the Caribbean some place. Like Antigua or somewhere. I don't know. Anyway, you give 'em your credit card number and then you place bets. It's all legal. At least, the government can't figure out a way to stop it."

"I've heard about them but I'm not much of a gambler."

"Mostly they're owned by the big conglomerates, the Vegas companies. One or two might be a little suspect. There are mob rumors about some of them but mostly it's legitimate, I think. They use the same odds you find every morning in the paper. There's this one site— Double down.biz—has a lot of golf action. You can get three to two on Tiger to win the Open. They also do what they call daily races, head-to-head bets. Today one of the races is Ian Person vs. Jimmy Wildheart."

"So?" I asked.

"What's going to happen is that a lot of people sitting at a lot of different computers in a lot of different cities are going to be betting $1,000, $2,000, up to $5,000 on Ian Person to beat Jimmy Wildheart today, head-to-head. Maybe a thousand different guys at a thousand different laptops going to a lot of different sites. All of a sudden, it's real money. A thousand times a thousand is a million bucks. Pay out a ten percent commission, you're still clearing nine hundred grand. You see what I'm getting at?" Stormy took another draw on his cigarette.

"Yeah, but if Jimmy Wildheart wins . . ." I said.

"He won't."

"How do you know? This course sets up pretty well for him."

Stormy just laughed, a bitter, disgusted chuckle. "Justus Litchard had a talk with Jimmy." He flipped another half-smoked cigarette away.

"What do you mean?"

"Man, don't you get it? Litchard told Jimmy that if he doesn't finish worse than Ian, something bad is going to happen. To him or to someone he loves. You understand?"

"Oh, come on. How is that possible?"

"Believe me, it just is."

"Is Ian involved?" I asked.

"Absolutely not. But it makes you feel dirty just the same. What's going to happen is Ian's going to play his best today. Put up the best score he can. It's the U.S. fucking Open, for God sakes. If Jimmy sees it's going to be better than anything he could shoot, well, he'll just try to get it as low as he can, too. But, if it looks like Ian might go for a big number, Jimmy will make sure he goes *higher*, one way or the other."

"Can't Ian do something?"

"Like what? Jimmy ain't going to cheat. He's just going to play bad," said Stormy. "Worse than Ian anyway."

"He's that afraid of Justus Litchard?"

"You bet your sweet ass he is. Everyone is. Justus Litchard is crazy, man, the scariest son of a bitch ever played. Jimmy Wildheart's not thinking about winning the U.S. Open right about now. He just wants to get out of Pinehurst with his fingers and thumbs still working. You understand what I'm saying? Man's got a career."

"Litchard's connected?" I asked.

Stormy exhaled disgustedly like he was explaining quantum physics to a garden slug. "Already told you that one, pards."

"Can he get to anyone?" I asked. "Litchard, I mean."

"Truth is, I'm not sure," said Stormy. "Usually, what I hear, it's the players in the middle. You know, the lurkers. Like Jimmy and Ian. And it doesn't happen often. Maybe three, four, five times a year. They load up on one match and, one way or another, Litchard makes sure it comes out the way they want it to. If you're asking me could the guy get to someone like Tiger Woods, the answer is, I don't know."

"You mean someone, like at the Masters, could be coming down the stretch and dump a shot into the water at the fifteenth . . ."

"No, I don't believe that's what happened," said Stormy. "Tiger'd be a pretty hard guy to threaten. He's got his own bodyguards. He just lost that one. My guess is Tiger would be too much trouble for them to go after. Besides, everything I know about him, you could break every bone in his body and he'd still try to beat you. I'm guessing they'd stick to the smaller fish. Make a million here and a million there and no one's the wiser. Don't get greedy. Of course, if I wanted to make a really big killing—pardon the expression—I'd make sure someone lost when he was a mortal lock to win."

I rested my hand on Stormy's shoulder.

"There's Ian," he said. "Later." He picked up the heavy bag, adjusting the weight so the strap sat just right on his shoulder. He draped the towel over the clubs and caddie-walked in a quick, bouncing step, to catch up with his man, who was striding so fast toward Heartbreak Hill you could almost see the steam coming out of his ears.

When I got back to the press center I made a call to Justin Pound on my cell phone. Since Killets, I'd been ignoring his messages. I just wasn't up to it.

"Pound."

"Justin," I said. "It's Nick Oliver."

"Oliver." I could hear him stop rustling slide sheets in the background. "You OK?"

"I guess," I said.

"God, it's just awful about Killets," he offered.

"Yeah."

"Do they think it was the Bogeyman?"

"The *what*?"

"The Bogeyman. That's what they're calling the guy in the tabloids in London," he said. "The British Open is the next major. The tabs are all over the story. Our overseas circulation is up two hundred and fifty percent."

"Great."

"You want me to send someone else down?"

"No," I said. "Not unless you really think it's necessary. I can probably handle it."

"Figured you'd say that," Pound said. I could tell he was relieved but I couldn't tell if he was relieved because he wasn't going to have to send someone else into a bad situation or he was relieved because he didn't have to spend the money.

"I'll get you the shipping instructions for Sunday night," he said. "There might even be someone coming back who can hand carry it. I think Webster is flying out then. When are you going to go digital?"

"Soon," I said. "I can get the early stuff processed here. There's a lab running film every night. That way you'll only have to process the Sunday take."

"Sounds good," said Pound.

"Justin?"

"Yeah?"

"What arrangements have been made about Jenny?"

"Dudley Sommers is on his way down there. He's going to bring her back when the police and the coroner's office release the body. Of course, there has to be an autopsy. Poor guy's pretty broken up," Pound said.

"Can you transfer me to someone in research? I need some background on a player," I said.

"Who?"

"A guy named Justus Litchard."

25

He was a broad man with meaty shoulders and thick, skillful hands. His left eye fluttered nervously. Fifteen years earlier Justus Litchard had been a promising boxer forced into retirement after just a few professional fights when he nearly lost an eye in a car accident. At least, that was what the biography published in the tour's media guide in the section entitled "Other Prominent Members" said. Those were the players who, when they did manage to get their name on a leaderboard, everybody's first reaction is, "Who's that?" I learned the real truth about Litchard from the archivist at *Current*. It was true enough that Litchard had been a promising light heavyweight and he did almost lose an eye but it was in a bar fight and not a car wreck. The fight happened in a place called the Pleasure Inn in a rough part of Daytona. About a year later, after a couple of plastic surgeries smoothed out his face and settled down the twitching of the eye caused by nerve damage, a man was assaulted, crippled for life, out behind the Pleasure Inn. Someone dropped a sack over the man's head, then knocked him unconscious. He was dragged behind a dumpster and tied in a sitting position to a telephone pole with some duct tape. Then the assailant or assailants dropped a cinderblock on his shins over and over again until there was nothing between his knees and his ankles but fleshy mush and bone chips. People in the bar said the victim was the same guy who attacked Justus Litchard with a broken beer bottle.

On the first tee, Litchard would be introduced as being from Boca Raton, Florida, but he'd actually grown up on the streets of South Philadelphia and still spent most of the year there. He owned a rough and tumble bar in South Philly but no one ever caused a problem in Justus Litchard's joint because it was rumored to be a mob place. Litchard himself was low-rent muscle who had become a better-than-average golfer in his spare time. It was Litchard who convinced Joseph "Joey Flowers" Sabella, the boss in Philly, that he could be more use playing on the tour than beating up deadbeats and hustling golf games in Vegas and Atlantic City. Joey Flowers knew he could fix basketball games by buying off kids from the projects and football games by bribing the zebras. But golf? This would have been a whole new product line. I knew, if Stormy was right, it must be a pretty lucrative one. And Justus Litchard was the key to it all.

As near as I could figure, in the time Joey Flowers had been running his golf scam, the only problem he had was keeping Litchard out on tour. To begin with, Justus Litchard was almost always in danger of losing his card. He was a decent player who saved himself most weeks with his short game. That, and cheating now and again. So, there was the problem of keeping him from getting caught and, when he did get caught, keeping him from getting booted off the tour. And there was the fact that Litchard was a heavy drinker, a carouser, and a brawler. He'd ripped a woman's dress nearly off and then tossed her in a pool at a party in Tucson and, another time, he shoved a man's head through a Golden Tee video game in Cincinnati. Litchard was violent and impulsive but, even by a conservative reckoning, he had made Joey Flowers in excess of $11 million so far. He was worth a little inconvenience.

On his way from the practice ground to the first tee, Litchard stopped to look at the large scoreboard filling up with names and black and red numbers from the morning rounds. He saw where Jimmy Wildheart had shot 72 while Ian Person finished with a one-under-par 69, one of only three rounds under par among the morning players. The edge of Litchard's mouth drifted up into a small grin. It was a good start to the day. His boss had already cleared seven figures. He ducked under the ropes, afraid he might be late getting to the tee.

Litchard was paired with the Masters champion, Francisco Pietro, and a Swede, Nils Spjutsson, who wore tight, bell-bottom pants and whose only English phrases were Bible verses and references to Christian saints.

"Play well," Pietro said to the other two as he was being announced and the crowd welcomed the winner of the year's first major.

Litchard grunted with a golf tee clamped between his teeth. "In His name," the Swede said, nodding his head.

All three drove it into the fairway but Pietro and the Swede were a good thirty yards ahead of Justus Litchard. For all of Litchard's size and strength, he was a puny hitter. The timing of his golf swing was just not good enough to get all the power that resided naturally in his thick, muscled body.

I took a position up the fairway, shooting back with my 600 mm lens. Because Pietro was in the threesome, there were a half dozen or so photographers walking inside the ropes through the hardpan waste area to the right of the fairway. Were these the people I was supposed to watch for Jacob Pierce? I couldn't bring myself to believe it. Besides, it wasn't them I was interested in, or the Italian, for that matter. It was Litchard. With the other photographers there, at least I wouldn't stand out too much. Besides, with a few pictures of Pietro thrown in the take, it would look to Justin Pound like I'd been out working and not just shadowing someone of little consequence, at least as far as *Current* magazine was concerned.

Litchard appeared distracted through the lens. He tore some blades of grass from the fairway and tossed them up in the air even though there wasn't a breath of wind. He angrily waved off a couple of marshals who were barely in his field of vision. Since he had hit balls for almost an hour before his tee time, Litchard's shirt was already soaked with sweat. He pulled a short iron from his Gucci embossed golf bag—a lucrative contract he got thanks to Joey Flowers. His approach was short and right of the green. It hit in the embankment and trickled off into a collection area. Litchard slammed the club against the bag and let it drop. Up at the green he managed to putt up the slope to within three feet of the cup and make that one to save his four. Spjutsson and Pietro both made birdie threes to open.

It became obvious, even to Litchard himself, that Pinehurst No. 2 was too much golf course for him. He couldn't drive the ball far enough to hit the kind of iron shots that would hold the inverted saucer–shaped greens. Litchard found himself either putting up huge embankments or trying to finesse impossible flop shots from tight lies to the hard, fast greens. As quick as the greens were, they weren't nearly as fast as most U.S. Opens. So severe are the contours at No. 2 that, had they been at 12 or 13 on the Stimpmeter, even the best players in the world wouldn't have been able to finish by dark.

On the eighth hole, a par 5 that was being played as a par 4 for the Open, Litchard hit a long iron approach that rolled to the very back of the green, 50 feet away from a pin cut at the front edge. The green on the eighth falls off steeply on the left and the crowd isn't allowed up that side. Nor is there anyone behind it since the green descends in that direction to the nineth tee. The only place for gallery was inside the line of longleaf pines on the right, far away from the green itself.

Litchard was already five over par and barely able to contain his fury. The Swede had driven it into the rough on the left, muscled it up short of the green, and praised the Lord. Pietro had missed to the left of the plateau green and his ball had come to rest in a drainage area. He was waiting for a ruling from the USGA referee walking with the group while Spjutsson wedged his ball up to four feet. I was standing back along the ropes, watching Litchard through my 600 mm lens. His ball was in the area of the green where players walked off to go to the nineth and it was already spiked up badly. Litchard marked his ball. Then he tapped down the marker with his mallet head putter. While Pietro, Spjutsson, and the referee were discussing the situation in the drainage area, Litchard took a couple of steps to one side, bent over and fixed a pitch mark, then tapped that down with his putter. As he leaned on the putter, he pushed it forward slightly and his coin suddenly materialized in that spot, away from all the spike marks. I couldn't believe what I was seeing. While Pietro was taking relief, Litchard was moving his ball mark. Then he calmly strolled forward along the new line, picking up pebbles and fixing other marks.

After getting relief from the drain, Pietro hit a towering flop shot that cleared the 10-foot-high embankment. It landed 7 feet short of the pin and rolled to within inches of the hole, so close he was able to tap in with the leading edge of his lob wedge while his new caddie, Jingles, pulled the flagstick for him.

Litchard watched disinterestedly, calm and cold. Five over par after seven holes of the U.S. Open on a golf course where he was clearly overmatched, and yet Justus Litchard was cheating to the best of his ability in front of a USGA official, two playing partners and their caddies, three volunteer scorers, and a hundred or so spectators just so he wouldn't have to putt over a couple of spike marks. He was doing it because he could. Cheating was as big a thrill for Litchard as competing.

When he was finally ready, Litchard rolled his first putt far enough past the hole so it took the down slope beyond the cup and rolled off the front of the green. He heard laughter from a few spectators on the dirt path back in the pines and he glared at them. Embarrassing himself was not what Justus Litchard had had in mind. He putted back up the slope at the front of the green, burning the right edge of the cup, then tapped in for yet another bogey, picking the ball out of the hole and, in one motion, throwing it toward the woods were it hit one of the trees with a thonk. The USGA official said something to him but Litchard just stormed off the back of the green, walking almost directly over the spot where his ball had originally been, to the nineth tee. The left side of his face was twitching violently.

I decided to leave Litchard's group to get a couple of shots of Tiger Woods, hoping to keep Justin Pound satisfied. I rested the 600 mm lens attached to the monopod on my shoulder, picked up the other camera body with the 70–200 mm zoom, and turned to cut through the tall trees toward the 16th, about where I figured I might catch up with Woods. Hidden back in the trees, Colt Reeves was sitting in a golf cart with a USGA RULES sign taped to the front. He had a pair of Nikon binoculars on the seat beside him and he was scribbling something down on a sheet of paper clipped to the steering wheel in the spot where a scorecard usually went. I wondered if Reeves had seen Justus Litchard cheat, too, and I wondered what he was going to do about it.

26

Not a goddamn thing, that's what.

At the end of the day, I expected to see Justus Litchard's name on the big scoreboard followed by a DQ for disqualified. Instead, it was followed by an 81. Litchard had finished his opening round eleven strokes over par. Pietro had hung in there, though he hadn't played particularly well, with a two-over-par 72. Nils Spjutsson had shot a one-over-par 71 and was tied with Billy Ray Toomey, praise be to Jesus. The leader after the first day was Tiger Woods, who shot 68. I'd caught up with Tiger's group in time to get a shot of him holing out from the bunker on the 16th (his 7th, since he started on the back nine) for a birdie three. The 16th was the other hole on the golf course the USGA had converted from a par 5 to a par 4 for the championship. Tiger made some good fist-pumping pictures so, between that bit of luck and a few shots of the Masters champion scrambling, I was in pretty good shape for my first day's work.

After Tiger made the turn, I packed my cameras away in my locker behind the big scoreboard. I wanted to ask Juli to have dinner but she was busy helping the USGA media people round up players for interviews. She knew the players well and the USGA was relying heavily on her. The first day was always hectic since it was difficult to decide what score would be low enough to merit a trip to the press center. As the day wore on, Tiger wound up being the main story but the press officials, unsure where the lead would fall, wanted to shuttle in every golfer at par or better. Juli had thrown herself into the job, performing on automatic pilot. I could tell by the look on her face that Killets's death had hit her hard and I suspected I probably had the same look.

When something happens to someone you know, it rubs off on you. Killets was Killets. She wasn't my favorite person in the world but she didn't deserve to have someone slowly squeeze the life out her, unable to fight for herself, helpless to move, unable to speak. And she didn't deserve to be tossed away, her body covered with old, bald Bridgestones like she was nothing more than a piece of garbage.

After I turned in my film to be processed, I walked back to the Aberdeen Inn and lay down for a minute. Between the emotional stress and walking in the oppressive heat, I felt drained and fell asleep almost immediately. When I woke up, I showered and changed into slacks and a clean golf shirt. I decided to grab a sandwich and a beer at Poogan's and go to bed early. Justus Litchard would be playing in the morning on Friday with the Swede and the Italian again. Rigging a sporting event—even just a small part of one—wasn't the same as murder, of course, but Litchard was a bad guy, of that much I was certain. It made sense to keep an eye on the devil I knew.

By evening the inside of Poogan's was jammed with people with U.S. Open badges and bags stuffed full of overpriced, poor-quality souvenirs. I managed to squeeze down the stairs into the basement bar and found a seat. I asked the bartender for a pint of Harp and a menu. He swabbed the wooden bar in front of me and put down the cold glass. I took a long gulp of the beer. The air conditioning was pouring out of the ceiling and the beer was almost cold enough

to make my teeth hurt. It was the perfect antidote to the
day's heat. Energy began returning to my body. Across the
bar, in a dark booth, I could see Justus Litchard and Colt
Reeves. They each had a beer bottle in front of them. Their
conversation was quiet and deliberate. First Reeves would
say something. Then, after a pause, Litchard would speak.
After another pause, Reeves would answer. They went on
like that, talking as if they were exchanging responses in a
chat room. Neither seemed angry. Neither saw me. Their
conversation was cold and businesslike. I wondered if
Reeves was warning Litchard about what he had seen, what
both of us had seen, on the eighth green. After a few minutes, Reeves slid out of the booth, picked up his straw hat,
shook Litchard's hand, and slipped off into the crowd.

Litchard held his beer bottle up to his lips and scanned
the noisy bar. He looked like he was expecting someone.
After I finished my beer, I ordered another and maneuvered
in a little closer. A waitress came over but he sent her away.
His left eye was twitching. It looked like a nervous tic except he didn't seem the least bit unnerved. He was drinking
slowly, taking tiny sips and watching the stairs. Maybe
Reeves was coming back and I didn't want him to see me.

The noise level in the bar seemed to rise suddenly like a
tidal wave, and down the stairs came the Masters champion,
Francisco Pietro, with a woman on each arm. He ushered
them through the crowded room. When he saw Justus
Litchard he threw up his hands.

"Ah, there," he said. "I was waiting up the stairs. I apologize. I did not know you are down here."

Litchard motioned for him to sit down.

"This is, what is your name, my dear?" he asked the
blonde.

"Jessica."

"Jessica," said the Italian, drawing out each syllable as

if he was whispering her name into her neck. "And you again? I'm so sorry." He looked at the brunette.

"Bonnie."

"Of course, Bonnie," he said. Pietro looked at Litchard. "Jessica and Bonnie," he said proudly to Litchard. "My nieces."

"Francisco," said Litchard, "I need to speak with you—alone."

"For a moment only," said the Italian, covering his heart with both hands. "As you can see, I'm very busy."

"Excuse us," Litchard said. He directed the women toward the bar and then pointed at the seat across from him for Pietro to sit down.

"It was a rough day, today, no?" Pietro said, sliding into a seat as the tone of his voice changed to serious business.

"Yeah, a bitch," Litchard said, talking quietly. "You know me, right?"

"Yes, of course, I play golf with you today," Pietro said.

"You know who I am?" Litchard's voice was getting hard.

I could hear him, brittle and cold. Something in it sent a shiver through me.

"Tomorrow, you're playing Billy Ray Toomey," he continued.

"You are confused," the Italian said. "He will be in the group in front of us. We are playing again with Nils who speaks only of God."

"No, Francisco, the book," Litchard said, exasperated. "The match is only for betting. Toomey's score for the day against your score."

"Of course," Pietro said. "For the gamblers. But who cares?"

"That's just it, Francisco," Litchard said, his voice getting softer and stronger at the same time. "I care. And friends of mine care. They care very much. What I'm telling you is you're going to lose to Billy Ray Toomey tomorrow. I don't care if you lose by one stroke or ten but you're going to lose."

"Perhaps," said the Italian. "Perhaps not. Every day it is something new. Like at the Augusta Masters."

"Not tomorrow," Litchard said, thumping the table with his middle finger.

Pietro finally understood. His face reddened. "And if I don't?" he asked angrily.

Justus Litchard laid his hands out palms up. "Sometimes people get unlucky."

"Are you threatening me?" Pietro asked, talking a little too loudly.

Litchard folded his hands between his thighs underneath the table. He leaned in closer and got quieter, so I could barely hear him. "No, no. Nothing like that. But you know, Francisco, I knew a guy once, he was a very unlucky guy. I ask him, did he ever get a beating, I mean a real beating? Sometimes people don't know until you show them, you understand? It's just that I wouldn't want the Masters champion to be unlucky. Maybe have a bad car accident. I knew a guy once got broadsided at an intersection. Very sad. Car came out of nowhere. Guy wound up a—what do you call it—paraplegic. Yeah. His wife had to change his diapers the rest of his life. It would be a goddamn shame. "

Pietro's face was flushed. "How dare you?"

A short, balding insurance salesman from Atlanta in a red striped U.S. Open golf shirt and a blue U.S. Open floppy hat walked over to the table where Pietro and Litchard were sitting.

"Mister Pietro," he said, holding his Thursday gate pass out in front of him along with a black Bic pen he had borrowed from a waitress, "I was wonderin' if I couldn't bother you for an autograph? It sure would make my day. I'm here from Atlanta with my wife and, see, she's Italian, too. We were at Augusta on Sunday, see . . .".

Pietro said, "Go away."

The stunned insurance salesman was about to rephrase his question, thinking Pietro must not have understood the simple request.

"No," the Italian held up his hand like a traffic cop. "Don't speak to me. Go away. Leave me alone. Can't you see I'm busy?"

Completely mortified, the man turned and walked back around to where his wife was sitting. "Do you believe that?" he asked her. "What an asshole."

"Who does he think he is?" she said.

Litchard grinned. "You ask around about me," he said to Pietro. "I think you'll find I'm a serious man."

Pietro was becoming visibly enraged.

"Francisco," said Litchard. "Calm down. You might even win the goddamn Open. Never can tell. All you got to do tomorrow is be one shot worse than Billy Ray Toomey. That's all. I'm going to be very disappointed if you're not. And most people, they don't like to disappoint me. It's only Friday. Plenty of time to make up a couple of shots. Say, we don't have a, you know, a language barrier here, do we?"

Litchard rose from the table, looking bigger than six-foot-four, and put his hand out. Pietro wouldn't shake it. Across the bar, the man from Atlanta saw the Italian refuse to shake Litchard's hand. Litchard turned and began moving away through the crowd. The insurance salesman tapped Litchard's arm as he walked past.

"That Italian, he's a rude son of a bitch, ain't he?" said the man.

"He's not so bad," Justus Litchard said, recoiling from the man's touch. "He's just having a bad day tomorrow." Then he disappeared up the stairs, grinning to himself.

I decided to follow Litchard and tossed a ten down on the bar to cover my tab.

Litchard walked down Market Square, past the leaded windows displaying golf memorabilia in the old Harvard Building. Then he turned to the left up Magnolia. I jogged a few paces to try to catch up to him. He was probably going to turn up Chinquapin and cut in front of the spa to get back to the Carolina Hotel but I wanted to be sure. Maybe I'd hang around, make sure he didn't come out later that night, just in case Justus Litchard was the one, the one who had killed all those women. The one who had murdered Jenny Killets.

When I came around the corner at Market Square I could see him on Chinquapin. By the time I got to the corner where the Aberdeen Inn Bed & Breakfast was, he had disappeared up the street. I began jogging again to try to get a glimpse of him. I walked between the white brick pillars, one of the original entrances to the old hotel, but still didn't see Litchard anywhere. I heard the crunching sound of someone stepping on dead magnolia leaves and whirled around. There he was, his hands in his pockets.

"You following me?" Litchard asked.

"What?"

"I said, are you following me?"

"Of, of course not," I stammered.

"That's good," he said. His eye was twitching above the scar on his cheekbone. "Because I thought I saw you out on the golf course today. And then I thought I saw you at Poogan's. And now here you are. I'm looking at you again. But I expect I'm not going to see you anymore. Am I?"

"Can't imagine why you would," I said.

"Good. Just so we understand each other." He walked right up to me and bent his face down so close I could smell the beer on his breath. His scar seemed to turn crimson. "I'm

Justus Litchard." He spit out the words. The sinews in his neck were popping out. His hands were knotted into thick fists at his sides. Slowly, coolly, he raised his right hand and patted my cheek, like I was a child in a stroller. "Just so we understand each other." He put his hands in his pockets and began walking toward the hotel, whistling the Frank Sinatra song *One for My Baby*.

27

The first night of a major championship is always a late night in the media center. Played on one of the longest days of the year, Thursday of a U.S. Open never seems to end. The Open has a huge field that goes off two tees, the front and the back, and Open courses, with their heavy rough and fast, hard greens require a lot of deliberate thought. There's always plenty of hacking out and laying up and debating what clubs to use from places on the golf course players never anticipated being. And, because of the peculiarities of Pinehurst's No. 2 course, there's a lot of three-putting and decision making around the greens, too. There's just too much at stake in the National Open to get in much of a hurry.

If the players are slow, the writers are slower. Everyone is looking for that cute phrase or undiscovered fact that will set them apart from the rest—at least in their own minds. The daily columnists end up laboring well past sunset, tapping out their witticisms on obsolete laptops provided by newspapers that are reluctant to cover their expenses. They toil as all modern writers do, in the hopes of one day becoming a television personality so they won't have to write at all. If F. Scott Fitzgerald were alive today, he'd be a regular on *20/20*.

It was close to eleven o'clock by the time the last writer, Jonathan Eggleston of the *Akron Beacon-Journal*, put his laptop into a faux black leather briefcase given to him by the Kings Island Golf Classic and stretched his arms above his head, finally ready to leave. A security guard would be on the premises all night, mostly to protect the photo equipment stashed in the lockers. Juli gave Eggleston a tired wave, making certain he was gone before she, too, left. If it had been anyone but him, she would have walked back to the hotel with him. But not Eggleston. With a complexion that perpetually seemed in need of soap and water, Eggleston hadn't paid for a round of golf, a golf shirt, golf clubs, or balls in the better part of 27 years. No piece of graft, no matter how small, could escape him. He was currently working on his fourth marriage. Wives No. 2 and No. 3 had been topless dancers, which inexplicably convinced him he was one hell of a fine-looking man. The walk back to the Carolina would only take five minutes and Juli would gladly risk bodily injury rather than walk five paces with Jonathan Eggleston.

So, when Juli finally left the media center, she was last and she was alone. When she turned up the road toward the Carolina, the hairs on the back of her neck stood up. She had the feeling someone was watching her.

She looks so good when she walks. So good. So good. Go ahead. Walk fast. Look confident. Don't be a victim. Her legs are so long. What a great ass. She won't be strutting like that when I finish with her. No. No. Her eyes will beg me. Beg me. Beg me. This one will cry. I know this one will cry. I'll see her tears. I'll touch them with my fingertips. I'll lick them away. Before it happens. Before the end.

His hands were pressed against the rough bark of a tall, wide pine tree. He could feel a spot of sticky sap on one palm.

I am the shadows at night. I am the shadows again. Her time in the shadows is coming.

28

O n Friday morning there was a knock at my door at the
B&B. Not a gentle, are-you-awake, 5 A.M. kind of knock,
but a firm, get-your-ass-up kind of knock.

I wrapped a bath towel around my waist and opened
the door an inch to take a peek. I saw FBI special agent Trent
Long. He slipped a folded piece of paper to me through the
crack and pushed me back as he muscled the door open.

I ran a hand across my head to calm my morning hair,
what there was left of it. "What the hell time is it?" I asked,
looking in the hallway behind him and then shutting the
door. The ceiling fan was making its wobbling and crank-
ing noises. There was no breeze at all coming through the
open window. I could hear the garbage truck down the street,
lifting a dumpster with a hydraulic moan and then dropping it back down with a hollow clank.

"Almost six," he said, walking straight to my clothes
duffel as he put on a pair of latex gloves.

I looked down at the paper in my hands. It was a search
warrant.

"What the hell are you doing?" I asked him.

"That's a warrant. I'm searching," said Long.

He stuck his hands into the furthest corners of my duffel bag then carried it over to the bed, turned it upside down,
and emptied out the contents. He picked through my clothes

like he was going through a pile of garbage, piece by disgusting piece. He opened the bureau drawers and did the same.

"My camera cases are in the trunk of the car," I offered. "They're mostly empty, except for the case with my strobes."

"Someone's down there looking through it now. The car's been impounded. We're going to tow it away," he tapped a finger on the paper I was holding. "It's in the warrant."

Long opened the closet door. I hadn't hung up very much. I never did. Just my blazer, a couple of pairs of slacks, a couple of shirts. Nobody cares if a photographer looks all wrinkled. Long felt through the pockets of the coat, finding the two Sharpies I'd bought at the drugstore. He opened them and sniffed the tips, then tossed them on the night stand, apparently satisfied.

"Me? You think it's me?" I said.

"I think you fit the profile," he said. "And I put a helluva lot more stock in our profilers than I do in that crap about you being able to *see* things. You ask me, if you *see* anything, it's because you already knew it."

I sat back on the edge of the bed next to the pile of clothes. The top sheet and slip cover were on the floor where I'd thrown them in the middle of the hot, uncomfortable night. I watched him rummage through my camera bag. And I wondered why he was there alone. Agents travel in packs. His buddies must have been down at the car.

"Look what I found." He held up a pair of white gloves made out of loosely woven cotton.

"They're for handling transparencies," I said. "So the oil from your fingers doesn't get on the film."

"The freak we're looking for wears gloves," he said. "I know a lot about you, Oliver, and I don't like much of what I know." He took the folded-up search warrant out of my hands and stuck it back in his jacket pocket. "I know you were staying a few doors down from a woman who got killed in Augusta and I know you were staying almost next door to a place where a woman was found dead in Hilton Head."

"Jesus Christ, Long, I'm the one who put the story out there in the first place," I said.

"Maybe you're the one who wanted the story out there in the first place. Maybe you like reading about yourself. Is that it? Move," he said, then lifted up the mattress to see if there was anything underneath. He let it fall back on the box springs with a thud. "What's the matter, wasn't anyone paying attention to you?"

I didn't know whether to be angry or scared. I stared out the window where the sun was beginning to brighten the hazy morning sky.

"I read the report about Charleston. Someone died there, too, didn't they? And you got in the papers then, too, didn't you?"

"I didn't have anything to do with that," I said. Two men had died. Friends of mine in Charleston, good friends, had been involved. It happened not long after Juli and I were divorced. One body disappeared. The other death was ruled self-defense. I tried to help the police and my friends. That was why Juli, at least, thought I could help now.

"I know about the fight, too," he said.

"That was a mistake," I said.

"It was about your ex-wife, wasn't it?"

"Yes," I said.

"That what happened in Charleston?" he asked. "Somebody get personal about your ex?"

"No," I said. "Juli has nothing to do with this."

"You have trouble controlling your anger, don't you, Oliver?" asked the FBI man.

"No," I said. "When do I get my car back?"

"When we're finished with it. We're taking it down to the Cadillac dealership to go through it. Someone will be in touch."

Long did another cursory lap around the room to see if there was anything he'd missed. He stopped at the desk and began unplugging my laptop.

"I'm going to have someone look at the hard drive, if you don't mind," he said, coiling the power cord around his hand. "That's in the warrant, too."

When he satisfied himself there wasn't anything he'd forgotten, Long put the laptop under his arm and left as abruptly as he had appeared.

I showered and shaved. My face looked old in the mirror, not like the young man I remembered. Not the one who lived in Charleston with Juli before it all went bad. That seemed so long ago. So much had happened. The white shaving cream set off my eyes, faded blue in color, sad, the whites turning yellow with age, the skin around the sockets soft and drooping and creased and sleepless. Clearly Long was able to convince a judge he had probable cause. I could have gotten Killets into a car with me. Maybe that was it. And when they looked at the hard drive, they were going to see all the searches I'd done. It would look like I was collecting stories about the murdered women. And the GHB. They were going to find the formula for GHB, too. Shit.

I knew when Long saw the stuff on my laptop, I was going to become his prime suspect, if I wasn't already. I was just as certain Justus Litchard was involved somehow. If I was going to keep an eye on Litchard, it only made sense that Long was going to keep an eye on me.

When I got to the press center, Juli was sitting at her desk having a cup of English Breakfast tea and staring into nowhere. There were newspapers spread out in front of her. She had been clipping stories about the first day of play to post on a bulletin board and Xerox for reference packets for the writers.

"You OK?" I asked. I sat down in a seat next to her, reserved for a USGA press officer who hadn't shown up yet that morning.

"No, I'm not," she said. "Poor Jenny, I can't get her out of my mind. It's so sad. And frightening at the same time, you know?"

I took her hand and squeezed. She squeezed back.

"I saw Dudley Sommers this morning," Juli continued. "He looked like hell, Nick, he really did. I think he actually loved Killets."

"Maybe so," I said.

"Poor Jenny," she said again. "When I think about it, about how she died, it makes me sick to my stomach. I can't bear to think about her last few minutes on earth. She must have been so scared. So alone."

"I don't think she knew what was happening to her," I said.

Juli looked at me for a long time. "It makes you wonder," she said, "about everything."

"I know."

We were quiet, just holding hands.

"Nick, I'm scared."

"I am, too."

It can all end so suddenly. You think you have choices but maybe it's just an illusion.

"Juli," I began and then stopped to take a breath. "The FBI agent, Long, he searched my room this morning. He impounded my car. Took my laptop. I think I'm pretty high on his list."

"They searched your locker, too," she said.

"It figures."

"They opened every single box of film and every single

plastic canister," she said. "They asked me to watch. For veri-fication, I guess. David Hailey was there, too. They said they were looking for some kind of drug."

"GHB," I said. "Talk to the commissioner. Tell him if he wants my help to keep Long away from me. I can't have that guy following me around everywhere."

"The commissioner isn't going to be able to tell the FBI what to do," she said.

"Juli, I think I might be on to something," I said. "I can't be looking over my shoulder all the time."

She slid her hand out of mine. "What is it?"

"I can't tell you. Not yet."

"I'll see if there's anything he can do," she said.

"Thanks." I said. We both wanted to say more but we decided to leave it alone. "I better get going."

"I've got to finish putting the Monday clips together," she said.

When I opened my locker, a hundred and forty empty green film boxes fell out.

29

Billy Ray Toomey hit his 3-wood for his second shot over the green on the par-5 10th, his first hole of the day, and took four strokes to get down for an opening bogey. Francisco Pietro, Nils Spjutsson, and Justus Litchard were in the threesome directly behind him and watched it all from the fairway.

Pietro's face was ashen, as if he had the flu. He didn't have to ask around much to find out Justus Litchard was someone to fear. Even Peter Hammett, Pietro's agent, had heard the stories about Litchard and what a crazy bastard he was. Back in the fairway, Litchard seemed relaxed, even confident, though he was sure to miss the cut. Spjutsson didn't want to lose any more ground to Woods, who was teeing off on the first hole at just about the same time. The Swede felt he needed to get off to a good start. He was only three shots behind but whenever Tiger was involved, there was always the fear he could blow the doors right off everyone else in the field. He'd done it before. Spjutsson knew he couldn't afford any mistakes. He couldn't have cared less about Billy Ray Toomey up ahead. All he was thinking about was making a birdie.

Litchard found the left rough off the tee and was forced to lay up about 120 yards from the green. After a good tee shot, Pietro thought he could reach the green with a 2-iron and waited for Toomey to finish. Spjutsson's drive had come to rest in a divot. He pronounced it God's will and laid up near Litchard's ball. After Toomey's group left the green, Pietro ripped a 2-iron low and hot that landed in the front bunker, burying under the lip. Litchard missed the green with a wedge, also finding the bunker. Spjutsson knocked it ten feet from the hole with just enough spin to hold the green and make his birdie four. Pietro left his third shot in the bunker, barely moving it out of its plugged lie. Both he and Litchard wound up with bogey sixes.

All day long, Pietro, Litchard, and Spjutsson were able to watch Billy Ray Toomey because Toomey was playing with Dutch Herndon, the slowest golfer in the known universe. The players on the tour said you could cut through the shaft of Dutch Herndon's 5-iron and count the rings to find out how long his round had taken that day. Pietro and Litchard had no problem knowing what score Toomey made on each hole but just in case, Litchard asked the scorer stationed at the exit of every green, then repeated the score loud enough for Pietro to hear.

By the time they got to the par-3 nineth hole, their 18th, Billy Ray Toomey was in with a six-over-par 76. Pietro, the Masters champion, was already seven over par and preparing to shoot a 77 unless he got damned unlucky and made a hole-in-one because there was no way in the world he was going make a putt for a two, of that much he was certain. Litchard, who once again was going to fail to break 80, had the honor on the last tee. He hit a 9-iron left of the green onto a pile of pine needles. Spjutsson had been sensational until the previous hole, where he made his only bogey of the day. He had gotten all the way to four under par for the tournament, tied with Tiger Woods for the lead. The Swede made the sign of the cross on his chest and forehead and then hit a 9-iron eight feet left of the cup. Pietro took out his

9-iron and tried to miss the green to the right but inadvertently pulled the shot. The ball covered the stick all the way, landing 12 feet behind the hole. It took one bounce forward and then began spinning back at the cup like someone was dragging it on a string.

"Sit," yelled Pietro and Litchard, almost in unison.

The ball sucked back toward the hole, barely missing the pin a second time. It dipped ever so slightly as it rolled across the edge of the cup before spinning back off the front of the green. Pietro dropped to his knees, echoing his famous celebration that April at the Masters. To the applauding spectators near the tee, it seemed like Pietro had just played his way out of the U.S. Open with a particularly unlucky round of golf. But Justus Litchard knew better. He knew, right at that moment, the Italian felt like the luckiest man in Pinehurst. Had his ball gone in the hole for a one, he'd have bought himself a bucketful of broken bones.

"Figlio di puttana, she was close," Pietro said as he got to his feet.

I'd taken plenty of shots of Spjutsson. I had Pietro on his knees. And I'd even walked with Woods for a few holes, so, for the second day, I felt like I'd done enough for *Current* and Justin Pound. All I needed to do was drop the film to be processed and I could spend the rest of the day trailing Litchard. I started walking back toward the clubhouse and the press center.

For two days, I'd watched Justus Litchard through my 600 mm lens, sometimes so close his face was the only thing in the frame. I'd gotten to know his scar, the smile that turned up at one side, the nervous way he milked the grips of his clubs before he pulled the trigger. I'd watched him cheat. Had Spjutsson and Pietro seen it, too? Confronting Litchard was something no one wanted to do. Just look at Colt Reeves. At the end of the day, it was easier to ignore a guy who wasn't going to break 80 than it was to challenge the crazy son of a bitch in the scoring tent. What difference could it have made to Pietro anyway? He had a much bigger problem with Litchard than a little penny ante cheating. No one in their right mind wanted to have anything to do with Litchard. He was a scary guy, all right, but capable of murder? I felt certain of it.

The 8th and 16th holes of the No. 2 Course parallel each other and I took the spectator crosswalk to the other side of the 16th, cut behind the 17th green, and walked inside the ropes in the waste area of the uphill 18th. At the green I saw Jeremy Howe near the scoring tent. He had a TV camera and lights set up between the bleachers and the clubhouse so he could interview players coming off the course. Just as I arrived, some unlucky gofer drove up in a golf cart, shuttling the stone-faced Pietro and his sullen caddie, Jingles, back to the clubhouse from the 9th hole. The Masters champion had bogeyed the nineth for a 78, finishing ten over par for two days, and seemed destined to miss the cut. He couldn't wait to clean out his locker and get out of town but he knew he couldn't avoid an "exit" interview with network television.

Pietro sat down in a chair and a sound tech pinned a microphone to his sweaty golf shirt. Howe sat on a nearby stool, seemingly unaffected by the vodka fog swirling around him. When the blonde woman taking the camera shot signaled she was ready, Howe leaned his bulk forward.

"Francisco," he began, "it was a frustrating day of golf."

"Yes," agreed the Italian. "I just never got anything going, you know? You look at the score and you think, it is awful, but it isn't so awful, really. A bounce here and a putt there and I could be very close. It is the way the game is. For example, the last hole, I almost make a one and finish with a four instead. Very difficult."

"Was there one hole that proved pivotal?"

"Not so much. But the greens, they are very difficult."

"What's next then for the Masters champion?"

"For me, it's back to Florence for two weeks and then get ready for the Open championship."

"Ah, the Old Course and the old gray toon," Howe said.

"And greens where it is possible to putt and chip," Pietro added, smiling.

"Thanks for sharing some time with us," said Howe.

"You got it," said the Italian.

As the tech unhooked the microphone from Pietro, Howe stepped closer.

"Bloody tough out there today," he said.

"Ridiculous," Pietro said. "It's a fucking crime, this is what it is." He kicked the microphone wire away, spit on the ground, and walked off.

"The Italian's running a little hot," I said to Howe.

"I dare say a seventy-eight will do that," Howe said. "Did you see much of him today?"

"Most of the round," I said. "It wasn't pretty. You mind if I leave my cameras here? I need to run into the clubhouse for a minute, use the facilities."

"Why don't you put them over there where they won't get trod upon." Howe indicated a spot by his lights.

"Thanks," I said and laid my equipment out of the way. I walked into the clubhouse, down the hall decorated with black-and-white photographs of Pinehurst in the 1920s and '30s, and into the locker room. By the time I got there, Pietro and Litchard were standing eyeball to eyeball, logo to logo. There were six or seven other players in the large room, some sitting on benches changing shoes, some watching television, others making airline reservations with the tour travel agent, who had a table set up in a corner. Most pretended not to hear or see anything. It was none of their business. And no one wanted to have a problem with Justus Litchard if they didn't have to. The locker room attendants, on the other hand, were spellbound.

"You pig. You dirtbag," Pietro said. "I'm going to report you to the police."

"You're not going to do anything," Litchard said.

"I'm going to tell the commissioner what kind of garbage he's got on his tour," Pietro told him. "Figlio di puttana. You son of a bitch."

"Yeah?" said Litchard. He grabbed a surprised Pietro by the front of his shirt and the back of his neck and began rushing him toward the wall of extra wide wooden lockers. The one next to John Daly was open and Litchard and Pietro were picking up speed as Litchard extended both arms and rammed the Italian into it. Then he managed to almost slam the door shut, leaning on it with all his strength. "Who you gonna tell now, you fucking bastard?" Litchard said, leaning on the door with his back and shoulder.

Litchard gave it one last shove, then walked over to his own locker and began calmly emptying it out. After a moment of stunned silence, one of the attendants helped Pietro to his feet. During the entire altercation, the only time Daly looked up was to make sure they weren't going to run into him, knock over his Diet Coke.

I turned around and went to retrieve my cameras. When I got back outside, I saw Stormy at the top of the stairway that led down to the bag room. He was waiting for Ian to arrive for his late afternoon round.

"You won't believe what I just saw," I said. I told him about Justus Litchard stuffing Francisco Pietro, the Masters champion, into a locker and slamming the door on him.

"He's not the first one. That's one frightening guy," Stormy said.

Litchard's bag was standing off to the side. "Jingles around?" I asked.

"Already gone," Stormy said.

I went to Litchard's Gucci bag and pulled out the putter, taking off the padded cover. I reached in my pocket and took out my money clip. Juli had given it to me when we were dating. It was a St. Jude medal mounted on a clip. I touched the medal to the bottom of the putter and it stuck. Litchard's marker must have been steel, too, and he moved it with a magnet in the sole of his mallet head putter.

I put the cover back on the putter, slid it back in the bag, and walked back over to Stormy. "Your man played great yesterday," I said. "A sixty-nine is right in the thick of it."

"Yeah, we did good, I guess," he said. "Glad it's over with though. I don't ever want to have another thing to do with that goddamn Litchard. What were you looking at in his bag?"

"Nothing," I said. "Here he comes now."

Justus Litchard came down the hallway, nodded to Stormy, and hoisted the big, professional Gucci golf bag onto his shoulder. He was carrying his golf shoes in a green felt Pinehurst shoe bag. Two security guards held the doors for him so he could maneuver his way through. A couple of kids ran up to him for an autograph but he ignored them and started walking toward the players' parking lot.

"Not now," he barked, scaring them away.

I figured Litchard was headed back to the hotel to get his things and clear out of town. I told Stormy I'd see him later, retrieved my gear from the 18th green, and thanked Howe. I walked as quickly as I could to the press center and packed everything away in my locker. I put a body and a couple of small lenses in my camera bag and started for the hotel to pick up Litchard's trail. I wasn't sure why I brought the camera with me. Habit, I suppose.

"Did Justus Litchard check out yet?" I asked the desk clerk at the Carolina, showing her my media badge. The air-conditioning inside gave me a chill and I shuddered. She typed his name into her computer. "I need to catch him. For an assignment," I explained, putting the camera bag on the desk. She looked at the photographer's badge hanging around my neck.

"Not yet," she said.

"Thanks."

I walked over to a winged back chair half hidden behind the bell stand and sat down with a copy of *Travel & Leisure* I picked up from a table in the lobby. By six that evening, I still hadn't seen any sign of Litchard but I had learned more about the Wickaninnish Inn on Vancouver Island, the Hotel de Crillon in Paris, and family vacations in Tuscany than I ever wanted to know. I admired the way the art director displayed photographs and thought, at the moment, it would be a helluva lot safer shooting hiking trails and waterfalls in Kauai than it was working for Justin Pound and *Current*.

When I finally saw Litchard, he didn't have any suit-cases or golf bags in travel cases. He wasn't going anywhere, except to the Old Dornoch Room off the lobby to get a drink. I wondered if he was meeting someone. Was he fixing another match? Or maybe hunting for another victim? After a moment I walked slowly by the front entrance to the Old Dornoch Room and saw Litchard at the end of the bar. The room was beginning to fill with noisy fans talking about Pietro's collapse and the rest of the day's golf but he seemed to be alone and with a hard enough look on his face to make certain it stayed that way.

"Did you see the eagle Charles Howell made at the

fourth?" said an overweight man with a cap tilted back on his head, the brim dark with sweat. "What did he hit, three-wood, six-iron? These kids are amazing. What's he weigh, about seventeen pounds soaking wet?"

I didn't want Litchard to know I was there so I backed across the lobby, getting far enough away so I could see him but not let him realize he was being watched. I was taking his warning seriously. People were walking between us, stopping to chat with one another, tell stories, make plans for the evening. The voices were loud and the conversations jumbled together.

"What are you doing here?" Juli appeared out of no-where.

"Don't do that," I snapped.

"Sorry. Didn't mean to scare you."

"Justus Litchard," I nodded in the direction of the Old Dornoch Room. "In the bar."

"Did you hear about the fight?" she asked.

"Hear about it? I saw it."

"Really?"

"Stuffed Pietro right in a locker." I told her what I knew about Litchard, everything Stormy told me and everything I'd learned from the researcher at *Current*. The only thing I didn't mention was about coming face to face with him the night before. "Can you get me in his room?"

"No."

"Come on, there's got to be a way," I said. "If he's the one, he'll have some GHB someplace or at least the stuff he needs to make it. Wasn't that what Long was looking for in my locker?" I slid a couple of steps off to the side. Someone had stopped right in my field of vision. Litchard was still at the bar, taking his time over what looked like a vodka.

"He alone?" she asked.

"Yeah."

"How long has he been in there?"

"Just got there and he looks like he's planning on being there for a while."

"This seems like a bad idea."

"What the hell, we might actually learn something. Come on, Juli, there's got to be a way. Flash your tour credential. Tell them you have to leave something in his room. Parking passes. I don't know. Look official for God sakes."

"The first thing the desk clerk will do is get the manager."

"What if you tell them he's your husband? You just got in town and you want to go up to the room, freshen up, then meet hubby for dinner?"

"No luggage."

"Airlines lost it."

"What if they ask me for identification?"

"Perfect."

I took Juli by the arm and we marched out of the Carolina. One of the bellmen in plus fours and a white golf shirt opened the door for us.

"Where are we going?"

"Press center." I was walking as fast as I could. Juli was having trouble keeping up. The sun was just setting and it was going to be another hot night.

"What for?"

"You're going to make yourself a guest badge. Mrs. Julia Litchard."

We'd use their digital imaging machine, the Kodak-whatever-the-hell-it-was, the one in the corner of the press center, behind the curtain. It fixed pictures on an array of badges. Media. Photographer. Messenger. Guest. By the time we got there, most of the volunteers who worked behind the counter had left for the day. There were a few writers still tapping away on their laptops at their seats in front of the big scoreboard, mostly noting that, with Tiger Woods in the lead, the Open was all but over.

"Juli." It was Todd Parkinson, the head USGA press officer, a former captain of the Yale golf team and a veteran of the New York City public relations wars, where he had served with distinction in the front lines of Cavendish, Cleek & Gougelmann, a firm that specialized in damage control of corporate scandals. "Thought you were gone for the night."

"Forgot something," Juli said. She sat down at her desk and shuffled through some papers. I wandered over to my locker and watched her from behind the big board that had the names and scores of everyone in the field on it. She chatted and laughed with Parkinson, touching his arm. When he finally walked away Juli ducked behind the curtain and came back out in a matter of minutes.

She nodded at me and headed for the exit.

"Juli?" It was Parkinson.

"Yes?" she said.

"See you in the morning?"

"Sure. I'll be here early."

"You be careful," he said.

"Right." She walked outside. I caught up with her on the path leading back toward the hotel. Even in the dying light, I could see she was slightly flushed.

"Here. Happy now?" She put the credential in my hand. It was a guest pass for Julia Litchard and it had Juli's picture on it. I handed it back to her.

"That'll work."

When we got back to the hotel, I looked in the Old Dornoch Room and Litchard was still there, alone at the end of the bar, reading a menu.

"Looks like he's going to order dinner," I told Juli. "Get the key from the desk and I'll go up."

It was too easy. The desk clerk was young, probably

just working there for the summer while she studied hotel management at the community college. Juli told her she was Justus Litchard's wife and she'd just arrived in town and wanted a key to the room. She showed the girl her guest pass with the picture ID. The girl called Litchard's room but when there was no answer, she seemed perplexed. Juli looked impatient and sighed, and the clerk punched some numbers into a machine, ran a key card through it, and handed it to Juli.

"Five thirty-seven," she said.

"Thank you." Juli's expression said, *it's about time.* I was waiting around the corner, looking at a window display of resort real estate I couldn't have afforded in my wildest dreams.

"I don't think you should do this," she said as she gave me the key card.

"You stay here and watch Litchard. If he leaves the bar and starts upstairs you call the room. Let it ring twice, then hang up. I'll clear out. If he leaves the hotel, whatever you do, don't follow him. Understand?"

"Sure."

I stood there a moment.

"Aren't you forgetting something?" I asked. She leaned up and kissed me on the cheek.

"No. The room number."

"Oh," she said, slightly embarrassed. "Five thirty-seven."

"Thanks. For the kiss, I mean." I smiled.

"Just go, if you're going."

On the fifth floor I got off the elevator, turned to the right, and walked almost to the end of the hallway. A few doors away, Vijay Singh and his wife and son came out of their room, presumably going to dinner. I nodded at him and he ignored me. I was certain he'd never even remember seeing me. As far as he was concerned, I didn't even exist.

When the hallway was clear, I went in. Justus Litchard's bed was creased and the pillows were propped up against the headboard. The television remote was on the nightstand along with an empty Budweiser can and a small travel alarm clock. There were four other empty cans in the trash bucket.

I began opening drawers. His clothes were folded neatly, almost military-style. If he had the ingredients and the equipment to make GHB, it wouldn't be easy to hide. If he made his own, he'd need distilled water, gamma butyrolactone, and either sodium or potassium hydroxide. I couldn't imagine someone traveling with all that. If he made it somewhere else and just brought a vial of liquid with him it could be hidden almost anywhere. I dug around in his empty suitcase on the luggage stand in the closet. His dirty clothes were in plastic laundry bags on the floor. His shaving kit contained a bottle of aspirin and a prescription bottle of Zocor for high cholesterol. I shook the Zocor bottle to hear the rattling of the pills inside. I knew GHB could be a powder, too. There was a bottle of aftershave. I took off the top and sniffed it. It smelled like English Leather. GHB has no odor. I remembered Long taking a whiff of the Sharpies he found in my jacket.

There were two 30-pound dumbbells on the floor by the window. On the writing table were two sets of car keys—one to a courtesy car—and a cell phone. I looked at the minibar. It could be in there, I thought. I tugged at the door but it was locked.

The telephone in the room exploded. It rang one more time. I don't know why but I picked it up.

"Hello."

There was silence. Then I heard Juli's voice, quick and scared.

"He just left the bar."

A sense of panic swept over me and I slammed down the phone. I looked at Litchard's cell phone and impulsively slid it into my pocket. I didn't even bother to check the hallway before I came out. No time. I started to walk to the elevator. No. I doubled back to the stairway. Behind me, back down the hallway, the elevator doors opened and there was Justus Litchard. I pushed into the stairway, went down one floor, and walked halfway across the hotel to another elevator.

When Juli saw me in the lobby, the worry melted from her face.

"Jesus," she said. "You're white as that wall over there. Don't ever do this to me again."

"Did he go up alone?"

"Yes. But when he walked by the front desk, the clerk recognized him and asked if Mrs. Litchard had found him yet. He said, 'There ain't no Mrs. Litchard.' And just kept on going. The clerk didn't say anything, though. I think she was afraid she might lose her job."

"Come on," I said. "I need a drink."

As Juli hid her face from the desk clerk, we walked across the lobby and into the Old Dornoch Room, taking a table in the corner. I pulled the small cell out of my pocket.

"What's that?"

"His cell phone."

A waitress stopped at the table. She had pencils in her hair and pulled one out like she was picking a dandelion.

"I'll have a pint of Harp."

The waitress just kept staring at Juli, who kept staring at the cell.

"Juli?" I said.

"Cosmopolitan," she said without looking up. When the

waitress had gone Juli looked back at me. "What the hell is the matter with you?" she whispered angrily.

I opened the phone and scrolled down to Messages. I hooked up to the voicemail. It said, "You have one saved message." I listened to it.

A voice said, "We did good on Toomey. Nothin' Saturday. We got one more to lay down Sunday. This will be the big one. Have dinner on me. I'll call again tomorrow when we got the race." The voice was talking about which two players would be paired against each other for the final-round wagers.

The phone told me if I wanted to return the call, I should press eight. I pressed eight. It said the number was not available.

I pushed END and went back to the menu. I scrolled down to Phonebook and pushed OK.

"Juli," I said, "write this down."

There were only initials, no names, in the list. I read off the initials, followed by the numbers. She was writing, looking up nervously and writing again.

"How are you going to get the phone back upstairs?" she asked me.

Then it rang.

Juli nearly jumped up from the table. I looked at it like it was a hand grenade about to explode. Jesus.

It rang again, making a little singsong noise. I thought about answering it.

The phone went silent. The screen said there was one missed call. It gave the main number of the Carolina Hotel. Justus Litchard was calling me. I thought, *oh shit*.

I closed the phone, picked up my pint glass of Harp, and went to the bar.

"Excuse me," I said to the bartender. "I ordered a pint of Guinness." I held up the lager.

"Sorry, sir." He took it away. With my right hand, I let the phone drop onto my foot, catching it with my toe. I set it down on the floor and kicked it under the barstool next to where Litchard had been sitting. It was half hidden behind a stuffed U.S. Open souvenir bag.

"Sorry again," said the bartender, handing me a Guinness.

"No problem," I said.

As I sat back down at the table with Juli, I heard the singsong tone of Justus Litchard's phone one more time. The woman at the bar looked all around her, then looked down. She got off the stool, picked it up, and answered the call.

I don't know what Justus Litchard said to her, but the woman's face turned pale.

30

Saturday was the day Jimmy Wildheart, the world-class also-ran, became The Man.

He had recovered from his opening round of 72 with a virtually unnoticed second round of three-under-par 67, making him one under par through 36 holes and three shots behind the glamour pairing of Tiger Woods and Nils Spjutsson. But Saturday was about as normal for Pinehurst in June as sunbathing was in Yellowknife in January. Overnight a Canadian cold front blasted through, rubbing up against the heat and humidity in front of it, creating window-rattling thunderstorms. Temperatures dropped so precipitously I woke up shivering in bed, closed the window, and pulled the chain to stop the ceiling fan. I took a threadbare blanket off the top shelf in the closet, wrapped up in it like a cocoon, and tried to regain a little warmth. It felt more like northern Michigan than North Carolina.

Even worse, all morning there was a steady, misty rain, cold and dreary. The golf course is built on sand, though, and the water rarely puddles. As the day wore on, the rain turned into a ghostly Scottish mist, blowing a wet fog sideways behind an aching cold wind.

For Jimmy Wildheart, this was nothing more than a fine winter day in West Texas, and he played like it. He instinctively guarded his balance, shortened his swing, widened his stance. It was as though God had laid his hand on Jimmy Wildheart and said, "Son, you are about to win you a United States Open." Jimmy went out in a stunning five-under-par 30 and added a 33 on the back to tie the U.S. Open single round record of 63, seven under par for the day, eight under for the tournament, on a day when no one else could feel their hands. Even the old timers in the press room said it was the greatest round ever played in a U.S. Open. Better than Jack. Better than Tiger. Better than Johnny Miller.

Wildheart was two twosomes behind Tiger Woods and Nils Spjutsson because, although he was three shots off the lead, going into Saturday there were only seven players under par in the whole field. Wildheart was playing with Davis Love III. Woods and Spjutsson were last off. In between were Ian Person and Vijay Singh.

Maybe even more surprising than Jimmy Wildheart was Tiger Woods, who was launching his drives wide right all day. As the round wore on Woods became increasingly cold and distracted, walking with his head bowed, his arms crossed on his chest underneath a rain jacket, and his hands tucked in his armpits. He could read scoreboards, too. As he fell further and further behind, he became easily distracted by TV cameramen, backed off shots, and slammed clubs to the ground. The portable microphones picked up his anger. He finished with a six over, 76, two over par for the tournament.

Nils Spjutsson, who kept looking at the sky like he was Job trying to make sense of a merciless God, was even worse. Intimidated by Woods from the outset, the Swede was sucked down the drain with him, eventually shooting a 79 for a five-over-par total through 54 holes. Of the players who began the day under par, only Ian Person and, of course, Jimmy Wildheart stayed there. Ian shot a one-over-par 71 and was two under for the championship, a full six shots behind Wildheart.

The weather was so miserable few spectators stayed the entire day, particularly once Woods fell apart. After Tiger's triple bogey at the eleventh, people started scrambling for the transportation buses, looking for a hot shower or a bar with gas logs in the fireplace. It had been a cold, miserable day and Sunday promised more of the same.

Jimmy Wildheart was a journeyman player and a pretty decent quote but he was no Tiger Woods in the history department. The TV ratings would be in the toilet. And, considering the weather forecast, the crowd would probably stay away, too. The sense of gloom spread throughout the press center. No one wanted to write the Jimmy Wildheart Open. The only real story in golf was Tiger Woods, and Wildheart just beat him by 13 strokes. Plus, there was no heating system in the giant media tent and some of the writers moaned about being able to see their breath.

The only good thing that happened to them all day was when they finally got to talk to Wildheart. For most of them, it was the first time they'd ever heard him utter a word. But, when it came to talking to the press, Jimmy was no rally killer. In the mass interview when they asked him if he'd be able to handle the pressure on Sunday, he said, "It ain't like I seized the opportunity out there today. It sort of seized me. I feel like I'm just a bunch of walking nitrogen with a hot putter and a cold, cold heart."

Juli didn't see much reason to hang around the press center Saturday evening. Parkinson and his USGA types in their blue shirts with the eagle logos had everything under control now that it was almost over. She fielded a few questions some writers had about Jimmy Wildheart and the Red Raiders of Texas Tech but most of the younger newspaper guys were writing the collapse of Tiger Woods. The older ones were writing the greatest round in U.S. Open history and talking about Miller and Oakmont. Mostly the work was doing itself. She could make it an early night.

I stopped at her desk while she was stuffing papers into her briefcase.

"Did you see the *Dunbar Pilot* this morning?" I asked her. It was the local paper that usually published three times a week but was coming out daily because of the Open.

"No, I didn't do the clips today," she said.

"Here." I showed her a copy, folded back on itself. I pointed to a small item at the bottom of page eight.

It said Marcus E. Darnell, age forty-nine, was found dead of a suspected drug overdose at 3312 Marigold Street in a section of Dunbar known as the Forgotten City. The article said it was the second body found in that section of Dunbar in the last three days. It said that, up until three years ago, Darnell had worked for the county school system as a janitor. And there was a picture.

"I saw that man two nights ago at Eli's Inside Club," I said. "He said he saw the man who killed Killets. Stormy was there that night, too, with Jeremy Howe."

Juli nodded. "Did you tell Long?"

"Haven't had a chance. Besides, I'm afraid the next time I see Long, he's going to slap a pair of cuffs on me," I said. "You ready to head back to the hotel?"

"Yeah, I'm pretty beat." I could tell it was all beginning to wear on her. "I think I'm just going to order room service and try to get a good night's sleep. I feel like I haven't slept in weeks. What about you?"

"I guess I'm going to keep track of Litchard," I said. "According to the message on the cell phone, he's going to be putting the screws on someone to . . ." I stopped talking when Parkinson came up.

"Juli," he said, "could you help Dana? Copier four is down again."

Juli sighed. "Sure," she said. After he was gone she turned back to me. "It's a paper jam and they think they need to call NASA. You don't think Litchard's going to lean on Jimmy Wildheart, do you?"

"It's the only one that makes sense," I said. "The odds would be huge. They could make a fortune if Jimmy was to shoot 80 tomorrow."

"You be careful," said Juli. "Don't do anything stupid."

"Don't worry," I said. "Besides, it's not the fix that worries me. It's what happens after. What if killing women is how he celebrates?"

31

The note slid under the door. There was a knock right after it. Juli got out of bed. She had fallen asleep watching *The Man Who Knew Too Much* but had awakened in the middle of the night to reruns of *Gilligan's Island* and couldn't get back to sleep. It was past midnight. She was wearing a thin negligee and the air was cool in the room with the window slightly open. When she got up, her nipples hardened.

She picked up the envelope, stuck her finger under the flap, and broke it open.

"Meet me at the Pine Crest ASAP. Don't use phones. Not even cell. Someone is listening." It was signed "Nick."

She pulled on a pair of blue jeans, still wearing the negligee, and combed her hair back quickly.

It was time. I knew she would come. I knew it. The note. When it's over, you have to go back to get the note. Go to her room. Get the key from her. Go to her room. I hope she doesn't bring it. It would be a reward. She would be gone but she would be there, too. Watch me. Watch me squeeze out her life with my hands. When I'm finished I'll go there just to smell her perfume. Her scent will belong to me, just like her soul. Life and Death, together at last.

There she is. She looks good in her jeans and running shoes. The jacket on top but I know what's underneath. I'll touch her again. And again.

Now is the time. Now is the time. She's coming to you. Use it. Turn her, squeeze her. She'll never know. There's no one around. No one will see. It's late. Now is the time. Now.

There she is. There she is. Yes.

Juli came out of the front entrance of the Carolina and turned left. She walked quickly along the brick path. It was cold, a penetrating cold, and she wrapped her jacket tightly around her against the misty rain. It would only take a few minutes to reach the Pine Crest. She had to hurry. Nick might be in trouble.

She was almost to the dark end of the parking lot, near the white pillars by the spa, when a car turned on its lights and pulled up alongside her, so close it made her jump.

"Dammit, you scared me," said Juli.

"Sorry," he said. The window was open. The cold mist was hitting his face.

She stood there, looking at him.

"You shouldn't be out walking in the middle of the night," he said. "It's not safe. Besides, it's raining."

"I'm not going far."

"Get in," he said. "I'll take you."

"Thanks." Juli walked around the front of the car. The headlights were bright enough she had trouble seeing as she climbed inside, into the dark. It was odd. The inside light didn't come on when she opened the door.

"It'll only take a minute to get to the Pine Crest," he said. Then she knew.

She fumbled for the handle. Too late. When he saw her begin to turn, he grabbed her shoulders and spun her around. He threw his right arm around her neck and squeezed as hard as he could. He pushed her head forward with his other hand. The hold was choking her and preventing air from reaching her lungs or blood from getting to her brain. She kicked but only hurt herself. He was too strong. She tried to tear at his arms with her fingernails but he was wearing a wet rain jacket she couldn't rip. The fight began to drain from her faster than she thought possible. She began to see light and dark. No color. Then just shapes. Then not even that.

She went limp in the crook of his arm and he leaned her up against the passenger door and stroked her hair gently.

Here. Here. Drink this. Put your head back. Don't let it dribble out of your mouth. That's it. Drink it down. Hope you're thirsty. Don't cough it up. That's it. Drink. This will make you feel better. Much, much, much better. You'll like it better this way. Really, you will.

32

There was still one day to go in the National Open but the cold, chilling weather had driven everyone inside. The carnival atmosphere from the beginning of the week had been replaced by the dreary reality. The weather had turned bad and Tiger Woods wasn't going to win. I never did find Justus Litchard. I looked in the dining rooms and the Old Dornoch Room. I called 537 but there was no answer. I looked in the Holly Inn and the Magnolia. I walked to Poogan's Pub and checked upstairs and down and went to the Pine Crest. Litchard wasn't in the bar there, either. It was nearly 1 A.M. Sunday morning and I knew I'd lost him and I was afraid of what it might mean. I was certain Jimmy Wildheart was going to be the next target in Litchard's gambling scheme. But what about after that? I needed to find out where Wildheart was staying so I called the Carolina on my cell phone and asked to speak with Juli Oliver. I couldn't stand the thought of Litchard out there, roaming in the night. Hunting.

There was no answer in Juli's room. A chill, a panic, surged through me. Ohmygod.

I jumped off the porch of the Pine Crest and began running toward the Carolina. The roads were wet with the cold rain. I ran up Dogwood, turned hard right down Market

Square, passed the art shops at a full gallop. I slipped when I turned left onto Magnolia, tearing the knee out of my khakis, but I jumped up and kept going, turning right onto Chinquapin, still running even though my legs were burning. I turned into the headlights of a car parked at the back of the hotel lot near the spa and put my hand up to cut the glare. Then the lights went out.

The car door opened and Colt Reeves got out. I walked toward him. He was saying something in a voice I couldn't hear, as if he was mumbling to himself. For a second, I thought he must be drunk.

"Reeves," I said, getting close to him now. "Have you seen Juli?"

A smile came over his face, an odd smile, the grin of someone who was in a near state of rapture. He exploded into me, knocking me backwards with his shoulder, throwing me off balance, and I sat down hard on the ground with my arms behind me. Before I could get to my feet he was on me. A kick to my body forced all the air up through my throat and out of my mouth and I felt like I was going to throw up. Somehow I was on my feet but I didn't see the blow that came from underneath, jolting my head backwards and lifting me up. I felt the one that crashed into my left temple but it turned everything into a buzzing white like snow on a TV screen. Then everything was black.

Colt Reeves picked Nick's body up and dragged it to the trunk of the car. He loaded him in, then slammed it shut. Reeves looked around. He was still lucky. The parking lot was deserted. It was late, cold and rainy. No one was around. It happened so fast. Maybe it wasn't luck, after all. Maybe he was just good. He was better than all of them. Reeves grinned.

*You fucking idiot. You moron. Didn't I tell you to be care-
ful? How could you be so careless? Now you've got to get rid of
them both. You understand? Both. And you still have to come
back for the note. Don't forget the note. You're such a moron. Go
ahead. Have your little fun with her. Come back before morning.
I'll deal with you later.*

Reeves got in the car and pulled out of the parking lot,
took the turns through the village, and headed for the traffic circle. He was being careful about his speed. The last thing
he needed was for a Pinehurst cop to pull him over. It was
hard to stay calm, he was getting so excited. It was a quiet
night. The cold and wet had seen to that. *It's dead tonight*,
thought Reeves. And that made him laugh. It was a perfect
night for him. For him, it was Mardi Gras.

He took the Midland Road exit off the traffic circle. The
speed limit was thirty-five and he stayed right on it. It's a
four-lane road, like a tunnel at night through tall pine trees,
left and right and even in the median. Everything was wet
from the rain. His headlights bounced off the reflective paint
on the side door of a Dunbar cop car hiding in the trees,
waiting to catch a DUI swerving outside the lines. Reeves
checked the speedometer. Perfect. The cop car pulled out
behind him anyway. There was a dead possum in the road
and he didn't move to miss it. Both tires on the right side
thumped over the carcass and the smell of death shot up
through the air vents.

"Fuck," Reeves said, spitting out the word. The cop followed him for a mile or so, then swung into the passing lane
and went around him, going too fast. Reeves sighed. Juli
moaned in the passenger seat. The GHB was working. Reeves
reached over and stroked her hair. Then he put his hand
between her legs and squeezed hard.

Reeves took Midland Road underneath the U.S. 1 by-pass, then started climbing up the hill into the town of Dunbar. The town was bisected by a set of railroad tracks, and he took the first left that crossed over the tracks, drove up to May Street, turned left again and then right onto Youngs Road. Within a couple of minutes he was passing horse farms on both sides of the road. Reeves drove for a mile or so, saw a dirt road off to the right, slowed down, and turned in. He continued down the rutted, sandy trail until he saw another, even more deserted-looking trail. It led back into a stretch of open fields fenced off by creosote-soaked split rails. He pulled his car up on some grass under a dogwood tree that glowed brightly in his headlights and turned off the engine.

Juli was completely under the influence of the GHB. She was blinking. Her eyes were looking around but nothing seemed to be registering. She had no idea where she was or that she was about to die. Not yet.

Oh, God. It was black. I couldn't even see my hands. I could feel the swelling in my face and I couldn't seem to catch my breath. The car was bumping and thudding over rough ground. Not gravel. More like sand. Every time it dropped, my sore ribs bumped into something hard and metal. I felt around. The car jerked and I put my hand underneath me to cushion the blow against my ribs. It was the spare, the doughnut. He'd taken all the carpeting and the boards out of the trunk. Blood stains, I thought. DNA. The doughnut was fastened down with a wing nut and it kept poking into my side. I unscrewed it far enough to reach underneath the tire. There was a packet of tools wrapped in plastic. One of the tools was a tire iron, the modern kind, just a few inches long. It would have to do.

The car stopped. I could hear Reeves get out. He was mumbling to himself again.

Make this fucker sorry. Make him pay. Make him pay. He'll be sorry. This is for you. This is for us.

I heard the trunk lid unlatch but it didn't open all the way, just a crack, just enough for the trunk light to pop on. It seemed like a police spotlight to me. I gripped the tire iron in my right hand. I was on my left side; my back was turned to the rear of the car. I didn't think he'd kill me right there. When he reached for me, I'd swing around. Maybe catch him in the side of the head. I could feel him looking at me through the small opening.

The trunk lid rose slowly.

"Anyone home?" Reeves said. "Still out? Well, you never could take a punch."

That was when I threw my right arm around, turning my body to put all the force I could summon behind it. And I missed. Completely. He grabbed my arm and pounded it against the edge of the open trunk. My wrist hit the metal latch and the tire iron fell out on the ground. I tried to turn and kick him but he grabbed my shirt and with one great, tearing yank pulled me out of the car and threw me down on the ground. He kicked me in the ribs again and I curled up, trying to catch my breath. I knew I was about to die.

Come on, dogshit. What's the old joke? Hit the ball, drag Fred. Hit the ball. Drag Fred. Here. Let me stomp on that for you!

I thought he broke my hand when he stepped on it. He kicked me in the back, in the kidney, and a wave of nausea overwhelmed me. Then I thought I was going to lose consciousness. I could feel myself being dragged across the ground.

Nick began to moan. Reeves pulled his foot back and kicked him hard in the ribs and again in the face. Nick's nose exploded. Even though he was unconscious, he continued to moan. The killer leaned him up against a fence post, pulled both his hands roughly behind him, and tied his arms together, wrapping duct tape around and around and around his wrists. When he opened the passenger door of the car. Juli fell out onto the ground. Before he picked her up, Reeves reached into his pocket and pulled out a pair of rubber gloves. He blew into each one and then stretched them over his big hands, whistling while he put them on, making sure the fingers went down to the end.

She wants it. She wants me. Can't you see?

"I see," Reeves said out loud. He dragged her close to where Nick was tied up. He began taking her clothes off. "I'm not stupid."

Juli looked up at Reeves. Her eyes told him she knew what he was doing but she was unable to speak. She tried to scream but nothing came out. Her jaw wouldn't move. She wanted to kick, to run, to fight, but her limbs wouldn't respond. She was completely at his mercy. He smiled at her. He touched her hair with his hand. Gently.

He pulled her jacket off.

"It's not too cold, is it?" he asked. "No, I guess it isn't."

Rip it open. Rip it open.

He tore the front of her negligee with a powerful yank. Her breasts were firm, the nipples hard in the cold rain. Her hair was wet and he smelled it. Reeves felt her breasts with his gloved hands. He twisted them hard. Juli just watched him. Her head was too heavy to lift.

Reeves took off her shoes. He unbuttoned her blue jeans. He picked up her legs by the ankles and began tugging the pants off.

Nice and tight. Nice and tight.

Juli's panties came halfway down her thighs as the jeans came off. Reeves tossed the pants away then roughly took the underwear the rest of the way off. He spread her legs apart, put his gloved hand on her, and sighed.

He walked over to where Nick Oliver was tied to the fence post. He crouched down beside him and pulled a knife out of his pocket. He slapped Nick with the same hand he'd used to touch Juli.

"Wake up, asshole," said Reeves. He slapped the side of his face gently a couple more times. Reeves put a ball gag in Nick's bloody mouth and tied it tightly behind his head.

I couldn't focus. I remembered Justus Litchard, talking to the Italian. *Have you ever had a beating, a real beating?* My mind wouldn't stay in one place.

"Know where you are?" Reeves asked me.

I could only moan. My mouth wouldn't work. I couldn't speak, couldn't call for help.

"Know what day it is?" he bent down and asked me. His face was so close I could smell his breath. I could feel the rain. I couldn't feel the cold but I was shivering.

I couldn't move my arms and my eyes didn't see well. One didn't seem to work at all. I wondered what he'd done to my eyes. I knew I needed my eyes. My tongue was swollen and dry.

Know what day it is? It's cut your dick off and shove it down your throat day, that's what it is.

"Wake up, asshole." Reeves tapped the side of my face with his knife. I could see the evil in him. I'd seen it before but hadn't understood it. I'd gotten it confused, all mixed together. And it was going to cost us our lives.

"Hurt much? It does? Oh, that's too bad. Well, it won't hurt much longer. I promise you that. Look over there," Reeves said, pointing with his knife.

I turned my head and saw Juli lying there nearly naked in the rain. I tried to tell him to leave her alone but only muffled grunts came out. I knew we were going to die.

"You love her, don't you?" he said. "Well, you can't have her. She's mine now. Completely. In the end, she belongs to me. They all belong to me."

I grunted again. I think I started to cry. I don't know. It mixed with the rain and the blood on my face. I was suddenly cold. Very cold. Then, oddly, the fear was gone. I had become one of the dead. What more could he do to me? Reeves crouched down and began to whisper in my ear.

"This is what I'm going to do. I want to you know. The poor thing, she can't feel anything at all. You don't have to worry about that. She won't feel any pain. I promise. Not like the pain you're going to feel. I'm going to fuck her one last time. She thought she could deny me. Now, she knows how stupid that was." Reeves grabbed me by the hair and yanked my head back.

Right? Right? Is this the best you can do?

"She moaned for me," Reeves said. "Did she ever moan for you? I bet she didn't, you little piece of crap." Reeves stood up and kicked me in the side. I heard something crack and I almost passed out again.

"Stay with me," he said in a quiet voice. "Stay with me. I'm going to go over there and play with our little sweetheart for a while. Then I'm going to put my hands around her neck. I'm going to squeeze until there's no blood in her brain. Until her brain tells her heart to stop beating. Until she's mine. Then I'm going to take this knife and I'm going to cut her wide open. I'm going to pull out her intestines and dump them in your lap."

I tried to curse him, to say something, but only moans came out. It was a struggle to stay conscious. I knew I was slipping away.

"Let's see, how about if I make the FBI think you did it?" Reeves laughed. "What did you think of that little piece of lens tissue I left in Hilton Head? Too much? I didn't want to do it every time. I just wish I'd thought of it in the beginning. Never occurred to me until I saw you at the Masters. Of course, you look a little beat up. Don't guess I can let them find you like this. Wonder what the FBI will think if you just disappeared—forever?"

That's it. That's it. They're all yours. It's open season now.

I watched him walk over to Juli and kneel down beside her. He rubbed her cheek with his gloved hand.

"Ready for me now?" he asked her.

A shadow flew in front of me. Something real, something solid. It drove into Reeves full force, hitting him square in the back using a wooden rail like a battering ram. Reeves arched in pain and yelped as he pitched forward on the ground. I saw Stormy standing over him. He lifted the railing over his head but it was too awkward and heavy to bring down with any force and Reeves scrambled away easily, getting to his feet. He charged at Stormy. They locked together and rolled over and over on the ground, flailing at one another, unable to deliver any kind of deadly blow. Reeves raised up with something in his hand, it was too dark to see what, and brought it down hard. Stormy just laid there, his legs motionless.

I was kicking, trying to get free. My eyes were stinging and I wanted to yell. Reeves turned around in a circle, looking in every direction.

Do it. Do it. Hurry. No one can stop you. No one.

He walked back toward Juli. I watched him standing over her. "What'll I do with the caddie? Well, I'll worry about that later. First things first," he said just as his head exploded like a water balloon hitting a cement wall.

FBI special agent Trent Long walked toward the body lying on the ground. He held his gun loosely down at his side. When he was satisfied Reeves was dead, he took his raincoat off and spread it over Juli.

"EMS is on the way," he said to me, cutting through the tape on my arms. "You're going to be all right."

I dropped my head and passed out.

33

I woke up in a bed in Moore County Hospital. I couldn't remember how I got there but I couldn't forget why. My ribs were taped up so tight I could hardly breathe. No air was going in or out of my nose. My head ached and my face felt like it was covered with bandages. Juli was asleep in a chair next to me. When I saw her, I couldn't help myself. I took a deep gasp of air and pain shot through my body.

The telephone rang. Juli's eyes opened. She smiled when she saw I was awake.

"Can you talk?" she asked me.

"I guess so," I said. My voice was thick from lack of use and maybe from the painkillers they must have pumped into me. I reached my hand over and took the phone.

"Hello," I said.

"Oliver. Pound," came the voice.

"Justin," I said.

"Just how am I supposed to get another photographer there now?" he said. "A joke, it's a joke."

"I can't," I replied, handing the phone back to Juli. "Hang it up." And she did.

The doctor, a Jamaican, came into the room. He told me I was a lucky man. That I'd been beaten up very badly, had a concussion, several broken ribs, a broken nose, and two lost teeth. He said he was going to keep me in the hospital for a couple of days. He said after I healed a little, I'd need reconstructive surgery on my nose and, after I got a couple of implants to replace my teeth, I'd look as good as new.

"Can't we aim a little higher?" I said. He patted me on the shoulder and turned to Juli.

"And how are you feeling?" he asked.

"I'm OK," she said.

"You make that appointment?" he asked.

"Yes."

"Good. You'll like her very much. She's very good in this kind of situation."

"Thank you, doctor."

He gave her hand a little squeeze.

"Doctor," I said. "What about Stormy?"

"Mr. Monday?" he said. "Mild concussion. He's fine. We released him early this morning. In fact, we couldn't get him to stay. He said he had a job to do." The doctor patted a file folder against his leg and walked out.

"Nick," she said, bending down close to me, "about Colt . . ."

"Don't," I said. "You couldn't know."

Juli helped me take a sip of water through an elbow straw. "Where do you think Reeves kept the GHB?" I asked, leaning back down.

"He had it on him," she said. "It was in a Visine bottle. He'd just squeeze some into a drink. In my case, directly into my mouth, I guess. When they searched his home in Columbia they found a regular laboratory in a room off the garage where he regripped golf clubs."

"How'd Stormy find us?"

"I asked him to watch you," she said.

"Howe was right," I said. "You are a mother hen."

"Stormy says you're a damn sight harder to look after than Jeremy Howe ever was."

It hurt to smile. "What about Long?" I asked.

"I tried my best to get him to back off and leave you alone. I'm pretty glad he didn't," she said.

"Me, too."

There was a rap on the door. It opened and Gavin Webster poked his head inside.

"How's the patient?" he asked. Juli and I looked at one another. We both knew immediately all he wanted was the story.

"Get the fuck out of here, Webster," I said. "I mean it."

He looked down and backed away. As the door closed, Juli was about to say something. I put my fingertips on her lips. The touch seemed to pass right through the wall between us. "Let's not talk about any of it now," I said. "We'll talk later. There's plenty of time for talk."

That afternoon the last twosome was standing on the first tee of the No. 2 Course at Pinehurst. It was still cold and rainy. Umbrellas lined the right side of the fairway behind a green rope, stretching out like a brightly colored laundry line. Jeremy Howe was near the starters' tent, preparing to walk with the last group. A network technician was putting a fresh battery in the pack around Howe's ample waist. The rain was already causing his microphone to drift in and out.

Ian Person and Jimmy Wildheart were waiting to be announced and told to play away in the final round of the U.S. Open Championship. Donnell "Stormy" Monday had a bandage above his left eye that was covering eleven stitches. He was wetting the edge of a golf towel with water from a green cooler. He'd use it to wipe the dirt off Person's irons. Stormy unzipped the large pouch on the side of the golf bag and counted the towels. He was carrying six and he hoped that would be enough to keep his man's grips dry all day.

At the front edge of the tee box under a black umbrella with block letters that spelled GUCCI, Justus Litchard was staring straight at Jimmy Wildheart, who refused to return his look.

Person was introduced first. He was fighting his nerves. He was aging out and he knew it. In all probability, this would be the last, best shot he'd have at a major championship. He hadn't slept at all and he could barely catch his breath. The last chance is even harder than the first. You know how much is at stake. He had a lot of ground to make up on Jimmy Wildheart—probably too much—and he couldn't afford to make any mistakes. Person hung his opening drive out way to the right. It sailed over the line of red and green and blue and yellow umbrellas and went deep into the pine trees.

When Wildheart was announced there was a smattering of applause except for the Texas Tech twins, Sandi and Soozi, who cheered and whistled from two hundred yards down the fairway. He hit a high 3-wood with a little draw. While the ball was still in flight, everyone on the tee seemed to begin moving forward. Stormy, Person, the scorer, Judge Thomas who was acting as the USGA referee, a shove of photographers led by David Hailey, two Pinehurst policemen, Jeremy Howe, and a television cameraman. Everyone seemed to move except Jimmy, who just stood there watching the ball curve against the gray sky, steady as you please. A perfect arc. It landed just in the right side of the fairway, giving him an ideal angle into the green. He exhaled deeply, picked his white tee off the ground, and slipped it into his pocket. He knew he could win this goddamn thing. Just knew it.

When he had walked as far as the front of the tee box, Justus Litchard called out to him in his thick voice, "You play smart, Jimmy, you hear me? Be real smart."

Litchard didn't see Trent Long and the three state troopers behind him until it was too late.

"What's this all about?" he said, as one of the troopers hooked a pair of handcuffs on Litchard's wrists while Long took the Gucci umbrella and held it up over them.

"It's about ten to twenty, I'm figuring," said Long, who nodded at Jimmy Wildheart. A few paces farther up the fairway, Stormy looked back over his shoulder at Justus Litchard being led away in cuffs. Something deep down made him feel good about losing.